5 2016

RAIDERS OF THE LOST BARK

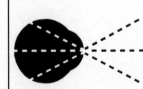

This Large Print Book carries the
Seal of Approval of N.A.V.H.

THE PAMPERED PETS MYSTERIES

Raiders of the Lost Bark

Sparkle Abbey

THORNDIKE PRESS

A part of Gale, Cengage Learning

GALE
CENGAGE Learning®

Farmington Hills, Mich • San Francisco • New York • Waterville, Maine
Meriden, Conn • Mason, Ohio • Chicago

Copyright © 2016 by Carter Woods, LLC.
The Pampered Pets Mysteries.
Thorndike Press, a part of Gale, Cengage Learning.

Thorndike Press® Large Print Clean Reads.
The text of this Large Print edition is unabridged.
Other aspects of the book may vary from the original edition.
Set in 16 pt. Plantin.

LIBRARY OF CONGRESS CATALOGING-IN-PUBLICATION DATA

Names: Abbey, Sparkle, author.
Title: Raiders of the lost bark / by Sparkle Abbey.
Description: Large print edition. | Waterville, Maine : Thorndike Press, 2016. | Series: The pampered pets mysteries | Series: Thorndike Press large print clean reads
Identifiers: LCCN 2016030506| ISBN 9781410494221 (hardcover) | ISBN 1410494225 (hardcover)
Subjects: LCSH: Pet grooming salons—Fiction. | Dogs—Fiction. | Murder—Investigation—Fiction. | Large type books. | GSAFD: Mystery fiction.
Classification: LCC PS3601.B359 R35 2016 | DDC 813/.6—dc23
LC record available at https://lccn.loc.gov/2016030506

Published in 2016 by arrangement with BelleBooks, Inc.

Printed in Mexico
1 2 3 4 5 6 7 20 19 18 17 16

DEDICATION

To our Pack. You are the best street
team ever, and we are
so grateful for your support.

NOTE TO READERS

If you're looking for Laguna Hills Regional Park, please note it only exists in our imaginations, along with the ARL glamping event. While our fictional park allows domesticated pets, wilderness parks closest to Laguna Beach do not allow pets other than horses for a number of reasons. We all know wild animals rely on scents to determine territories — hunting, breeding, and their home. When our pets "mark" their territory, it alters the habitat for the wild animals. Since dogs are natural hunters, their natural hunting instincts spring into action when they smell or see rabbits, squirrels, and other natural prey. And if that's not enough, keep in mind, all the wilderness parks have bobcats, mountain lions, and rattlesnakes, which put our pets at a high risk of injury and death. If you're interested in visiting an Orange County park, which we highly encourage, check out the OCparks website for a complete listing of parks that allow dogs in camping areas and which ones do not. ocparks.com

CHAPTER ONE

The idea sounded like fun. A week of camping at the Laguna Hills Regional Park with your beloved pooch. Or in this case, a week of "glamping." Glamorous camping. Think oversized, celebrity RVs, king-sized beds, and Persian rugs. I like to refer to glamping as experiencing the outdoors on a silver platter — service, luxury, comfort. Well, it is Orange County. You didn't think we'd actually sleep in polyester tents and smelly sleeping bags from the local sporting goods store, did you?

Here's the catch — if I attended the event, I had to spend a week with a blackmailer.

Betty snickered. "*Glamping Under the Stars By the Sea.* Sounds like a prom theme."

"Yes, it does."

My feisty assistant, Betty Foxx, tapped the gold-leafed, engraved invitation I held. "I'm not about to pass on an opportunity to cozy up next to a hunk all night. What about you,

Cookie? You ready to let down all the brown hair you keep hogtied to the back of your head?"

No, Betty wasn't the blackmailer, although she had been pushing me hard for the past couple of weeks to attend the "Five Paws-Up" Laguna Beach Animal Rescue League fundraiser. I was referring to that sneaky, no-good, pet chef, Addison Rae.

I scowled at Betty and smoothed my ponytail. I'd traded the beauty queen routine for my tomboy style years ago and hadn't looked back. I liked my laidback style. It sure beat evening dresses and two-sided tape.

"You've got to let it die. I'm not going. Stop pestering me about it." In the past month, I'd had all I could take of Addison and her "favors." Just thinking about her got my hackles up. Only the good Lord knew what I might do if she walked through the boutique door.

I tossed the extravagant invitation in the wastebasket and returned to stocking the doggie neckties. I'd make a generous donation, volunteer a couple of extra days next month at the ARL, and call it good.

"Why are you being a stick-in-the-mud?" She immediately retrieved the invitation and tucked it safely in her pocketbook, which was stowed under the counter.

"It's June. Tourist season. You of all people know it's not the ideal time to close the shop."

Bow Wow Boutique catered to the pampered pets of our beachside town whether resident or visitor. May through mid-September was the busiest time of year, with Christmas coming in a close second.

Don't get me wrong. My desire to keep the shop open wasn't because I needed the cash. Lucky by birth, I came from the Texas Montgomerys. We had an abundance of two things — money and a love for competition. While I didn't advertise my family's wealth, the same could not be said about my competitive nature.

Despite my built-in excuse, Betty wasn't convinced. I didn't need to see the suspicion in her sharp gray eyes or her arched vengeful red-lipstick colored eyebrows. (I follow the don't ask, don't tell philosophy when it comes to Betty's eyebrows.) I could feel the heat of her questioning gaze across the boutique. I braced myself for the inevitable interrogation from the eighty-something know-it-all clad in her purple silk lounging ensemble most women would call "pajamas."

"Cookie, ever since your handsome fiancé

stomped on your heart and then handed it back to you in pieces, you've become *boring,*" she sang out the last word in her best Oprah imitation. "Where's that gutsy chick who'd close the boutique without a second thought so we could solve a crime like Rizzoli and Isles?"

Wow. Nothing like kicking a girl while she was down. I ignored the sharp ping of truth about Grey Donovan, my on-again, off-again fiancé. We were presently off-again. I was pretty certain our relationship was permanently flat-lined. Yes, Grey had broken my heart. But the truth of the matter was, I had played a larger part in the demise of our relationship with my rash actions and lack of trust. But enough about that. No sense dwelling on the past.

It didn't take a detective to know Betty wanted a reaction from me. I loved her for it. If she wanted to think I wasn't willing to participate on the adventure because of Grey, that was fine by me. That reason was easier to explain than the truth.

I looked down at my graphic tee which read "Rescued Human", faded jeans, and motorcycle boots I currently wore. "Am I supposed to be Rizzoli?"

Betty's white sneakers squeaked against the hardwood floor as she made her way to my side. "Look, each day I wake up with something to look forward to. Sometimes it's coming here. Most times it's taking my Raider boy to the dog park like that bossy cousin of yours insisted. But tomorrow, I'm looking forward to sleeping in a gigantic RV and being waited on hand and foot by my very own butler. And finding a little bit of trouble. Since when do you pass up the chance to babysit me?"

I sighed. She did need to be kept on a short leash at times. "I don't want to close the boutique for a week." I checked my watch. "Come on. It's six o'clock. Lock the door and let's get out of here."

Before either of us could make our way to the front, the boutique door swung open, the chimes chirping. We looked toward our last-minute guest. Betty automatically called out a warm greeting. I, on the other hand, choked on mine.

Wouldn't you know it? The "real" reason I wanted to avoid glamping under the stars strolled toward us as if she didn't have a care in the world. Or my mama's future in her hands. I sent a quick prayer to the good Lord that I didn't do something I'd regret later. Just so you know, in the past, He hadn't been quick to grant that request.

"If it isn't my favorite blue-haired chef,"

Betty announced, completely unaware that she was kissing the fanny of a black-hearted blackmailer. Side note — Addison really did have blue hair. In my humble opinion, it was hideous, which meant Betty adored it.

I dropped the paisley tie I clutched in my fist before I ripped the silk fabric into pieces.

"I'm so glad I caught you before you closed." Addison's reedy voice sounded thinner than usual. Like she was out of breath from rushing to catch us before the shop closed.

The girl was a con artist. The only running she did was to catch her next victim.

"Mel, is it true?" she asked. "You're not coming tomorrow?"

"Sure is," I ground out. I broke down the empty cardboard box with more effort than it needed. Better the box to be on the receiving end of my ire than Addison.

"You have to go. It's only because of you that I even got the job for the event." She weaved past a shelf of dog beds. She spoke with the most annoying false tone of gratitude; surely even Betty had to have picked up on it.

"That was awfully nice of you, Cookie."

Or not.

"I didn't get you the job," I corrected. "I *recommended* you."

14

I brushed past Addison, making my way toward the counter. The two quickly started to gossip like schoolgirls. My heart kicked up a few beats when I realized Addison's unexpected visit today could possibly be her last. The sooner Betty left, the sooner I'd complete my business with Addison and she'd be out of my life.

I propped the flattened cardboard against the wall and focused on closing out the register. After a quick tally, I stuffed the day's worth of cash into a red night-deposit bag and locked it.

"Hey Betty, drop this off at the bank. Don't dillydally." I didn't need a witness for what was about to go down next.

She grabbed the deposit bag I held toward her, then snatched her oversized pocketbook off the shelf. "Don't you worry about a thing, boss. I've got pepper spray in my purse, and Detective Hottie on speed dial."

Good Lord. The bank was three blocks down the street. If I'd thought for a moment she was in any real danger, I'd drop it off myself. I wished her fun on her glamping trip and in turn, she shot me the evil eye. She muttered something about me being a party-pooper just loud enough for me to hear as she walked out the door. I waited until the white-haired rabble-rouser was out

15

of sight before I turned my full attention on Addison.

I crossed my arms. "What do you want now?" I thought I saw Addison flinch at the edge in my voice.

She fingered the pet tags hanging on a display rack. "Still can't talk you into joining us tomorrow?" She looked at me sideways, her thick blue hair falling across the side of her face.

I shook my head. "Still not interested."

"But you worked so hard to help me out," she cooed.

"Save the theatrics for an audience." I brushed past her toward the coffee bar. The last item of the day was to rinse out the coffee pot. "I held up my end of the agreement."

"Agreement." Addison nodded. "I like that."

I refused to call it blackmail in front of her, even though that's what it was. "What would you call it?"

"A friend helping out another friend." She casually waved her hand through the air.

I scoffed. "We are not friends." If we were, I'd stop her from looking like a taxicab in those black-and-white checkered shorts, and yellow scoop-neck tee.

She shrugged. "Under different circumstances, we could have been. We're similar, you and I. We're enterprising women who refuse to be people pleasers. We're both highly ambitious." She flipped her hair and continued. "That complicates life, being ambitious. But it's our fuel to succeed."

Good grief. She acted like she was stumping for my vote. "You're wrong. We are nothing alike."

"Just because you want me to be wrong, doesn't make it a fact."

What I wanted was to tell her what I really thought of her and her blackmail scheme, but it wasn't the right time. I may have held up my end of the bargain, but Addison had yet to follow through with her end. And until then, I needed to keep my cool.

I gently set the empty pot on the counter. "Where are the letters?"

She snapped her fingers. "That's what I forgot." A nasty smile tugged at the corner of her small mouth. "I didn't bring them with me."

I bit the inside of my lip to keep from shouting. "Why not?"

"I have one more favor to ask of you. As a friend."

"No. No more. I've introduced you to everyone you wanted. You're the pet chef for the ARL fundraiser. There's nothing left for me to do."

She smiled. "But you still haven't written the foreword to my cookbook."

I could feel my temper slipping. "And then what? Sell your *Pampered Pet Cookbook* here? But that won't be enough for you, will it? What next? Get you on Top Pet Chef?"

She snapped to attention, momentarily sidetracked by the possibility of national celebrity fame. "Can you do that?"

"No." I spat out the word like it was poison in my mouth.

"I'll tell you what. You write that foreword and bring it to the campground tomorrow. If I like what you've written, which I'm sure I will, I'll give you the letters."

"I have zero credibility in the chef world."

Addison's eyes narrowed as she weaved a tangled web of manipulation around me. "But you have enormous credibility in the pampered pet world. You've built up a trustworthy reputation." She pushed her lips together. "You do know how to write a foreword, don't you? All you have to do is tell the readers why they should purchase my cookbook. An anecdote works best to create that emotional connection. I'd suggest writing about how you bounced back from the public humiliation of being kicked out of the Miss America pageant, and how you see that same determination in me."

I was going to kill her. I crossed my arms to keep myself from strangling her skinny neck. "That's never going to happen."

She waved a hand dismissively. "Fine, fine. It was just a suggestion. Write something boring."

Write something boring? It was as if she didn't take the cookbook seriously. "Again, I'm not a chef. Certainly, you know someone else more qualified."

"Do you want those letters or don't you?"

"How do I know you'll keep your word?"

"You don't." She laughed lightly. "But you want those letters so badly, you're willing to take the chance."

I closed the distance between us, until our noses almost touched. I smelled the mint on her breath. Surely she could feel the rage on mine. "You'd better keep your word or you'll be sorry. You can only push me so far. Do you understand me?"

A quick movement caught my eye. I jerked my attention to the front of the store. Great! Callum MacAvoy, afternoon news reporter looking for the fast track to the evening news, had his busybody face pressed against my front window, watching Addison and me argue.

I took a deep breath and stepped back. With a short nod toward the front door I said, "You need to leave. Neither of us wants the nosey reporter poking around in our business."

Addison turned and waved at MacAvoy. "I don't know, he's very attractive. I thought you were going to get him to do a story on my rise to fame?"

I don't think I'd ever met such a self-absorbed blackmailer before. Not that I have an abundance of experience to compare her to, but honestly. You expect a level of evil . . . but narcissism? MacAvoy waved back, and took that as an invitation to come inside. Lovely.

"Leave. Now," I whispered to Addison. "Or the 'agreement' is off."

Addison hiked the strap of her purse over her shoulder. "See you tomorrow, Melinda Sue."

As they passed each other, they exchanged a hello. Mr. TV watched her leave, then turned his attention to me. "What was that about?"

I ignored his question. "I almost didn't recognize you without your pushy microphone and cameraman. It helped that you had your face plastered against my window like a lightning bug on a windshield."

He flashed his trademark TV-ready smile, strolling toward the back of the store. "Who says I don't have my microphone?" He watched me for a minute, his green eyes calculating how far he wanted to push me. "That looked intense. Who was that?"

There was no reason to lie. "Addison Rae. I left you a message about her a couple of weeks ago. The pet chef I suggested you do a story on."

He shoved his hands in the front pockets of his trousers. "Interesting. That's why I'm here. I had a couple of questions before I followed up on your hot tip."

He didn't fool me for a second. "You didn't need to see me. You could have just as easily called."

"True. But then I would have missed that fascinating exchange. I'm curious." He rocked back on the heels of his leather loafers. "Why would you want me to run a high-profile story on someone you don't like?"

Well, hell's bells. "I never said I didn't like her."

"You don't even treat me with that much disdain, and you don't like me. What did she do?"

"You're reading way too much into this. Aren't you late for . . . something?" I strode to the register and grabbed my tote from under the counter.

He shook his head. "Not at all. I've got all night."

"Well, I don't. I have to go home and pack." I grabbed him by the shoulders, turned him around, and gave him a shove toward the door.

"Running away?" he tossed over his shoulder.

"Hardly. I'm attending the ARL fund-raiser."

I know. I know. I said I wasn't going to attend. But after that last exchange with Addison, I didn't really have a choice if I wanted those letters.

"I didn't see your name on the guest list," he said.

Under normal circumstances, his persistence wouldn't make me uneasy. But the last thing I needed was a hungry reporter with a nose for sniffing out trouble to think there was a story of any kind in his territory.

"I'm Betty's plus-one."

I guess I needed to let Betty know I'd changed my mind. She was getting a room-mate after all.

"What in Sam Hill is that?"

"That's a V-B-R." Betty, dressed in an

22

army-green jumpsuit with multiple pockets across her chest, waved her hand like a *Price is Right* model.

I dropped the large duffle bag I'd brought outside and told my bulldog, Missy, to sit. "I hate myself for asking this, but what's a VBR?"

"A Very Big Rig."

Of course it was.

"What do you think? It's our home away from home for the next few days. Isn't it delicious?" Betty bounced on the toes of her white tennis shoes.

Delicious wasn't the first word that came to mind. It was a behemoth of an RV that took up over two-thirds of my street. I mean there's luxury, and then there's *luxury*. This was over the top, yet perfect for an Orange County glamping trip.

Sleek, pearl-black paint glistened in the California morning sunshine, promising a lavish lifestyle on the road. Missy sighed and lay on the pavement as Betty and I stood at the end of my driveway.

"Where did you get it?"

"Hudson Jones, the program director for the event, emailed a list of companies that rent rigs —"

"Rigs?" She was really getting into the RV lingo.

"Recreational vehicle. Motorhome. Coach
—"

I held up my hand. "I get it. I get it. Please tell me you didn't drive that here."

She puffed out her chest. "Of course I did. That Hudson Jones guy offered me a driver, but I told him to bug off. I'm a great driver."

"No, you're not." I'd ridden with Betty a handful of times. After each jaunt, I'd kissed the ground, thanking the Lord Almighty I was alive, and swore I'd never accept a ride with Racecar Betty again.

"Don't be a hater, Cookie. If it makes you feel better, Valerie insisted I take lessons."

"With who?" My skepticism was alive and well.

Betty lives in an adorable bungalow on her daughter, Valerie's, property. I've spent some time with Valerie. I wasn't impressed. She was more concerned with how Betty's actions would reflect on Valerie's social climb to the top of the Orange County social ladder than her mother's well-being.

"The RV rental place. If you had signed up for the party like me, you could have taken lessons too. Oh, I have a matching jumpsuit for you inside."

"No, thank you. I've driven a motorhome before. Granted, not a mammoth thing like that. How big is it?"

"Forty-one feet. I could have gotten a

forty-eight footer, but that seemed overkill, ya know?"

"You don't say."

Betty peered up at me, shielding her eyes from the bright sunshine. "Cookie, you never said on the phone. Why'd you change your mind?"

I grinned. "Let's just say you wore me down."

"I think it has to do with that pet chef."

For many reasons, I'd kept Betty unapprised about my dark relationship with Addison. One being, Betty couldn't keep a secret if you paid her. The last thing I wanted was for the real reason Addison had come to Laguna Beach this summer to get out. And I definitely didn't want word to get back to Texas to my mama and daddy.

"Do me a favor, don't get too close to Addison."

"No way. I'm sticking to her like glue. She's going to make sure we all eat like kings."

She was the pet chef. She'd make sure the dogs ate like kings. "As long as you keep it to food."

Betty laughed. "Cookie, you're not jealous are you? First Caro and now Addison. Don't you worry. There's plenty of me to go around."

25

I was not jealous of Caro. Sure, my feisty red-headed cousin and I weren't technically speaking to each other, but that had nothing to do with jealousy, and everything to do with Caro taking offense to me expressing my opinion of her yellow-bellied, good-for-nothing, coward of an ex-husband. Not that she'd asked for my opinion. But I'd shared it anyway. And in the process, we'd had "words." Truth be told, I missed Caro very much. And as soon as I got my brooch back from her, I planned on apologizing.

Let me start at the beginning. The feud was rooted in our disagreement of who was the rightful owner of a multi-jeweled brooch. A twenty-two carat gold basket filled with fruit-shaped precious stones wasn't only monetarily valuable, but was also emotional real estate. It had belonged to our Grandma Tillie — the calm in our crazy lives as young girls. She'd left the heirloom to her "favorite granddaughter." I knew Grandma Tillie meant me. That said, Caro believed just as strongly that meant her. From that day forward, we were at odds. My inability to keep my opinion about her ex-husband, Geoffrey, to myself only exacerbated the problem.

As for Addison, within ten minutes of arriving in our laidback town, she'd managed to destroy the unsteady relationship my mama and I had recently started to rebuild. Those damn love letters.

"Enough chitchat. Raider is waiting inside. I need to let him out to do his business. Now, stand back and don't offer him any treats. Your sassy cousin said to only give him a reward when he obeys."

"I guess he's going without," I murmured under my breath.

Betty shot me a look.

I shrugged. "Just calling it like I see it." Betty had rescued the rascally Saint Bernard pup a few months ago. I'd been worried she'd get hurt if she didn't learn how to control him. Her barely five-foot self would snap in two if she didn't teach him three simple commands — sit, stay, and down. I'd recommended she work with Caro, a local pet therapist.

Ever since, Betty's believed she and Caro are best buddies. Betty even interfered in a recent murder investigation thinking she was "helping" Caro and homicide detective Judd Malone, AKA Detective Hottie.

"I'll have you know he's been a very good boy. He hasn't knocked me over in two months."

"That's something, I suppose."

Betty pulled out a dried apple ring from

her pocket. "Now, watch this."

She opened the passenger door, then quickly jumped to the side. Raider sat at attention at the top of the four steps, tail thumping on the marble tile. Thick slobber dripped like ropes from the sides of his humongous mouth. I was impressed. I'd never seen him sit for longer than two seconds. Missy jumped up and barked.

"Stay," I said. She obeyed, but didn't take her eyes off Raider. I didn't either.

"Wait," Betty commanded. She stepped back, making room for him when he exited.

The Saint Bernard scooted his butt closer to the edge of the top step until his large front paws hung over the ledge. His face begged her to offer the dried apple.

"Good grief, he's going to fall out. Hurry up and give him his treat."

"Good boy. Come." Betty slapped the side of her thin leg.

Raider didn't wait to be told twice. He bounded out of the motorhome with one leap, landing inches from Betty. Missy shifted until she leaned against my leg.

Betty tossed the dried apple ring straight up; Raider snapped it out of the air with one bite.

"Good dog." Betty buried her face in his furry neck. "Good boy."

"He's come a long way. You both have."

"I told you he was a good dog. He just needed someone to believe in him." Betty's face beamed with love and pride. I was relieved she'd been taking Caro's advice.

Betty stepped back into the RV and grabbed his leash off the passenger chair, then snapped it on his collar. She walked him to my front lawn. He marked just about every bush and the mailbox post before he ran out of urine. There was something to be said for female dogs.

"Are we ready to go?" I picked up my duffle bag full of T-shirts, socks, a couple of pairs of jeans, and toiletries.

Betty pulled a rag from under the passenger seat and quickly wiped the drool off the floor. Once she was finished, she loaded Raider into the RV. He trotted toward the back and jumped on the leather couch. He sprawled out, claiming his territory. Missy and I entered next. We both stood there for a moment, taking in the interior. I was awestruck. It was as elegant and lush as any mansion in Orange County.

Leather couches, reclining chairs, a fireplace, a sixty-inch TV, and a ceiling fan. And that was just the living area.

Betty stood behind me. "Isn't that a hoot?

We're going to have fun, Cookie. Don't you worry."

I tossed my bag and favorite black cross-body handbag on a reclining chair. "Let's get settled and head out."

After a few adjustments, rearranging the dogs, and convincing Betty she wasn't driving, we were finally ready to leave. I buckled my seatbelt with a decisive snap before I started the RV.

"Wait!" Betty jumped up and pulled a plastic Saint Bernard bobble-head from her purse. She spit on the rubber cup on the bottom then smashed it onto the dashboard.

"Let's rock 'n roll, baby," she sang out, pumping her fist in the air.

I burst out laughing. "What does that even mean?"

She shrugged. A mischievous smile lit her face. "I have no idea. I've always wanted to say it."

I shook my head. "Sit down and put on your seatbelt."

After triple checking I wasn't about to cause a five-car pileup, I pulled away from the curb and headed toward Laguna Hills.

Had we known about the pileup we were about to encounter, we might have thought twice about glamping under the stars for a week and stayed home instead.

Chapter Two

We rolled to a stop at the park ranger's station. Our massive RV dwarfed the park office to dollhouse size.

"I'm telling you, this is the wrong place. Look at it. It's brown. Dead. This is not glamorous." Betty sucked in a deep breath through her nose. "Gag. It even smells like death."

Earthy. Dusty. A faint lingering scent of campfire smoke clung to the air. But in no way did it smell like death.

She'd been convinced we were heading in the wrong direction when I didn't hang a right on El Toro Road. I'd explained I was not about to drive a forty-one foot motor coach through the middle of Laguna Hills. I didn't care about shaving ten minutes off the route. I cared about getting us there in one piece.

That said, Betty was right about one thing — it was far from glamorous. California was smack dab in the middle of the worst drought in history. I expected a brownish landscape. I didn't expect a vast dry canyon with a smattering of sycamore shade trees and cacti clusters.

I wasn't much for dirt and dust either, but what made me want to turn the bus around and head home was the big brown sign that read, "Warning! Mountain Lion Country. A Risk!"

Where the hell's bells were we? I thought I'd left the big cats back in Texas.

The park ranger strolled toward the RV. I rolled down the window.

"Good morning, ladies. What can I do for ya?" His tenor voice shot into the vehicle like he was about to spring a joke on us any second. I guess the punch line was welcome to Laguna's version of Death Valley.

"We're here for the ARL event. Betty Foxx and guest, Melinda Langston."

With his head down, Ranger Elliott, according to the name tag sewn on his drab green uniform, pawed through multiple pages of paper clamped in a wrinkled mess on the clipboard he held. "Do you ladies have dogs with you?" He never looked up. Just kept mauling through his lists.

"Two. We've already provided licensing and vaccination information to the ARL."

32

He made a couple of notes on his paperwork, then looked up. "Take the first road
to the left and follow the signs." His brown
eyes hinted at some unspoken joke as he
handed me a packet of papers. "You can't
miss it." The last part he'd said with a hint
of sarcasm. The whole interaction totally
threw me. I wondered what it was all about.

"About that sign," I started. He looked in
the direction I pointed. "Are there really
mountain lions here? Is this safe for the
dogs?"

Betty unfastened her seat belt and lurched
toward me. I leaned back just in time as she
stretched across me, sticking her head out
the window. "Forget the dogs, what about
us? Am I going to get dragged out of my rig
in the middle of the night?"

He jutted his chin. All humor and sarcasm
evaporated into the warm air. "Ma'am, your
dogs will be safe as long as you keep them
on a leash and stay in the area specifically
marked for your event. There is one marked
trail for your group. All other trails are off
limits. If you're caught on those trails with
your pet, you'll be asked to leave. No excep-
tions. You're more likely to encounter a
rattlesnake than you will a mountain lion."

"I hate snakes," Betty and I said simulta-
neously.

"Don't forget to pick up after your dog. Just because this is the outdoors, it doesn't mean you can leave your pet's waste. By doing so, you'd upset the delicate balance of the ecosystem at the park." Once he finished his lecture, he tipped his hat, turned his back, and returned to his shack.

I was offended. Doubly offended. First, he called me "ma'am." I was barely thirty. Second, he assumed he needed to explain the need for me to clean up after my dog.

Betty grumbled, returning to her seat. "I didn't like that guy the minute I saw him. He's got small eyes."

I tossed the papers to Betty. "What does that have to do with anything?"

"It's a fact. Most serial killers have small eyes."

"You're making that up."

"Maybe. But you thought about it for a minute." Her merlot-colored eyebrows bobbed up and down.

I stared at her for a couple of seconds. "Ranger Elliott has an attitude, but he's not a killer."

"If he goes all *Friday the Thirteenth* on us, remember I called it first."

"If that happens, we have bigger issues than you being right." I put the RV in drive and pulled away from Ranger Bad Attitude.

Great, not only did we have to keep an eye out for mountain lions, but snakes as well. This day just kept getting better. Not.

We followed the paved road for half a mile. The hillside was nothing but brown dead grass and dirt, with a smattering of dull green shrubby trees. I was beginning to get worried. Betty, on the other hand, was ready to abandon ship.

"We've been had," she huffed.

We turned a corner and suddenly it was like we were characters in the movie *The Wizard of Oz*. You know that part when the movie changes from black and white to color? We were seeing it in real life. I don't know how they'd managed, but someone had laid lush thick sod in the middle of a four hundred yard semicircle of dry, dusty ground, transforming the landscape from sprawling dirt to plush green grass. Seriously, this grass was barefoot worthy.

A mix of RVs and large white canopy tents staked their claim around us. Planters spilling over with vibrant flowers were placed at each campsite. White Christmas lights were wrapped around tent poles, and paper lanterns were strung between the sleeping quarters, with multi-colored flags hanging from the tent ropes.

I'm not going to say it was breathtaking,

but the kaleidoscope of colors was a striking contrast to the brown wasteland. I sighed heavily, relieved I wouldn't be glamping it up in a dirt bowl.

"That's amazing!" Betty shot up. Or at least she tried to; her seatbelt yanked her back against the seat with a loud thwack. "It's a mirage."

A handful of people and dogs milled around the open grass area. They seemed to be enjoying themselves; the dogs were playing, and their owners smiled as they gestured toward the RV and tent sites.

"Why would you be hallucinating? It's the camp."

The heavy canvas sides of all the tents were pulled back, revealing hardwood floors, thick red Persian rugs, and king-sized beds with fresh linens. Vivid colored throw pillows and Moroccan lanterns strategically littered the floor.

"Why didn't you sign up for one of those?" I asked.

"How was I supposed to know the tent would be just as swanky as the RV? Besides, you weren't even coming, so you don't get a vote. Pull in and let's get out."

"Hang on. What's our camping number? It's on the paperwork Ranger Bad Attitude gave us."

Betty rustled through the paper. "Twenty-three."

That was easy enough to find; there were five empty spots left, and ours was right on the end. I backed us up and pulled onto the long slab of dirt meant to be our camping site.

And here I'd thought Betty had overdone it with the size of the RV she'd rented, but from the look of the other campers, ours was on the small size. I put the RV in park, and set the emergency brake.

I looked at Betty. "Now what?"

"What do you mean, now what? We get out, snoop around those tents, and find out when we eat."

Hey, don't get me wrong, I was all about food. I loved a good roasted hot dog, broiled fish, and baked potatoes. But even I knew you couldn't just park the motorhome without some final touches.

"Don't we need to level this thing? What about our water, waste, electricity? You got the rundown. What do we do? How do we hook it up?"

"I didn't pay attention to any of that once I knew there'd be someone here to do it for me. Come on."

I rested my head against the steering wheel. Why? Why did I do this to myself?

While Betty grabbed the leashes, I double-checked that I had the cookbook foreword I'd thrown together at the last minute. The envelope was right where I'd tucked it inside the duffle bag. I know I was being obsessive, but I couldn't help myself. I was so close to ending this whole sordid affair. Pun intended.

Betty handed me Missy's leash. I slipped my crossover bag over my head and Betty grabbed her straw handbag.

"Are you going to carry that around all day?" I asked. It was big and looked heavy.

She clutched her bag against her chest. "A woman of my experience is never caught without her handbag."

Well, all righty then. I guess she was carrying her purse.

We all tumbled out of the RV, the dogs especially eager to explore. I closed the door behind us and locked it, slipping the key in my bag.

"Let's find the program director. What'd you say his name was?"

"Hudson Jones. Nice guy. You can't miss him. He's a cutie patootie for a short guy. Wears a tan fedora and khakis."

"I'm just curious. Do you judge all men by how good-looking they are?"

"Not at all," she deadpanned.

I waited for the smart-alecky comment to follow up her denial, but she silently returned my stare.

"Just so we're clear. I don't believe you," I said.

We followed the stone pathway to the opposite end of the camp toward the largest canvas tent, with an oak sign out front that read, "Headquarters." Our fellow campers called out boisterous greetings at our odd-looking foursome. We had to be the talk of camp: the tall lady and short bulldog, and the senior lady with the drooling St. Bernard puppy. We definitely stood out.

Missy was happy to walk at a normal pace. Raider, on the other hand, wanted to take the campground by storm. I had to hand it to Betty; she was doing a decent job of keeping him under control. Her time with Caro had paid off.

A set of four oversized blue paisley planters filled with snapdragons and chrysanthemums stood guard at the tent entrance. The heavy canvas doors of the headquarters tent were pulled back in an invitation to enter. Betty and Raider charged inside; Missy and I followed close behind. The dogs found a line of stainless steel bowls of water and immediately began to sample each one.

Standing before us was an average-looking

guy, of average height and average build, wearing khakis and a tan button-down shirt. His name was not Average Joe. He was Hudson Jones. And he was not short.

"Welcome, ladies." He pushed back his felt fedora and blinked dark black eyes. "How was your trip?"

"Longer than necessary." Betty shot me an exasperated look.

"It was fine. Is there someone who can help us with our rental RV? Neither of us know how to hook up the water or electricity."

"Sure, sure. Asher's out there somewhere. He'd be happy to help you." He rubbed the back of his neck. "That's too bad no one showed you that before you left the RV lot."

Betty had the decency to look sheepish. "I may not have been paying as close attention as I should have been."

He chuckled. "Short attention span?"

"You could say that," I said dryly.

"Let's talk about today. What are the plans? I heard there's going to be a s'mores feast tonight." Betty rubbed her hands together. Raider made his way to her side and laid down. Missy continued to sniff around the water bowls. She was looking for food.

"That's right. We've got a couple of fun

events for the dogs as well. At one o'clock, we'll start the games. We also have a spa. If you'd like to pamper yourself and your pet, you can sign up for massages and facials. There's also a group outing at three o'clock. We'll be taking a mile walk with our furry friends. Chase, our camp butler, will be around to anticipate your needs and providing you with beverages and snacks." His grand delivery reminded me of a game-show host.

"Sounds like fun. I was wondering if Addison Rae has arrived yet?" I asked.

"The chef? She's in the kitchen prepping. Do you know her?" His quizzical expression made me think I'd caught him off guard.

"Cookie got Addison the job," Betty chimed in.

"I didn't get her the job. I recommended her. And it's Mel, not Cookie."

"Gosh, you're the owner of the Bow Wow Boutique."

I offered a lame smile. "That's me." I don't think I'd ever heard a grown man say "gosh" before. I didn't know if it was sweet or creepy.

"Thanks for providing the prizes." He pointed to a large cardboard box behind him. "That was a heck of a great gesture."

He thrust his hand toward me. I shook it,

feeling guilty that he was excited about a donation I knew nothing about. Judging by the size of the box, Betty had been very generous.

I looked at Betty. "I hadn't realized we provided the prizes."

"Did I forget to mention that? You know my memory isn't what it used to be. Short attention span. Speaking of forgetting, I have something for you." She patted the oversized pocket on her chest. "Remind me to give it to you later."

It was probably a dried apple ring. I'd seen her stuffing her pockets with them before we'd left the RV.

About Betty's memory — it was fine. Until she didn't want it to be. I turned my attention back to Hudson. "I'm glad we could help. I'm looking forward to seeing what we donated." I ended on a light laugh, hoping he'd realize I wasn't upset with him. "This is Betty Foxx. She's the one who put the donation in motion. And these are our dogs, Missy and Raider."

"I'm Hudson, or Hud if you like, the program director. If you have any questions about what we're doing, find me. Don't be surprised if you see the media around. We got word late last night that Channel 5 is sending a reporter to the event."

42

I tried not to show my dismay. "Callum MacAvoy?"

Why couldn't he keep his perfectly shaped nose out of my business? I know, I know. I'm the one who told him about Addison in the first place. But really, why couldn't he have conducted that interview last week? Damn procrastinator.

He nodded with a smile. "That's him. If you see him, I hope you'll grant him a short interview."

Not on his life. "I'd be happy to. We won't keep you any longer. I'm sure we'll see you around."

"I'll find Asher and ask him to give you a hand." Hudson Jones tapped his fedora. "Don't forget, one o'clock for the food toss. Three o'clock for the trail walk."

"Wouldn't miss it." I was normally a horrible liar, but since Addison's appearance in my life, I was becoming alarmingly good at it.

I should have taken that as a sign of things to come.

We didn't need Asher after all. Once we left headquarters, the other RV campers were waiting for us and offered to help us connect to the utilities, and show us which buttons to push to extend our four (yes, you

43

read that right) slide-outs. Apparently, correct camping etiquette is to introduce yourself to your neighbors, offer assistance to those with less experience, and give tours of your RV. Personally, I think they were just nosey, but hey, so was I. I'm the last person to judge.

There's even a "Golden Rule." Yeah, it's the same rule my parents taught me — "Do unto others." But in this community, it seemed to be adhered to religiously. We heard story after story about saving someone's awning in a windstorm, tucking lawn chairs inside when it rained, or rolling up car windows. All to be a part of a greater solution rather than a perpetual problem. Why isn't that the ideal in any community?

Like all good neighbors, no one outstayed their welcome. Betty and I promised to stop by each person's site later and take a tour of their motor home or glamping tent.

I needed to find a way to ditch Betty for a short time so I could deliver the cookbook foreword to Addison, and get my letters in return. Luckily, Betty and I had met a charming couple — Veronica Scutaro and her pooch Harry, a Japanese Chin.

Veronica seemed like a friendly fellow camper, and a possible new customer for Bow Wow Boutique. Although she lived in

Dana Point, she hadn't really shopped at the local merchants in downtown Laguna. Betty was about to change that. She'd never met a pet lover she couldn't convert to a Bow Wow fanatic. God bless her love for retail.

Harry was a black-and-white puff-ball clown. He loved attention. He was adorable, hopping on all fours like a bunny, begging for a treat. It was obvious he had his human wrapped around his tiny paw. Betty shanghaied Veronica after everyone else left, happily chatting her up about toenail pawlish and chew toys.

Missy wasn't much for long walks. As a bulldog, she easily overheated, so letting her nap in the air-conditioned RV made her happy and kept her safe. I promised her we would play the food toss game that afternoon. She promised me she'd stay awake for most of it. What can I say, the girl enjoyed naps as much as she liked food.

I grabbed the envelope from my bag, folded it in half longways, and shoved it in the back pocket of my True Religion jeans. I tugged my T-shirt down, ensuring I'd covered the evidence. After tossing my purse into a bedroom nightstand, I tucked my cell phone in my front pocket.

I slipped past Veronica and Betty who

were chilling on lawn chairs under the awing. Veronica was telling Betty about a missing butterfly bracelet that she believed to have been stolen a few weeks ago. There was no doubt in my mind Betty was concocting a scheme to somehow recover it.

I nodded hello to a number of my new neighbors as I trudged across the cushy grass in my Merrell hiking shoes. I preferred my motorcycle boots, but the hiking shoes were a comfortable substitute.

The kitchen was located in the middle of the campground. It was actually a large yurt with a round wooden platform, canvas walls, and a raised rooftop that included a domed skylight. Perfect for stargazing at night. That was, if one found themselves huddled in the kitchen area.

I was about to walk inside when my cell phone rang.

"Hello?" I answered without looking at the caller ID.

"Hi, darlin'." It was my mama, sounding all sweetness and light.

"This is a bad time."

She sighed heavily in my ear. "It's always a bad time. Especially lately. Stop being so contrary, it will give you wrinkles. Speaking of Grey, are you two back together yet?"

Since we weren't talking about my ex, I

46

ignored her attempt to pry into my love life. Or the lack thereof. I tried to find something humorous about the whole "Mama" situation. Instead, I got nothing but a bad mood, and it was all Mama's fault. That's not exactly fair, but it was the truth.

When I was twenty, rumor had it my mama had sex with a judge in order for me to final in the Miss America pageant. Mama referred to it as *The Incident.* At the time, I didn't want to believe it. Even after all these years, I'd held out hope that she'd just let me believe the worst about her because she liked the drama. I loved my mama, but she was a martyr at heart. To her, any attention was good attention.

Today, the truth would come out. And my mama was tucked away in our family home, unaware of the drama unfolding almost fifteen hundred miles away. It was better that way.

"Melinda Sue, are you still there?"

I stepped away from the circular tent. "I have to go. Love ya, Mama." I returned the phone to my pocket and took a deep breath to regroup my scattered emotions.

Shoulders squared, head held high, I entered the lion's den.

In the far back, Addison stood behind a long butcher-block table, prepping for the

47

day's meals next to a tall, dark-haired man with tattoo sleeves. Both were dressed in plaid short-sleeved shirts, jeans, and matching black aprons.

The yurt was filled with tension. I guess Addison brought out that trait in most people she had close contact with. On the surface, Addison was a pretty girl. Unfortunately, her personality was as toxic as a *Housewives* reunion episode.

She pulled out a black notebook from the large pocket of her apron and flipped the pages, then rattled off a list of ingredients.

"I thought tonight was the lamb kabobs?" The man's voice sounded strained.

"As head chef, I changed my mind. We're having lamb stew. You can make kabobs tomorrow. Stew is a better choice for the first night. We can cook on the open fire in front of the group. It will add to the experience."

I grudgingly agreed with her assessment. I made a mental note she'd said "head chef" and not "pet chef." Seemed she'd managed to wrangle herself a promotion. Addison was probably a fine cook. I'd even give her the title of "chef." She just sucked at being a human being.

Tattoo Man slammed a cookie sheet on the butcher-block counter. "Stew is not a gourmet meal. Besides, we don't have the proper ingredients. They weren't on your list for the shopping trip."

"As the sous-chef, it's your responsibility to anticipate what I need. Figure it out or I'll replace you. I'd suggest you make a list and find a way to get to the store." An ugly sneer formed on her face. "I heard Pepper Maddox is camping with us. She'd snatch up your job in a heartbeat."

Addison was about to unleash more venom, but when she looked up and saw me standing in the doorway, she pressed her lips together.

The sneer quickly transformed into a smirk. "Melinda. You decided to come after all."

There's nothing scarier than someone with a screw loose.

"You knew I would."

"I hope you haven't been waiting long."

"Just long enough to hear we're having stew for dinner."

Without breaking eye contact with me, she dismissed the sous-chef. "Redmond, start peeling the onions and potatoes out back. Be careful with the onions, they're dangerous for dogs."

"I'm fully aware of what the dogs can eat." Disgust clouded his eyes.

I couldn't blame him. I hated her too. Addison waited until he disappeared before she said, "Did you bring it?"

"It's the only reason I'm here." I pulled the envelope from my back pocket and held it against my chest. "Did you bring the letters?"

"Of course. But I don't have them with me right this second. I thought you wanted to keep the letters quiet? Was I wrong?"

I maintained a neutral expression and an even tone. "I want to get this over with. The sooner the better."

"I can't just leave, Melinda. I have a job to do. You, of all people, can understand that."

"I don't care. You've strung this out long enough. Let's go to your RV or wherever you're staying and get my letters."

Her eyebrows disappeared under her blue bangs. "Don't you mean your mother's letters?"

I sucked in a breath and forced myself to stay calm. "Right," I said through clenched teeth.

"To my father." Addison brushed her hands on her apron, in no big hurry to get moving. "I've read them, you know. Each one. More than once. You can't blame me. At first, I thought they were letters between

50

my parents."

My stomach churned, imagining what my mother may have written to her lover. Not only had she had an affair, she'd penned a written proclamation of her love for someone other than her husband. What the hell was she thinking? I didn't want to read the letters, and I didn't want anyone else to read them either. Especially my daddy.

I shook my head. "You're going to give me those letters like you promised or I'll find them myself."

Hudson Jones traipsed into the tent, interrupting us. "Hey, Addison. How are you coming with those sweet potato chips for the Toss Across Challenge?" He skidded to a halt right next to me. "Gosh, sorry. I didn't see you. Mel, right?"

I tucked the envelope in my back pocket. "That's all right." Lordy, I hope he hadn't heard me sound like a bad imitation of an angry mob wife.

He pushed back his hat and looked at Addison. "The game starts in an hour. Are you ready?"

"Melinda, why don't we meet up later? In the meantime, you should relax. This could be a fun weekend if you let it."

It galled me to no end that she sounded like the calm and reasonable person in the conversation. I ignored her advice about unwinding. "When and where?"

"After the game. We can take a walk along the trail. We'll meet at the first resting point."

Privacy. I hated to admit it, but it was a good idea. Betty wouldn't be hovering around, wanting to know what I was doing. Random people wouldn't barge into the middle of our tête-à-tête.

"Two o'clock." I spun around and stomped out of the tent past the sous-chef.

"I'll get them back. One way or another," I muttered.

CHAPTER THREE

In the words of Grandma Tillie, Betty "came out swinging her purse like a southern church lady" during the Toss Across Challenge.

No one, and I mean no one, other than Betty and Raider stood a chance at winning a game that involved a dog and his owner standing five feet apart, catching sweet potato chips. Raider didn't miss one. And Betty made sure everyone knew. Most people seemed to take her excessive celebration in stride. A few others weren't so forgiving.

I pulled Victory Dance Betty and Raider away from the group of other contestants she'd been bragging to. "You need to relax. You won a game. Oprah didn't gift you with a brand new car."

"Nah. She doesn't do that anymore. You need to keep up with your pop culture, Cookie."

I rolled my eyes. "Be a gracious winner and a good neighbor. Rein it in. Stop being a blowhard."

Betty blinked. "Oh." She looked over her shoulder at her new friends. An awkward silence fell over the group. She shrugged helplessly. "I was excited."

I gave her a quick hug. "I know. I've been there. Trust me. Just go back and tell everyone they did a great job. When you and Raider win the next game, keep your celebration to a couple of fist pumps, and hoots and hollers."

She regarded me seriously. "You're a good friend."

I smiled. "Don't let that get out."

She slipped her arm through mine. "I have a surprise for you. You're going to like it."

That was a change of topic I wasn't expecting. "You've mentioned that," I replied, cautiously.

Betty could have a pocketbook full of dollar bills or backstage passes to a Van Halen reunion concert. I always expected the unexpected where Betty was concerned.

"Come with me." She tugged on Raider's leash for him to stand.

I checked my watch. "I have to meet Addison . . . can you give it to me after that?"

"What are you meeting her for?"

I patted her hand. "It's not important. I shouldn't be long. Keep Missy with you, okay?" I handed her the lead. "I'll be back and then we'll do whatever you want."

She narrowed her eyes. "Really?"

I nodded. "Just give me an hour."

"What if I want to get a massage?"

"That sounds like heaven."

"We'll go horseback riding. I haven't done that for over twenty years."

I laughed. She'd change her mind three more times before I got back. "If that's what you want to do."

I left Betty and the dogs and rushed past our fellow glampers with a shout good-bye. My adrenaline was pumping out of control. This was it. For the first time since Addison rode into town on her larger-than-life broom of malice, I felt as if the end was within reach.

Finding the trail was easy. Since it was the only trail our group was allowed on, it was heavily marked and right off the roadway. The first resting point was about a quarter of a mile into the walk, which I reached easily within five minutes. I checked my watch — one-fifty-five. I wasn't that early.

I lifted my ponytail off my neck, sweating in the early afternoon heat. It was unseasonably warm. I shielded my eyes from the sun's glare. I cast about for even the smallest amount of shade. Nothing. In my haste to be early, I'd left my sunglasses and a hat at camp. I reminded myself to apply fresh sunscreen when I returned to the RV.

I paced back and forth for what seemed like an eternity. It was just me and the chirping birds. The absence of human chatter and hiking footsteps filled my ears. I slapped the envelope in my hand. Where was she? I began to have a sick feeling I'd been played. Again. I felt like complete idiot. Or as my daddy was fond of saying, I was dumb as a post.

Why in the world had I believed for one minute Addison would keep her word now? When she'd yet to prove an ounce of trustworthiness and reneged on our agreement at every turn. The blackmailer would willingly give her last breath to lead me on for one more day.

I kicked a rock into the sad green bushes on the side of trail. She'd never had any intention of handing over those letters. Heck, for all I knew, they really were love letters between her father and mother.

I ran my hand over my face. I knew that wasn't true. Addison had shown me the envelopes and one of the letters. I recognized my mother's handwriting. Plus, Addison knew things about that week during the pageant that only people who were there would know. Or who'd written about it in a letter. Like what restaurant my mother had eaten at the night the scandal had broken. What we were both wearing when we'd argued that night.

And most importantly, what I'd said to my mama when we were alone.

I checked my watch for the last time. Two forty-five.

She wasn't coming.

I charged back to the glamping ground, determined to ransack Addison's sleeping quarters if I had to. Once I'd learned where she was staying. Dang. Dang. Dang. I couldn't believe I'd let her get the best of me.

I was so focused on berating myself for foolishly believing Addison's lies, I almost ran Betty over in front of the showers and restrooms.

"Holy cow. I'm sorry, I was preoccupied." I steadied my petite assistant before she tumbled over.

"Are you trying to give me a heart attack?" She clutched her chest. "Where have you been?"

Her face was flushed. The dogs were

nowhere in sight. Betty was full of life and energy, not worry. My stomach knotted. I grabbed her delicate shoulders. "What's wrong?"

Betty's gray eyes were huge. "It's the pet chef. She's dead."

My throat constricted so tightly I barely got the words out. "What do you mean, dead?"

"Murdered, Cookie. Someone stuck a fork in her. She's done."

CHAPTER FOUR

I pulled Betty into our RV for a full-on discussion, not just the highlights.

Missy and Raider greeted us with barking and spinning. I bent down and loved on Missy briefly before she waddled back to her dog bed. Raider realized he wasn't getting a treat, so he moped toward the leather couch.

I tossed the envelope containing my foreword to Addison's cookbook onto the table. No need for that now. Addison was dead. I had so many questions. Who would have killed her? Where were the letters? How would I get my hands on them now?

"Melinda, you're shaking." Betty shuffled to my side. She grabbed my hands and held them firmly between hers.

I glanced down. Sure enough, I looked like I was on a caffeine high. Then it registered what she'd said. "You called me Melinda."

"So?"

I tilted my head slightly. I'm not sure I'd ever figure her out. "The last time you called me by name, you were trying to convince me that you hadn't killed someone."

She planted hands on her narrow hips. "Was I lyin'?"

Not that long ago, Betty had been a suspect in a murder during a Dachshund dash. It was the first time she'd ever called me by my first name. At the time, I had feared she was hiding evidence about the murder. I was half right. She had a secret, but it wasn't the worst-case scenario I'd concocted in my head.

She inched up on her toes in an attempt to look me eye to eye. She failed miserably, but I appreciated the effort. "I got to tell you something," she said with a quiet intensity. "Word around camp is that you did it."

I matched her tone, "Did what?"

"Work with me here. You killed Addison."

I stepped back, holding my hands in front of me in defense. "Oh, no. That's ridiculous. I may not have liked her, but I did not kill her. Who's saying that?"

She pushed her lips together silently, debating if she should rat out her new friends or keep her mouth shut. Let's just say no one would describe Betty as someone who "spoke less" and "smiled more."

"Let me explain. When I say word around camp, what I mean is, *eventually* people are going to think you were involved once word gets out that you were jealous of her and you didn't like her."

"I was *not* jealous of her."

"You didn't like her."

Because she was blackmailing me. A legitimate reason if I'd ever heard one. "What does that have to do with anything? If I was someone who rammed a fork in everyone I didn't like, I would have started much sooner than Addison. Besides, I was supposed to meet her . . ." *Oh. My. God.* I felt the blood drain from my face.

Betty pulled a notepad and pen from the end table. "Cookie, we need to get our stories straight before the coppers get here. I didn't tell anyone you were meeting that pet chef. What do you want me to say?" She set the paper on the counter, ready to write down whatever I told her to.

I grabbed the pen and slammed it down. "Stop that. Don't talk to anyone. We wait until Malone gets here, and then we spill our guts."

"He ain't coming here. This isn't Laguna

Beach. This is The Hills. The Laguna Hills police will be in charge."

I knew that. Since when was Betty the one who made sense? "We talk to them and no one else. I wasn't even around here. I was waiting for her on the trail."

I twisted my ponytail around my fingers, wracking my brain for anyone who could corroborate my alibi. No one, not a single soul, had walked that trail the whole time I'd been waiting. I rubbed my temples. At the time, I'd thought that was a good thing. Now I'd learned I was alone because everyone else was gawking at a dead body.

"Who found her?"

Betty looked down. "Well, about that. Before I tell you, promise you won't get upset."

"I make no such promise." I needed to sit down for this. I parked my backside on the edge of the booth in the dining area.

She sighed dramatically. "Fine. I was talking with my new friends and I sort of got distracted. I dropped the leashes at some point, and the dogs went for a walk by themselves."

I did a double take. Missy was curled up tightly, snoring away in her bed. "Go on."

"When I realized they'd wandered off, I went looking for them. It's a good thing I stopped by the spa to check on prices for that massage you promised me, because that's where I found the pet chef. Lying on the massage table with a fork stuck in the side of her neck. I think I'd rather see dead people who've been shot."

I didn't bother to correct her about the massage. My stomach turned as I realized where her story was heading. "But you obviously found Missy. Since she's right there." I almost managed to keep from raising my voice.

"Sure. She was here, lying in front of the door waiting to be let inside."

"With Raider?"

Betty shifted. "Well, he was missing for some time, but I found him in the kitchen tent, rootin' around for an afternoon snack. By the way, can you spot me some cash? A hundred should cover it. I need to buy a couple of legs of lamb."

At some point during her story, my mouth dropped open. I snapped it shut. "Did you call 911?"

"No. I told you, the dogs were fine."

"Not for the dogs. For Addison!"

Betty blushed. "Oh. I may have frozen and screamed like a little girl when I first saw her."

I swear I'm not a bad person, but I did

giggle just a little as I pictured what that looked like. I'm sure it was nerves that made me laugh. "Has *anyone* called 911?"

"Of course." Betty looked offended. "Veronica called. She's pretty calm under pressure. By the way, I think I'll pass on the massage you promised me."

I shuddered. I wasn't all that excited about the idea myself. "You need to get back outside. The police are going to want to talk to you."

"Not as badly as they'll want to talk to you," Betty countered. "I have one more thing to tell you."

There was a knock on the RV door. We both jumped. The dogs barked. Good campground etiquette required that we quiet down the dogs. For Missy, that was a quick command to be quiet and lie back down. Raider wasn't so easy. When the simple "sit" command didn't stop his deep bark, Betty pulled out a dried apple ring from her jumpsuit pocket. That worked like a charm. Raider sat and immediately shut up. Betty counted to ten out loud then held it out for him.

She looked at the door. "What should we do?"

I didn't have a good feeling. I pulled out my cell phone.

"Who you calling?"

I quickly thumbed through my favorite contacts. I had two choices. I stared at Grey's name for a long time. Yes, we'd broken up. But if he knew I was in trouble — serious trouble — he'd come. As an undercover FBI agent for white-collar crimes, he knew a thing or two about working with law enforcement.

The knock came again, louder. Then the doorbell rang.

We had a doorbell?

The barking started all over again. I snapped my finger and pointed at Missy. She stopped the noise and hung her head. Betty didn't waste time going through all the proper steps this time; she tossed Raider a treat and that was that. I was pretty sure Caro had counseled against rewarding bad behavior.

"I'll peek out the window and see who it is." Betty loved to play cat and mouse games, and peering from behind a window shade, spying on an unsuspecting guest, certainly filled the bill.

I returned my attention to the phone, focusing on my contact list. My other choice wasn't any better.

"Oh, it's that sexy reporter," Betty cooed.

Damn. MacAvoy has been nothing but a

pain in my side since the day I met him. I heaved a sigh of resignation. I didn't have any other option. I needed expert advice. There was only one thing I could do. I swallowed my pride and placed the call. I closed my eyes and waited for him to pick up.

One ring.

Two rings.

"Detective Malone," the no-nonsense man barked.

I opened my eyes.

"It's Melinda Langston. I need your help."

CHAPTER FIVE

There was silence on the other end of the phone.

"Do I let the reporter in?" Betty continued to peek out the window.

I shook my head no and waved her off. "Are you sorry you answered your phone?" I asked Malone, hoping for a little levity before I unloaded on him.

"Yes."

MacAvoy knocked again, only this time louder. "I see you, Mrs. Foxx. I just want to ask you a couple of questions," he shouted through the door.

Betty dropped the shade. "He's awfully persistent. Maybe he's here to ask me on a date?"

"Are you still there?" I could picture Malone in his black jeans, black T-shirt, and stoic face. It was possible he'd hang up if I didn't speed it up and get to the point.

"Yes."

I hated his one-word answers. And now that I had him on the phone, I quickly realized this was one of those times when my impulsiveness wasn't doing me any favors. Really, what did I think he was going to do? Hop in his silver Camaro, drive up here, and handle the investigation? "Do you know anyone working homicide in Laguna Hills?"

A deliberate pause. "Why?"

I switched the phone from one ear to the other, stepping away from the RV door. "Betty and I are in Laguna Hills glamping. It's an ARL fundraiser. The event has been advertised all over town. I'm sure you've heard about it."

"Get to the point." I imagined him rubbing his temple, wishing for patience.

I glanced over my shoulder to find Betty watching me. "Right. Well, the chef was murdered."

"Hang up and call 911."

"Someone's already placed that call," I said quickly. "I-I . . ." I wasn't even sure what I wanted. I just knew if Malone was on the case, he'd listen to all the facts.

"Ms. Langston, are you in trouble?"

Yes. *The person who was blackmailing me is dead and I have no verifiable alibi.* That didn't seem like a confession best given over the phone to a homicide detective. Instead,

I said, "I'm not sure yet."

"You have two choices. Hang up and call a lawyer."

I really hoped it didn't come to that. "What's my other choice?"

"Hang up and call that fiancé of yours."

I groaned. "You do know we've broken up."

"I can't help you. That's not my jurisdiction. Stop being stubborn and call Mr. Donovan." And with that, he hung up.

After I ended the call, I slid my phone across the kitchen table. I sighed deeply, unsure what move to make next. I smoothed my hair back from my face. It had been six weeks since Grey and I had spoken last. He could be in town, or he could be in D.C.; he wasn't mine to keep track of any longer.

It was a crapshoot if he'd even take my call.

Betty huffed impatiently. "Did Detective Hottie give you a name?"

I turned to face her. "Nope."

MacAvoy pounded on the door again. The mere fact that he asked for Betty most likely meant he knew she had found the body. We couldn't continue to hide. It was time to face the annoying reporter.

I grabbed my cell from the table. "Don't fall under his manipulative charm. The only

69

answer you give him is 'no comment.' Got it?"

Betty nodded. She fluffed her hair, brushed off the bodice of her jumper, then patted her various pockets, primping for MacAvoy's camera.

I swept past her toward the exit. "Keep your head high, look straight ahead. Don't make eye contact with him. Let's go find out what's going on."

She inched behind me and grabbed a handful of my cotton T-shirt. "I have one more thing to tell you."

"In a minute." I swung open the door. "No comment, MacAvoy."

Only it wasn't the nosey reporter.

It was two tall, plainclothes cops who blocked our exit. "Ma'am, Laguna Hills Police."

"I lost your Granny's brooch," Betty confessed at the same time as a cool blond police officer showed me her badge.

I don't know how long I stood there, door open, mouth open, gaze bouncing between Callum MacAvoy, the two cops, and Betty.

In the end, Betty won my attention first. "Did you just say you lost my brooch?" Yes, that came out a wee higher pitched than was comfortable.

"I stol—" Betty eyed our unexpected

guest. "I retrieved it from your cousin. I wanted to surprise you with it here. Don't you worry. I'm on the case. I'll find it. It's got to be around here somewhere."

I shook my head. "I don't understand. Why did you have it?"

"I hate to interrupt this riveting admission of carelessness, but we're here to investigate a murder," the female officer said, all business. "I'm Detective Lucy Finn, and this is my partner, Detective Thomas Lark. May we come inside? We'd like to ask you both a few questions."

Who decreed all homicide detectives were devoid of charm and good humor? I nudged Betty with my elbow to back up and give me room to allow the officers inside. "We'll talk later," I whispered to her. She had some explaining to do.

A smidge of satisfaction warmed my heart when the frumpy male detective shut the door on MacAvoy, denying him entrance. Did Mr. TV really think he could waltz inside and listen to them question us?

I led them toward the living area and offered them a recliner. Betty kicked Raider off the couch and we sat side by side. Raider trotted to the king-sized bed at the back end of the rig and made himself at home.

Detective Lark pulled a brown notebook

from the inside of his wrinkled suit jacket. He mumbled to Detective Finn. She rolled her eyes, reached inside her perfectly pressed blue blazer, and handed him a pen.

"I want it back."

He snatched it from her with a sullen, "Yeah, yeah." He flipped the pages of his notebook quickly.

Out of the corner of my eye, I saw the envelope meant for Addison on the table. My heart raced. I willed myself to not draw attention to it.

Finn nodded toward Missy. "Whose dog?"

"Mine," I said.

"The Saint Bernard in the back is mine," Betty said proudly.

"Which one of you is Betty Foxx?" Lark asked without looking up from his notes.

Betty raised her hand like she was in grade school. "That's me."

"You found the victim?"

"Sure did. Nasty business finding dead bodies."

That made him look up mid-scribble. He rubbed his scruffy jaw. "What were you doing at the spa?"

"Cookie and I were going to get a massage. I stopped by to get available times." She rested her bony elbows on her knees, bending forward for a closer look at the detective. Lord only knew what she was about to say next. "You know, I bet if you told them you were a cop, they'd fit you in for a shave. I got twenty bucks that says you're a good-looking guy under those gray whiskers."

I coughed back my laugh. I swear Detective Finn snickered, but her lips never moved.

Lark loosened his retro floral tie until it hung a good three inches below his Adam's apple. "Everybody wants Rick Castle — until there's a real dead body stinking up the neighborhood. Back to real life, Grandma. Did you make an appointment?"

"You're a prickly one. I like that, so I won't hold it against you."

His face remained stoic. "Gee, thanks. Can you answer the question?"

"The place was empty. Except for the dead pet chef. Did she really die from the fork? That doesn't seem possible. Once, we found a drag-queen-plastic-surgeon strangled with a dog leash in front of our pet boutique. Maybe the pet chef was strangled first, and then the killer stuck her with the fork. Ya know, since she's a chef."

I closed my eyes and shook my head. When Betty got like this, there was no stopping her. The best you could hope for was to slow her down or maybe detour the conversation. As for the story she was currently spinning, Betty hadn't found Dr. O'Doggle. My best friend, Darby, and I had stumbled across him. But to correct her would only encourage her to continue.

He had either tuned her out or had ignored her as a batty grandma spinning stories. "Did you touch anything?"

"No, sirree. We've seen enough dead bodies to know to never disrupt the crime scene. That makes people like you even crankier."

I shot Betty a look to stop offering information.

Lark lowered his notebook and raised his brows. He was paying attention now. "How many crime scenes have you seen?"

Either she didn't get what I was silently communicating, or she didn't care. I'm pretty sure it was the latter. Betty just kept on flapping her lips. "This is my second. But Cookie here, she's seen th—" I kicked her with the side of my foot. "What'd you do that for?" she squeaked.

"I can speak for myself." I didn't need Betty throwing me under the bus in her attempt to be helpful. I already had my own issues, thank you very much.

The detectives looked at each other. Finn

stood, pointed her long index finger at me. "How about you and I talk outside?"

Sure, that *sounded* like a question, but I knew from experience with Malone, it was an order. Wonderful. Who knew what Betty would say once she was alone with Lark? I told Missy to stay, and then followed Finn to the front of the RV.

She opened the door, ramming it into MacAvoy's shoulder. "I thought I told you to leave."

"No, you never said I had to go. Callum MacAvoy, Channel 5 News." He held out his hand. Announcing where he worked was unnecessary; the station logo was sewn on his blue polo shirt.

"Beat it." She pushed past him without a second glance.

He stepped in front of me. "I want to talk to Betty."

I stepped out of the RV, closing the door behind me. "She's busy." I skirted past him and rushed to catch up to Finn.

Mr. TV kept step with me. "What about you?"

I cut him with a get-real look. "No time."

The detective stopped and spun around, the grass squeaking under her boot. "Scram."

MacAvoy blinked rapidly. "Excuse me?"

75

She pushed back her blazer, shoving her hands on her wide hips, revealing her badge and firearm. "We don't give interviews to the media. If we have information to share, we'll hold a press conference. Now beat it before I call over one of my bored officers and give him something to do."

Malone's dislike of the media couldn't compare to Finn's. MacAvoy opened his mouth but must have thought better about what he wanted to say. He snapped his mouth closed. With a curt nod, he slinked away.

He'd be back like a bad rash. There was no question about it.

Finn led us up the stone pathway to the headquarters tent. I paused at the threshold. The area had unmistakably been transformed into a temporary police command center. I recognized the investigative crime scene tool box and supplies strewn across the large tables against the sidewalls. The same equipment used by Laguna Beach's finest. A handful of uniformed officers huddled together, their low murmurs carrying a sense of gravity.

Finn pointed to a small makeshift desk at the back of the tent. Heads turned as we made our way through the area. I worried what type of reputation she had with her co-workers that she commanded their attention so easily.

She pulled out a creaky wooden chair and motioned for me to sit. She positioned herself directly across from me, leaned against the desk, and crossed her arms, her face unreadable, her tone neutral. "What's your name?"

"Melinda Langston."

"How did you know the victim?"

"She's new to Laguna Beach. I've been helping her plug into the community."

Her gaze locked on mine like she suspected me of lying. "You're the one who got her the job."

I willed myself to hold still and not squirm like an ant under a magnifying glass on a sunny day. Any move I'd make, the loose-jointed chair would give me away. "I *recommended* her for the job," I corrected.

"How long have you known each other?"

I shrugged. "A couple of months maybe."

"Why'd you recommend her?"

I blinked. "Excuse me?"

"If you've only known her for six or eight weeks, why would you recommend her for a job?"

"I — ah — I . . . she asked me to?" Anyone who knew me at all knew that was an excuse, not a reason.

77

Finn studied me with an intensity that should have been reserved for those who committed heinous crimes. The thought that she might think I fit into that category made my chest tighten. I forced air into my lungs.

"Do you do everything people ask you?" she asked.

"No."

"But you did this time?"

"Yes."

"Were you also responsible for getting the original chef fired?"

"What?" My legs twitched, and the chair moaned underneath me.

Someone had been fired because of me? Who? When? Before I could fully process that bombshell, Detective Finn continued her rapid-fire questioning. "Did Mrs. Foxx have anything to do with the murder of the victim?"

"No."

"How do you know?"

"She liked her. She didn't have any reason to hurt Addison."

"Did you like her?"

"Not really."

"But you 'recommended' her for the job. Someone you didn't like?"

I sighed. "Yes. Liking someone doesn't

factor into it if they're good at what they do. Addison is — was — a good chef."

"Do you know anyone who'd want to kill her?"

Her sous-chef came to mind, but I wasn't in any position to throw stones. "Like I said, I didn't really know her all that long."

"Right. Just long enough to get her the job here, resulting in the original chef, Pepper Maddox, being fired. Do *you* have reason to want the victim dead?"

Pepper Maddox. The name sounded familiar. Wait, what did she ask me? "What did you say?"

The tension was broken by a commotion behind us. For the first time since she started questioning me, Finn broke eye contact and looked over my shoulder toward the front of the tent where the hostile voice came from. Curious, I turned around to see what the hubbub was all about. That was a mistake.

"That's her!" It was the tattooed sous-chef, Redmond, shouting to a couple of uniformed officers. And he was pointing at me. "She's the one who argued with Addison just before she was murdered."

I whipped around and looked at Finn. That gawdawful look was back. She pushed away from the desk, straightening to her full height, and looked down at me. "I'll ask you again. Did you have a reason to want her dead?"

I swallowed hard and lied. "No."

The lies just kept coming and coming. Eventually, I'd pay for them.

CHAPTER SIX

I've always lived my life as an open book. I'm impulsive, curious, and loyal to a fault. Often, my snap decisions don't necessarily work out in my favor, but I've always owned up to my mistakes. If I were to psychoanalyze myself, that's probably why I've detested liars and people who keep secrets.

Now I'm one of those people I've chastised for their refusal to tell the truth. The irony wasn't lost on me. It was possible I'd harshly judged others when I should have given them the benefit of the doubt. Well, maybe just the secret-keepers. The liars were liars. Enough said.

Detective Finn had dismissed me with the order to stick around camp when she realized I wasn't going to divulge useful information. Not that this was the first time I'd ever been told to not leave town. On the bright side, Finn didn't threaten to throw me in jail. Yet. Detective Malone liked to dangle that temporary housing situation over my head at least once every two or three months. Along with telling me to stop sticking my nose in his murder investigations. Blah, blah, blah.

When it came to Addison's untimely death, the truth of the matter was, what I did know would reflect negatively on me. The knot in my stomach tightened as I realized I was probably a suspect in Finn's murder investigation.

I left the interview with two thoughts: get those letters before the police found them in Addison's personal effects, and talk to Betty about the brooch. I returned to the RV to find Betty and Raider gone. I breathed a sigh of relief to see my envelope on the kitchen table. I tucked it away in my bag. I wondered if the cookbook would still go to publication since Addison was no longer alive.

Betty had propped a note on the dining table to let me know she went to look for the brooch. I couldn't begin to wrap my mind around how Betty might have out-foxed my conniving cousin. Caro and I had been stealing the heirloom from each other for years. She was a master at locking it up and guarding it with her life. I was usually a master at finding a way to retrieve it. When had my feisty assistant managed to nab the brooch?

With Betty out looking for the pin, I turned my attention to finding Addison's sleeping quarters and retrieving my mother's letters. I pulled on a ball cap and my favorite Dior sunglasses. I put Missy on her leash and took her outside for a short walk to do her business while I asked around about where Addison had been staying.

I was a little taken aback at the hushed conversations and stares as Missy and I walked by. I waved at an older couple with a bouncy Pom on a pink leash. They ducked their heads, pretending they didn't see me. Dang. Betty may have been on to something. Rumors in an RV community spread faster than a prairie fire with a tailwind.

The spa was the closest activity tent to our RV. Using Missy's need to explore as an excuse, I edged toward the entrance, hoping for a peek inside. *No can do.* Yellow crime scene tape restricted access for unauthorized persons. That would be me.

Missy sniffed a row of tree trunks next to the window. I drifted along, eavesdropping on the two officers standing guard at the spa doorway. Unfortunately, they were talking about the Guns 'n Hoses softball charity event next week.

Missy tugged on her leash, ready to move on. I leaned down and patted her head. "Sorry, girl," I whispered.

I was about to walk away when one officer said, "Did they find the dog?"

His partner grunted. "Not yet. If I was in charge, I'd line up all the dogs and check their paws for blood. But hey, I'm just a uniformed cop. What do I know?" He punctuated the last part by thumbing his chest.

It sounded like there were bloody paw prints at the crime scene. Did that mean the killer had a dog? Was that why Finn was asking about our dogs? My heart sank. At some point, Raider and Missy had been lost. Who knew where they went or what they'd gotten into?

I looked down at Missy. At first glance, her paws didn't look bloody. The minute we were back in the privacy of our motorhome, I'd give her a thorough once-over.

The two cops resumed their talk about which baseball team was better; the Dodgers or the Giants. I scoffed silently. Everyone knew the Texas Rangers were the best. While they argued good-naturedly, I took the opportunity to bug out before we were noticed.

Head down, I turned, and smacked into Hudson. Hard. His fedora and my ball cap fell to the grass. My sunglasses smashed into the bridge of my nose, making my eyes water. I bobbled my sunglasses as I steadied myself after almost tripping over Missy.

Shoot. Why did I have to literally run into the one person other than Betty who knew I was going to meet Addison today? Had he ratted me out to Finn and Lark?

We both apologized for knocking into each other as we reached for our hats. I quickly slipped my glasses back on and shoved my cap on my head. I wasn't normally one to tuck tail and run, but I needed to concentrate on Addison's sleeping arrangements, not hang around to possibly be questioned about a meeting with Addison.

I mumbled a quick good-bye and led Missy away.

"Hey, wait a minute," he called out.

I pretended I hadn't heard him and continued toward the firepit where dinner was supposed to be served in a few hours. I hoped the sous-chef might be there prepping for dinner. Surely he'd know where his boss had been staying.

"Hey, Mel. Stop. Are you okay?" Hudson shouted as he ran after me.

Darn. He just wasn't going to give up. I slowed my steps and turned slightly. Missy grumbled. I'm sure she was wondering what

85

the heck I was doing.

It was possible Hudson wanted to make sure I was okay. I sighed. How bad could a confrontation be with a guy who said gosh as often as I said hell's bells?

As soon as he caught up, I smiled apologetically. "Sorry, I didn't realize that was you calling me."

"Who'd you think it was? Those two cops you were spying on?"

So he wasn't as naive as I'd initially hoped. I shrugged sheepishly. "If they wanted my attention bad enough, they'd pull out the handcuffs."

"When your glasses fell off, you looked like you've been crying. Are you okay? It's been a rough day."

His concern caught me off guard. He really was a nice guy. I motioned with my hand toward my face. "I'm fine. When we bumped heads, my sunglasses got shoved into my nose. What about you? Are you okay?"

He looked at me funny. "Oh, gosh. I'm fine. Not a scratch on me."

I smiled. "I was referring to Addison. It seemed like you were friends. Or at least friendly."

He glanced around as if to make sure we were alone. Veronica and Harry waddled past. She waved at us with a huge smile on her face. We returned her friendly greeting. My wave was less enthusiastic in an effort to keep her from stopping to chat. As if sensing we were going to be a while, Missy lay down in the grass and rested her head on her front paws.

Once Veronica was out of earshot, Hudson said, "It's disturbing. I'm sure you realize we have a killer on the loose at camp. My glamping event has turned into a horror movie. Some of the guests are claiming the trip is cursed with bad luck."

"Are you thinking about calling it off?"

He shook his head. "No. I'm not superstitious, and I don't believe in curses. Besides, the police want us all to remain here. The events are planned. It's just best to keep on rolling."

I liked his attitude. "Whatever I can do to help, let me know." I paused for a minute, then asked as casually as I could, "Addison had mentioned she was the head chef, not just the pet chef. Who will replace her?"

"Red Hardy, her sous-chef, will take over. Pepper Maddox is here — I could give her the job back," he finished, absentmindedly.

That's where I'd heard her name. "Is it true that she was fired so Addison could have the job?"

MacAvoy appeared out of nowhere. "That's a great question, Melinda. I'd like to know the answer to that myself."

The sun disappeared behind a cloud, casting a shadow over us. It was as if even Mother Nature knew that MacAvoy was a wet blanket.

"Where'd you come from?" I asked with a sour look.

"I was walking down the road toward my RV when I saw you. I thought I'd stop. See what you two are discussing so earnestly."

"Nothing that pertains to you. It's private."

"Ah, but you're wrong," he said to me before turning his attention to Hudson. "I don't believe we've met face-to-face yet. I'm the reporter from Channel 5. You've been expecting me." He flashed a you-can-trust-me grin.

Hell's bells. Hudson had mentioned MacAvoy was there to conduct interviews. I sighed deeply. This could only go one way — badly.

The men shook hands. "Yes, of course." Hudson pushed the rim of his fedora back, taking a closer look at MacAvoy. "It's a pleasure to meet you. Will you be camping with us?"

"I will."

There it was, the "badly" part. There'd be no getting rid of him now. Missy stood and shook, reminding me she was still there, and bored. Bulldog drool slapped my jeans. Yuck. I patted her head and told her to lie back down.

Mr. TV edged closer to the program director. "Back to Melinda's question. Did you fire Pepper Maddox in order to bring in Addison Rae for the head chef position?"

Hudson cleared his throat. He had to be rethinking his earlier enthusiasm about granting an interview to the media. A lopsided smile tugged on his mouth. "Gosh, you shouldn't take campfire talk so seriously."

My eyebrows lifted. He needed to know the truth before MacAvoy cornered him into saying something he'd regret later. "If that's not true, someone should tell Detective Finn she got bad info, because she mentioned it when she was questioning me."

His dark eyes blinked in surprise. "You've been questioned by the police?"

I tried to play it off. "It's routine. The police will talk to everyone eventually."

He nodded, pondering what I'd said. "Pepper wasn't exactly fired."

"You're saying she quit? That's not the story Miss Maddox gave me earlier this afternoon." Mr. TV continued to be his annoying self.

Even though I was also curious to hear the answer, Hudson was such a nice guy, I felt the need to warn him. He obviously had no experience in dealing with the police or reporters intent on digging up a sensational story.

"Before you talk, you should know Mac-Avoy has been known to keep a digital voice recorder in his pocket," I interjected before Hudson buried himself by over-sharing or worse, spoke in half truths.

"No jacket today. No recorder." He held up his hands in a show of innocence. I didn't buy it for a second. He could have tucked a small recorder in his jeans pocket with little effort. The polo shirt, probably not so easily.

"Pepper was reassigned to a different event. But she was fine with it. In fact, she's here as a guest," Hudson explained.

"Are you sure she wasn't upset?" Mr. TV nodded toward the spa. "Some people take their job very seriously. Don't you agree, Melinda?"

Well, good grief. Why was he dragging me into it? I wasn't sure what he was implying, but I didn't like the feeling of impending disaster he brought to the group. He was up to no good.

"You're a reporter looking for a story. I have no comment."

He smiled, enjoying my churlish response. What can I say? He brought out the worst in me.

He acted like I hadn't even spoke. He just continued talking. "When I saw you with Addison Rae, you were arguing. But before that, you left me a couple of messages recommending her for a local news segment. In fact, you were adamant she'd make a great story. Now she's dead."

Again, with the contentious undertone. "And?"

Hudson studied our faces intently, mine harder to read behind my sunglasses, but he was still able to pick up on the tension. "I'm sure Mel is just as upset as the rest of us."

MacAvoy's eyebrow cocked questioningly. *"Mel?"*

I laughed at his bewilderment over Hudson calling me Mel, yet I refused Mr. TV the same familiarity. He needed to get over the fixation about my nickname.

I shrugged. "I like him. Where's your cameraman?"

"He's here. Are you ready to give me an interview?"

"You know the answer to that. Why are

you even asking?"

"One day you'll need my help."

"Don't hold your breath," I muttered.

Hudson rubbed his neck. "I didn't realize you two knew each other so well."

I pulled off my sunglasses to ensure there was no confusion as to how I felt. "He tried to pin a murder on my assistant, Betty."

"I just reported the facts. She was a prime suspect in the murder," MacAvoy argued.

"Please. Malone never seriously thought she was guilty."

Someone's cell phone rang. No one made a move to answer it.

"Malone?" Hudson asked.

MacAvoy folded his arms across his chest. "Homicide Detective Judd Malone. *Melinda* has him on speed dial."

I rolled my eyes. He was such a tattletale. The cell phone rang again. I knew it wasn't mine — wrong ring tone. "Someone answer your phone already."

"Damn." Mr. TV fumbled with his cell as he rushed to answer the call before they hung up. "Mac." He spun around, to give himself a semblance of privacy.

"We need to get rid of him," I whispered to Hudson. He nodded in agreement. I motioned toward the campfire area. We quietly headed in that direction, leaving Mr.

TV to finish his call in real privacy. Missy was excited to be moving along.

We hadn't taken more than ten steps before MacAvoy was walking next to us. He addressed Hudson. "My cameraman is ready. I'd like to record our interview now. Shouldn't take more than fifteen minutes."

We stopped walking. Poor Hudson looked trapped.

"You don't have to do it," I chimed in. "You should check with Finn or Lark first."

Mr. TV shot me a flinty look.

Hudson considered my suggestion. "Seeing that Mel has prior experience in these matters, I'm going to take her advice. Let me consult with the police on what they'd like for me to share. I'll come by and see you before dinner. What's your site number?"

"Twenty-two. Right next to Ms. Langston, I believe. I guess I'll see you tonight." He stalked off, presumably to meet up with his cameraman sidekick.

"Thanks for the pointers," Hudson said, as we continued to make our way to the campfire ring.

I put my sunglasses on. "No problem. Don't take what he says as gospel. I won't go so far to say he lies, but he does seem to interpret facts differently than regular folks."

"You don't like him?"

"It's not that I don't like him. He's a pain in the neck. I'm sure some of that is the nature of his job. In general, I haven't had the best of experiences with the press. They tend to enjoy misrepresenting the reality of a true situation for ratings."

"I see."

He had no idea, and I wasn't inclined to go into further details.

"Now that he's gone, enlighten me. What's the truth about the relationship between you and Addison?"

I could feel him looking at me, but I refused to meet his gaze. "What do you mean?"

"What that reporter said about you arguing with Addison. That was true. When you first arrived today, I walked in on an argument between you two, remember?"

Oh, I remembered. I was hoping he'd forgotten. I stopped walking and faced him. I slipped off my sunglasses. "Whatever you think you walked in on, it wasn't what you thought."

"So you weren't planning on meeting Addison after the game?"

I sighed. "That's true. But she never showed. Did you tell the police about that?"

He locked eyes with me. "No. But maybe

I should have."

The intensity of his stare made me a little nervous. "I didn't kill Addison. I know you have zero reason to believe me, but it's the God's honest truth."

We stood in silence. The birds chirped, and a warm breeze rippled over the lawn. I had things to do and standing around wasting time was not on my itinerary for the afternoon. It was almost four o'clock, and I wasn't any closer to uncovering where Addison had been staying.

"Who do you think did that to her?" He sounded so sad, a little choked up. Like he'd lost a loved one. Was he tearing up? Would he be this emotionally upset if he knew she was a blackmailer?

I shook my head. "I don't know. Do you know how she died?"

"I've heard a couple of theories."

I waited for him to share more. He didn't seem very interested.

"Was she staying in a tent or did she have one of those fancy RVs?" I asked, finally finding an opening that wasn't obvious.

"She liked the tents."

I had guessed an RV. "Probably picked one close to the kitchen."

He shook his head. "She liked her privacy. Number five. The far end of the circle."

I just bet she wanted her privacy. Didn't all blackmailers? "Is that the one behind the headquarters tent?"

He looked past me and pointed. "I was on my way to clear out her belongings."

No, no, no. "Why so quickly?" My voice pitched slightly higher.

"Excuse me?"

"I mean, don't the police need to look through her personal belongings? Or do you just gather everything and turn it over to them?"

"Oh, no. Her agent, Sunday Hill, will be here to pick up Addison's property this evening." He checked his watch. "In fact she'll be here within the hour."

My mind whirled a mile a minute, looking for a way to get into her stuff.

He cleared his throat. "That was one of the reasons why I wanted to talk to you. I thought you might want to help. With you being the only friend she had here. But now I realize that wasn't accurate, and you're probably not the right person to ask for help."

I almost fell over myself. I grabbed his arm, stopping him from walking away. "Hey, like I said a few minutes ago, I'd be happy to help any way I can."

I'd do whatever I had to in order to get

my hands on my mother's letters, even if it might be a little hard with Hudson looking over my shoulder. I'd cross that bridge when we came to it.

CHAPTER SEVEN

Hudson, Missy, and I stood just a few steps inside Addison's tent. I had to admit, I wasn't sure what to expect, but the degree of disarray was on a level I hadn't seen before. Ever.

"I didn't realize she was a slob. No wonder you needed my help."

Hudson shook his head repeatedly. "No. This isn't right. She was messy, but not like this." He took a few hesitant steps farther into the tent, scrutinizing the mess with a look of disbelief. "Gosh, someone did this." He faced me, flushed. "Do you think it was the killer?"

"I have no idea."

He pulled off his hat and ran his fingers through his hair. He was more upset than I'd have imagined. He acted like someone with an emotional entanglement. Even though he wore a bright gold wedding band on his left finger, I had a gut feeling that hadn't stopped him from getting close to the now-deceased pet chef. It got me thinking.

"You seem to know Addison pretty well."

He settled the fedora back on his head, then shoved his hands in his pockets nervously. "As the program director, it's my responsibility to make sure my staff is happy, settled in, and has what they need for a successful week."

Reasonable. But what was more interesting was that he immediately felt the need to explain their relationship. He was feeling guilty about something.

"Were you dating?"

He blanched. "I'm married."

Married or not, Hudson and Addison had something going on. But since I needed his help more than I needed to push the point, I dropped it. For now.

I knew the right thing to do was to notify the police. But I was torn. I wanted those letters first. I watched Hudson out of the corner of my eye. He looked like he was about to faint.

"Do you need to sit down?"

"No. I'm fine." He never took his eyes off the dresser drawers, half of which were hanging on by an inch, ready to fall to the hardwood floor any second. "Do you think this is the police's handiwork?"

Hey, anything was possible. But it was unlikely. "I'll tell you what, why don't you go get the cops and bring them over here? Missy and I will wait, just to make sure whoever did this doesn't come back and finish what they started."

"That's a good idea." But he didn't move. Could it be he was also looking for something that might prove they were lovers? Was Addison demanding he choose between her or his wife? What if Addison was threatening to go public, and he killed her to keep her quiet?

I dropped Missy's leash and told her to lay. She sighed, but immediately obeyed. Poor girl. This wasn't turning out to be a very fun adventure for her. I carefully meandered around the tent, gingerly lifting clothes and bed linens off the floor with the toe of my boot, working hard to not move any items from its original place.

"What are you looking for?" he asked.

I jerked around. He was still rooted in place. I took a chance with one of those half-truths I had warned him about earlier. "The same thing you are." I watched his reaction carefully. His eyes widened and the vein on his neck popped.

"Maybe the police already have her cell phone."

Ding, ding, ding. We have a winner. Photos. Text messages. Emails. Proof of an affair. As a blackmail victim, I knew Addison kept that type of evidence, banking on the day she could use it to get what she wanted.

Hudson, on the other hand . . . I just didn't peg him as a killer. "If she had the phone with her at the spa, the police have it now." Sorry, buddy. Them's the breaks.

"Oh. You know a lot about this."

"Don't take this wrong, but this isn't my first crime scene. I've worked with the Laguna Beach police on a couple of cases." Lordy, I was about to be struck by lightning any minute. I was playing fast and loose with the truth.

He looked at me with a mixture of awe and worry. "I see."

"Hudson, the sooner you get the police, the sooner we'll know if we can clean up or wait for the crime scene techs to do their thing here too."

He nodded. "Don't leave."

"I wouldn't dream of it."

I waited until he was far enough away and was certain that he wasn't coming back before I began the search for the letters in earnest. It made it a little harder to find what you were looking for when the place you were searching was already a mess. I picked up a T-shirt from the floor and used it to steady a drawer as I searched inside. Nothing.

Under the bed. Under the rug. Under the pile of clothes strewn across the floor. Nothing. I had quickly exhausted my options. I was about to give up, when I spotted her backpack shoved behind a recliner in the corner.

I double-checked that Hudson and the cops weren't about to burst through the opening to the tent. With the coast clear, I quickly grabbed the backpack and unzipped it. A dirty apron, recipe cards, a water bottle, event paperwork Ranger Bad Attitude must have given her, an area map, a thumb drive. Buried under all of that, at the very bottom, was a small stack of envelopes tied together with a faded blue ribbon.

My heart raced. My hands started to sweat. Who was I kidding, it wasn't just my hands — my whole body was sweating like I'd spent the last twelve hours in a sauna. I sucked in a breath as I pulled out the stack of envelopes. My pent-up air came out in a rush.

There was my mama's name in the upper left-hand corner. I recognized the large flowery handwriting immediately. I pressed the stack of envelopes against my chest and closed my eyes.

Missy gave a lazy growl. She never growled. Someone was coming. I whipped around and peeked out the doorway. I heard voices; they grew louder as they drew closer.

I frantically zipped up the backpack and shoved it back behind the recliner where I'd found it. I stuffed the envelopes inside the waistband of my jeans against my sweaty hip and tugged my T-shirt, stretching the material as I made sure it covered the evidence. When I lowered my arm to my side, I brushed the letters, but they didn't move. Perfect.

I squatted to pat Missy on the head and promised her a treat when we got back to the RV. While I was down there, I checked her paws. Good news; they were clean. Maybe a little grass-stained, but no blood.

I picked up her lead and waited. It wasn't but a matter of seconds when Hudson and Finn entered. I swear my heart was beating so loudly I was certain everyone could hear it

"Detective Finn." I attempted to sound chipper, but my voice squeaked in a way that, had my mama heard, she'd have hustled me off to voice lessons. Dang. Why

103

hadn't Hudson grabbed a uniformed officer?

Her alert eyes narrowed suspiciously. "Ms.
Langston. Interesting that I find you here.
Alone." She wasn't any more excited to see
me than I was to see her.

I cleared my throat and pointed to Missy.
"Nope. Not alone. Just so you know, not
my idea. Hudson asked for my help."

"Which you happily obliged."

Of course I did. My mama raised me
right. Judging by her skeptical look, she
didn't want to hear about my upbringing,
so I kept my lips pressed together.

Hudson adjusted his hat. "Gosh, that's
the truth. We noticed right away there was a
problem. Melinda suggested I grab you and
she'd wait here to keep anyone else out."

Finn's top lip curled up. "I bet she did."

"No one showed up. I guess that's good
news. So, is this your handiwork?" I asked.

"No. Who do you think did this?"

I shook my head. "I have no idea. I'd start
with the person who killed her." I backed
out slowly. "Look, I don't want to get in the
way. I know how you feel about me hanging
around. Besides, I need to take Missy back
to the RV. She's been in the heat for a while
and is ready for some shade time."

"Did you touch anything?" Finn barked,

stopping me in my tracks.

Hudson and I exchanged a look. "No."

I imagined the Boy Scout program director had his fingers crossed behind his back. Not me; I was so used to the fibs that now they just rolled off my tongue automatically.

The detective pulled her two-way radio from her belt and called for a couple of uniforms and the crime scene techs. Once she'd placed her order for the worker bees, the queen bee shooed us out of the tent. Unlike me, Hudson wasn't so eager to escape.

"But I need to gather her belongings for her agent," he said.

"The agent can wait."

"You tell Sunday Hill she has to wait," he muttered under his breath. "How long will this take?"

"As long as it needs to. You can have her personal belongings when I release them. Got it?"

I didn't wait to hear his response. I ran to the motorhome, Missy huffing and puffing the whole way.

"Hang on girl. You can make it," I cheered her on.

We breezed past a group of campers returning from the trail walk. I had to admit, I was surprised it had still happened.

I realized it had been quite a while since I'd seen Betty. I wondered where she'd disappeared to, and how much trouble she'd managed to fall into.

We reached the RV quickly. I unlocked the door, and we jumped inside. We were immediately hit with ice-cold air. It felt heavenly. Missy trundled to the water bowl and lapped up the refreshing liquid. She plopped her paw in the bowl, knocking it over.

"Missy." She looked up, water dripping from her jowls. "If you're that hot, I'll give you a bath."

I pulled off my cap and sunglasses, tossing them on the kitchen counter. I refilled her bowl before wiping up the mess she'd created. Once she'd had her fill, she waddled over to her dog bed and sighed happily.

I snagged a bottle of water from the fully stocked fridge and drank deeply. The refreshing liquid hit the spot.

I pulled out the stack of letters and gripped them tightly. I sighed, contemplating what to do next. Should I call my mama? Should I read them? Maybe I'd just burn them. Lord knew the decade-old letters had already caused enough trouble.

I untied the blue ribbon, letting it fall to the table. I picked up the top envelope tentatively and held it. I don't know why I was pretending I wasn't going to read the letters, because I was. I was going to read each and every one, because I was glutton for punishment.

I opened the envelope and gasped. What the hell was going on?

I frantically opened all seven envelopes. Each and every one was empty.

Even in death, Addison had managed to get the best of me. As my Grandma Tillie would say, "she's more slippery than a pocketful of pudding."

Who had my mama's letters? More importantly, why would they want them?

CHAPTER EIGHT

Betty burst into the RV in a cloud of dust, Raider hot on her heels. Like Missy earlier, he raced for the water bowl. I was glad I'd refilled it.

Betty didn't make it any further than the living area. "Cookie, what are you doing in here? I thought you'd be out solving that pet chef's murder."

She was covered in dirt from head to toe. Thin twigs and sticks poked out from her fluffy white hair, and black smudges covered her cheeks. It occurred to me she could have finally gotten her hands on Callum Mac-Avoy and had her way with him. She'd been begging for a date since she'd met him.

"You look like you've been wrestling a pig. Where've you been? I was getting worried." I grabbed the same kitchen towel I'd used earlier and mopped up the water Raider splattered on the floor before it ran into the dirt surrounding Betty's shoes and created a mud trail.

"I told you what I was doing. I'm looking for your granny's brooch." She patted her bottom; puffs of dust filled the air.

"Stop that. Sheesh. Take it off and shake it outside. Did you find the pin?" Please, let something have gone right today.

She shook her head, loosening a clump of dirt. It landed on the marble floor with a thunk. "But I'm not done. In fact, I have a theory. I think someone stole it."

That was crazy thinking. "What were you doing with it in the first place?"

"Well, I had an appointment with that sassy cousin of yours and she was late. Actually, she was being held by a crazy murderer, but I didn't know that at the time. Anyway, her friendly neighbor let me into Carol's house to wait —"

"Caro."

"What?"

I smiled. "Her name is Caro, short for Carolina."

Betty huffed. "I know that. Do you want to hear the story or not?"

"Of course."

"Then stop interrupting me. Where was I?"

"Caro's neighbor let you inside," I prompted.

Betty pulled a few sticks from her hair and dropped them. "That's right. She let me inside. While I was waiting, I got bored, so I snooped around the house and found the pin. She's not as smart as she thinks she is, let me tell you."

I was about to explain that she shouldn't be breaking into Caro's house and stealing jewelry, even if it was mine, but the look on her face stopped me. She was so proud of herself for outsmarting Caro. I knew from experience it was an exhilarating feeling besting my cousin.

The dust was making my eyes itch. I rubbed them as I tried to make sense of everything. "That was months ago."

"I was waiting for the right time."

"And you decided this trip was the right time? Why not bring it to the shop like a normal person? That seems like a right time to me."

"Well, that's just boring." She emptied out her pockets, piling dried apple rings on the coffee table. "But then I lost it. I didn't mean too. It was an accident. See, I shoved it in my pocket." She patted her hip, releasing a small dirt cloud. "But it must have fallen out. I just don't know when that happened."

I stepped closer to remove the remaining

twigs from her hair. "Where were you looking? In the trees?"

"That's ridiculous. I was looking under the bushes, in case someone accidently kicked it. I looked around the rig, at the campfire, the trail, the bathrooms. Oh, wait until you see the bathroom. Amazing. It looks like a spa. I'm really digging the whole glamping gig."

I pulled a clean hand towel from the drawer. After dampening a corner, I handed it to Betty so she could clean off her face. "How did you manage to be in all those places? We've only been here a few hours."

It was a little hard to tell under all the soot and dirt, but it looked like her face reddened. "I may have gotten sidetracked, looking places I wanted to see. Did you know Pepper Maddox was supposed to be the chef, but she got fired when you called Loni at the ARL and asked her to give the job to Addison?"

I didn't bother to correct her. It didn't matter anymore. "I've heard that a couple of times now."

"Did you know she's here and she wants the job now that Addison's dead? She was talking it up real big at the Toss Across game. Then I overheard her telling everyone who'd listen at the snack shack she'd get her job back or she'd get herself on the news and tell the world Hudson Jones's secret."

"There's a snack shack?" Could she have known that Hudson and Addison were having an affair?

"I guess that sous-chef, Redmond — everyone calls him Red — set it up. Smart thinking. But that's not the best part. You'll never believe who Pepper was yapping to. That sexy reporter you don't like."

That explained a lot. Mr. TV seemed to be everywhere lately.

Betty thanked me for the towel. She tossed it in the sink, then shuffled to the table and picked up an envelope. "What are these?"

I plucked it out of her hand. "It's not important."

"But that's your mother's name — Barbara Langston. Cookie, do you miss your mommy?" She laughed. "Has she been writing you camp letters?"

"You know Mama. Always has to be the star of the event." I gathered the empty envelopes from Nosey Nellie and stuffed them in my duffle bag. "We need to find that brooch. Have you asked anyone if they've seen it?"

"Sure, I have. That's what made me think someone stole it. You know, Veronica said a couple of weeks ago someone snatched her favorite bracelet right out her jewelry box. And her friend's diamond earrings were stolen that same week. Now your brooch is gone."

"But you lost the brooch."

"Don't rub it in."

"I —"

"What I'm tellin' you is, I think someone found it and kept it. It may be ugly, but any jewel thief would know it's worth at least a down payment on a house."

True story. "What are you suggesting?"

She rubbed her hands together. "The thief is here. We've solved dozens of murders. Solving a jewelry heist has to be a piece of cake."

We have not solved dozens of murders. If she ever said that in the presence of Detective Malone, he'd find a reason to arrest her just on principle. Luckily for her, Malone was thirty miles away.

"How do you propose we go about it?" I needed a reality check. I'd just asked Betty how to find a jewel thief. *I've officially lost my mind.*

"First, I'm changing my clothes. These are itchy and I'm starting to stink." She smelled her arm. "Yuck. I need a shower."

She dashed past me toward the bedroom and bathroom. She closed the door then yelled, "We need to visit the snack shack. That's where all the best gossip happens. And get a tour of everyone's place like they promised. You distract them on the tour and make small talk. I'll snoop around for that ugly brooch you love so much."

In theory, it sounded like a great plan. Until you got to the execution details. Like, how did you rifle through a possible suspect's belongings with them standing next to you and not look like you're a crazy person?

I found a broom in a closet and swept up the twig garden Betty had left behind. I agreed, we needed inside everyone's quarters. Not only to find the brooch, but to find out who had my letters. There had to be a way to linger behind everyone's digs to do a little harmless sleuthing. I swept the pile of dirt and twigs into the dustpan and dumped it all in the garbage.

"Cookie, I found your body soap in the cosmetic bag you had hidden in the back of the drawer. It smells like sugar lemon drops. Hope you don't mind me using some," Betty shouted through the door. Before I could answer, the shower turned on, drowning out what she was saying.

I smiled. Then again, maybe I was making this too difficult, and Betty was the perfect

person to carry out the plan. Who was going to think twice about a nosey Grandma
rummaging through your bathroom?

Maybe the day was looking up after all.

CHAPTER NINE

Betty emerged from the bedroom in khaki capris, a lumberjack plaid shirt, and sculpted raspberry cream eyebrows. I complimented her on the new outfit, only to be schooled on how it wouldn't hurt if I took a little time to update my own wardrobe. I reminded her I'd exchanged my motorcycle boots for hiking boots this weekend. Unimpressed, she suggested I change my graphic T-shirt for a top more "glamping-appropriate." It was as if she'd channeled my mama. It was only a matter of time before Betty would tell me to run a brush through my hair and freshen up my lipstick. Sheesh.

We agreed to leave the dogs behind. I was a little concerned about leaving Raider unattended. He was still a pup and had a hankering for chair legs, shoes, and used tissues. Betty assured me he'd be fine if he stayed confined to the bedroom. Since that's where she was sleeping, I went along with it.

Missy parked herself under the table, snoring and drooling. I doubted she'd notice we'd left until we came back. After double-checking we had everything we needed, we headed out to start our snooping tour.

For once, Betty wasn't exaggerating. The snack shack was the proverbial water cooler for campers. There were guests gathered under a large round canvas tent with the sidewalls rolled up. As we approached, people rushed to greet Betty with a hug and a smile, asking if she had any updates about Addison's killer. I guess finding a body was big news. It also made Betty an instant celebrity.

"You know all these people?"

"Sure." She patted my arm reassuringly. "I've tried to talk to everyone and assured them we're on the case and that you had nothing to do with Addison's murder."

"Why would they think I had anything to do with the murder? They don't know me."

"Well, I heard from Veronica, who heard from Asher, who heard from Red that you threatened Addison when you left the kitchen this morning."

Red was causing me grief at every turn. I needed to talk to him and find out why he kept throwing me under the bus. Judging by the way he was working the crowd, he was embracing his new role as head chef. That was a motive for murder in my book.

"For the record, I did not threaten her. And stop telling people we're going to solve this murder. Are you trying to get us thrown in jail?"

Betty couldn't help herself. Her intentions were good, but she didn't know how to subtly coax information out of anyone.

"Detective Hottie would bail us out."

Where did she get that crazy notion? "Don't bother wasting your one phone call on Malone. He'd let you sit in jail. Call a lawyer."

"What about the sexy reporter?"

I raised my eyebrows. "Do you have a story in exchange for your freedom? Because that's the price if you want his help."

We maneuvered through the crowd of hungry campers and exhausted pooches. Betty was in her element, roaming through the herd — part cheerleader, part politician — shaking hands and making empty promises.

A young man in his early twenties roamed through the crowd with a tray of half-filled champagne glasses. He had to be the butler, Chase. I grabbed a flute as he passed by.

Betty elbowed me in the side. "He's a little wet behind the ears to be serving alcohol, don't you think?"

I looked at her surprised. "Not at all. I thought you liked cabaña boys."

"Naw. I like cabaña *men.* That kid looks like he should be at home tuning up his bicycle so he can deliver the Sunday paper. I'll be back. I'm going to get us an invite to the Swansons' RV."

Betty disappeared. I had no idea who the Swansons were. I searched the group for Betty, but she was so tiny, it was nearly impossible to find her. I watched for her white hair. I finally found her inside the tent talking to the older couple with the Pom who'd snubbed me earlier. If they were the Swansons, I didn't think we'd be granted a tour of their RV anytime soon.

I drained my glass. The champagne was refreshing, but now I had the munchies. I shimmied my way toward the center of the venue. I noticed a small round table full of empty champagne flutes and set mine down with the others. I looked in the opposite direction, and spotted Red standing behind a food bar, directing traffic and barking out orders. With a perfected tempo, appetizers were quickly being pushed out to the hungry masses. A tray for the humans, and a tray for the pets.

If I had to put together a suspect list, he'd be at the top. He turned to shout at a short somber brunette with orthopedic shoes. She looked like she was about to cry. Or stab him with the large knife she clutched in her hand. I took my earlier declaration back. She looked like the prime suspect in a murder investigation.

Betty reappeared at my side, her face bland. "We'll need to find someone else to start our RV tour. You're bad news, buttercup."

I wasn't sure how I felt about her delivery that I was considered trouble. "Do you know the lady talking to Red?" I pointed toward the food bar.

Betty's face lit up. "Sure. That's Pepper. Let's go talk to her. I've got some questions."

That was Pepper Maddox? I wasn't so sure I wanted to introduce myself to the person I supposedly got fired while she was holding a chef's knife. "Maybe later."

Betty grabbed my elbow and dragged me toward the table. "Or now works too," I mumbled.

"Pepper," Betty shouted as her target started to walk in the opposite direction. Betty's thin voice couldn't cut through the excited chatter of the crowd. Pepper and her knife vanished out the backside of the snack shack.

As we reached the table, Red looked up. His eyes widened. "You." He pointed his finger at me.

I guess his mama didn't have the same rules of decorum as mine. Never point your finger at someone, and never rest your elbows on the table.

"Why aren't you under arrest?" he bellowed. His deep voice commanded attention. A few people turned to see who he was talking to.

"Probably for the same reason you're not. An argument isn't a motive for murder."

He crossed his tattooed arms. Even wearing an apron, the image he presented was intimidating. "You've got a smart mouth."

"You've got an anger management problem." Pushed up against a wall, I usually came out swinging. This was one of those times.

His face reddened. "You don't know what you're talking about."

We had a larger audience now. I couldn't walk away, knowing people might think I had something to do with Addison's death.

"Let me refresh your memory," I said. "I walked into the kitchen just as you slammed a baking sheet on the counter after Addison reminded you she was in charge. If I remember correctly, she banished you to peel potatoes and onions."

"She was an arrogant hack who let her title go to her empty head." Red pulled out an iron hook from under the makeshift bar he stood behind. "Maybe if she'd treated people nicer, she'd still be breathing."

Yikes. Why were the police wasting their time on me, when Red was practically begging to be on the suspect list?

CHAPTER TEN

I'm not gonna lie. When Red pulled out that iron hook, I expected him to leap across the table and take a swipe at me. A desperate move, I know. The snack shack tent wasn't a very private place for a murder.

Instead, he dragged out a large iron triangle from the same place he'd found the hook. I realized he was about to ring the dinner bell. All Betty's talk about horror movies was getting to me.

Betty settled next to me. "Don't back down, Cookie. He's just trying to scare you."

"The last thing I need is your help."

"Pfft." She grabbed another glass of champagne from the tray.

Red strode outside the tent. He struck the inside of the triangle for a solid twenty seconds. "Now that I have your attention," he shouted to the hushed crowd.

All previous signs of anger had vanished.

Standing before us was a poised and happy chef. If I hadn't seen the transformation myself, I'd have never recognized him.

A toothy smile split his lips. He wasn't what I'd consider a handsome man, but he looked less threatening when he smiled. "Dinner tables have been set up behind the kitchen. Follow the pathway lighted by paper lanterns. Service will begin in twenty minutes."

The hungry campers and canines quickly filed down the pathway, chatting excitedly about what could be on the dinner menu.

Betty frowned as we walked with the group. "I'm feeling guilty that I left Raider in the rig."

I felt the same about Missy. Here was the truth of the matter. Missy wasn't a refined diner. She snorted, grumbled, and breathed with her mouth open, which led to gas. Nasty, deadly gas. Not the best table companion for those who weren't head over heels in love with her.

When I imagined Raider at the table, chaos was right next to him. With Caro's help, his behavior had improved, but he wasn't necessarily ready to share his food bowl with other canines.

I put my arm around her. "We'll ask for a doggie bag."

She looked at me the same way I'd seen Raider look at her when she denied him a treat. "Raider might need two."

I tried to take her mind off her dog. "I'll bet you fifty bucks we have lamb kabobs tonight."

She scrunched up her face. "Why would I take that bet? You were in the kitchen earlier. You know what's on the menu."

I shrugged. "Maybe. There was an argument about what should be served tonight. I've got a fifty-fifty shot at being right."

She shook her head. "Nah. I don't like those odds. You know something." She paused for a minute. "Skewers would make a great murder weapon. Metal or wood?"

I laughed lightly. "I guess we'll have to wait and see."

We reached the dining area where four long tables were set up with Wedgwood casual dinnerware for twelve humans . . . and their dogs. Seating was first come, first choice. I dragged Betty to the backside of the last table.

"I want to sit at table one," she argued. "I'm starving."

"We don't want our back to the group. We'll sit here so we can see everyone. Who they sit next to. Watch them as they're being served."

She grinned. "Smart thinking. All that time you've been spending with Malone has paid off."

Actually it was the years with Grey. Thinking about him now, I missed him terribly. The urge to call him was automatic and strong. I felt the loss of his two cents in situations like this. My negligence at accepting his advice on similar incidents over the past few years was embarrassing. I'd been too pigheaded to stop and listen. I sighed. I was such an idiot.

Betty and I made our way to the table and chose the two open seats in the middle — Betty on the left, me on the right.

I grabbed the pitcher of water and filled our glasses. "When you see Pepper, wave her over."

"You got it! Too bad we don't have a secret code."

"We're sitting right next to each other. We do not need a code. Secret or otherwise."

Guests slowly picked seating, some distracted by their conversation, others concerned whether their dining partners and pups got along. Veronica and Harry sat at table one with the Suttons and their Lhasa Poo, Codi. The Swansons caught sight of me with Betty, and scrambled to sit at table two. And so it continued — we weren't anyone's first choice.

Table one filled quickly. Then table two. And so it went. We were passed over once, twice, three times. Until finally, a tall, handsome black man who looked like a soap opera leading superstar, slowly made his way past the first couple of tables.

"Asher," Betty cooed. "Yoo-hoo. Over here, Handsome." She patted the chair next to her. Asher flashed her a wide smile. He tossed a charming nod in her direction and made his way toward us, one sexy stride after another. I hardly noticed the dog he carried in the crook of his arm.

"That's Asher?" I sputtered. "*He* could have fixed our RV? But noooo. We got the whole town of stinkin' Mayberry."

"I'm hoping to get him to help me extend my slide-out later." She waggled her lipstick eyebrows.

Ugh. "Enough already. I have to sleep in there with you."

"We need a sign. You know, if I need some private time."

"You will not need private time." Lord have mercy on my soul. Surely, He'd spare me from being barred from the RV because Betty was getting busy with a stranger.

Asher and his pup joined us, taking the seat next to Betty. Poor guy had no idea what he was in for. Betty made quick introductions. She didn't call me Mel, but she didn't call me Cookie either. I was "the boss lady." Where did she come up with this stuff?

I quickly supplied my real name. Asher introduced us to Eddie, his short-haired, soulful brown-eyed, mixed-breed dog who sat on his lap, still as a fireplace statue.

Betty yammered on about their earlier conversation and his offer to help her look for her lost flashlight. I realized he must have come across her when she was looking for the brooch.

I glanced over the top of the glass I held and spotted Pepper conversing amiably with the Swansons at table two. She'd traded her chef knife for her frumpy Pekingese. I elbowed Betty.

"I see. I see. Hold your horses." She patted Asher's upper arm. I'm sure it was just an excuse to touch him. For once, I didn't blame her. "I'll be right back," she promised. Determination clear on her small face, Betty bolted straight for Pepper.

Out of the blue, Asher said, "You don't look like a killer to me, Mel."

Well, hell's bells. That was an interesting way to start a conversation. I dragged my gaze from Betty who was talking to Pepper

128

with a great deal of animated hand gestures. Apparently, Asher was not only good-looking, but believed in getting right to the point.

"I don't think so either. What does a killer looks like?"

"Angry."

That would describe Red — the one who'd stuck a hostile finger in my face. It was an obvious answer. Jealous, desperate — those were other options.

I offered my own opinion. "Or charming."

He chuckled dryly, as if I'd just told him a knock-knock joke he'd heard a thousand times. "Betty mentioned you've had some experience with catching bad guys."

"Did she?" What else had she been saying? His comments could be harmless and just his way of initiating conversation, but there was something about the hidden intensity in his eyes that my gut said there was more to it.

I changed the subject. "So you were helping her find her flashlight?"

"She was on her hands and knees looking round the spa when I stumbled upon her. She mentioned she dropped her flashlight." He shrugged. "I don't think she was looking for a flashlight. But whatever it was she was looking for, she was insistent she find it. It seemed awfully important to her. Or someone she cared about."

What was he implying?

He spoke with a slight accent I couldn't put my finger on. It was almost a mix of English and Australian. Or maybe it was fake. I was finding Asher Knox to be less attractive by the minute. There was something about him that didn't ring true. Maybe it was because it felt like he was implying Betty and I were involved in a cover-up of some type.

"Who's Betty dragging over here? It looks like she'd rather not come," he said.

"Pepper Maddox. I'm surprised you don't know her. She's also a chef."

He looked confused. "Why would I know her?"

"Oh. I just assumed. You and Red are friends . . . at least that's the impression I got. Pepper was originally the head chef."

He stiffened. "I met him for the first time today." He returned his attention to the two ladies heading in our direction. "Maybe Pepper will give us the inside scoop on dinner."

I was also hoping for an inside scoop, but not about food. Betty returned to her seat. Pepper picked a chair on the opposite side of the table. I introduced myself, Asher, and

Eddie. Pepper regarded me cautiously while remaining polite.

"This is Dim Sum." She held up her white mop with four stubby legs. I wasn't sure which end was the head and which was the tail. "He's only nine months old. He's still learning to socialize." He turned his squished face toward her and licked her right on the lips. Pepper smiled, transforming her face from mousy to radiant. The love of a dog never ceased to amaze me.

"Don't you have a dog?" Pepper asked me.

"I do. Missy. She's a bulldog, and tends to overheat easily. She had a long day so I left her in the RV where it's cool. Now that I have a better feel for what we're doing, I'll make sure she's able to attend meals."

"How long have you and Eddie been together?" I asked Asher.

He rubbed his dog's caramel-colored head gently. "He rescued me five years ago. He's a good-natured fellow. Smart as a whip."

Betty batted her eyes. "I'm sure he and Raider will become fast friends."

He flashed his charming smile. "You have a Saint Bernard, correct?"

"That's right. He rescued me, too. We already have so much in common." She leaned into his shoulder and sighed. If I were him, I'd keep a close eye on her

131

wandering hands. "Are you staying in an RV or tent?" Betty rubbed his arm.

"RV."

"We are, too. Maybe you'd give us a tour of yours tomorrow. Cookie here is thinking about buying one."

I was not. But if that story got us into his RV, I'd adopt it for the greater good.

He gracefully maneuvered away from Betty. "Not a problem."

"Oh, I'd love to come too," Pepper said.

"We can have an RV tour date." Betty clapped her hands. "Let's start at Asher's rig, and end at Pepper's."

"I don't have an RV. I'm staying in a tent."

"Even better. I'd love to see what we're missing out on," I chimed in. "Is nine too early?"

Everyone agreed that worked. Pepper and Betty were the most excited. I couldn't tell if Asher was just humoring us, or if he found the whole idea enjoyable. I guess it didn't matter. Our snooping tour was scheduled.

It was time to get us back on the topic of murder and lost brooches. "So, Asher, how did you know Addison?"

"I was a previous client." He picked up his cloth napkin and tied it around Eddie's neck.

"I didn't know she had clients," I said.

"She was your pet chef?"

He nodded. "Eddie has a very delicate digestive system."

"That's probably from his life on the street." Betty slipped a dried apple ring from her pocket and placed it in front of Eddie. He didn't so much as twitch a whisker.

Asher looked at her funny. "He's never lived on the street. Addison was teaching me how to cook for him in a healthy way. His previous owner only fed him cheap dog food full of fillers and preservatives."

Pepper's pale face brightened. "Do you live nearby? I'd be happy to offer my services as a pet chef."

I bet she would.

"I live in Dana Point," Asher supplied hesitantly.

A swing and a miss. Poor Pepper. He didn't seem interested in her "services."

"You said 'used' to be a client. What happened?" I asked.

Asher picked up the apple ring and smelled it. Apparently it met his approval, because he handed it to Eddie, who ate it immediately. "I don't want to malign someone who can't defend herself."

There it was again. A glimpse of pretentiousness lurking under the surface. Maybe it was his practiced facial expression or the humble tone that rang hollow. Usually, people who made those types of statements were just waiting to pick that other person apart. They just needed permission.

"What'd she do?" Betty hung off the edge of her seat. "Poison your dog?"

He blinked. "You have a very active imagination."

"You know it. I've helped solve a dozen murders, all because of my keen intellect." She tapped her head.

I kicked her under the table.

"You've got to stop doing that," Betty whined.

"You've got to stop telling people you've help solved a dozen murders." I smiled at Asher and Pepper. "We've sort of helped the Laguna Beach homicide with a couple of investigations. It's not as big a deal as she's making it sound."

"Is that so? How very interesting." Pepper shot me a nasty look. "So you're 'helping' the Laguna Hills homicide detectives now? Even though you're a suspect? You do have a way with ruining people's lives, don't you?"

If there was any doubt as to how Pepper felt about me, that was gone now. I'd hoped she'd either forgotten my part in her dismissal or had let it go. That was not the case.

"Let me start off by apologizing. I didn't know you were originally the head chef. Had I known someone had already been hired, I would have never recommended Addison for the job. I'm sorry." I caught Betty's twisted smile out of the corner of my eye. "And to be clear, we are not helping. And I'm not a suspect." At least, not that I'd been informed of. Yet.

Pepper narrowed her eyes. It was hard to tell if she was weighing the sincerity of my apology, or if she was deciding to shove it back in my face. She blinked away her indecision. "It's not the end of the world. In fact, Hud gave me a better gig. I'll be the head chef for the dog show later this year."

"That's great. I'm glad it worked out for you." I meant it, not only because it got me out of potential hot water, but because Addison's selfishness wouldn't rob Pepper of a new opportunity for success.

"Oh, look who's coming." A sly grin settled on Betty's face. Judging by the lilt in her voice, the person was male.

I leaned to my right to see around Pepper and immediately wished I hadn't. MacAvoy. He looked directly at me. Darn. There were still a number of empty chairs at our table. Plenty of room for him. Sure enough, Mr.

TV made a beeline for us.

Of all the empty seats, why'd he have to choose one at our table?

CHAPTER ELEVEN

Macavoy had changed out of his company shirt and put on a plain old green cotton T-shirt. He was still wearing that same idiot grin he always did when he thought he was about to get a scoop.

"Good evening," he said, with a disarming tone. "Ms. Maddox, it's wonderful to see you again."

Pepper blushed. Lordy, we were in trouble. She might dress sensibly, but she didn't have a good read for people. That might explain why she'd over-shared with a reporter about how far she was willing to go to get her job back. I studied Mr. TV and wondered if he was able to wrangle that information out of her, or if she'd randomly offered it.

"It's wonderful to see you, Mr. MacAvoy. Please sit here." She indicated the chair next to her and directly across from me.

He didn't waste time, he yanked the

wooden chair back and claimed his place. "I'd love to. Please, call me Mac." He held out his hand to Asher. "I don't believe we've met."

"Asher Knox." They shook hands quickly across the table. "This is Eddie."

MacAvoy held his palm toward the dog. Eddie gave it a quick sniff. He wasn't rude, but he didn't seem eager for attention from the stranger either. The dog was definitely a better judge of people than Pepper.

MacAvoy's gaze bounced between Betty and Asher. "Are you a friend of Betty's?"

"You got a problem with that?" My feisty assistant threw back her small shoulders, practically staking her boyfriend territory.

He cleared his throat. "Not at all." He directed his overworked charm toward me in the form of a tenacious grin. "Are you ready for that interview? I have questions about your relationship with the victim. We can take care of it tonight."

I unrolled a cloth napkin and placed it on my lap. "Sorry. I have plans to wash my hair."

"You can interview me, handsome." Betty slumped in her chair as she made googly eyes across the table. "Why don't we take a moonlit walk later tonight? After everyone's gone to bed."

MacAvoy jumped, ramming his knee into the table. "I thought dinner was to be served ten minutes ago?" he croaked.

Poor guy. Betty had to be playing footsies. I felt a tad bad for him. Not so bad that I wanted to help him. I enjoyed watching him squirm too much. "There's a lot to do now that it's just Red. We should probably cut him some slack."

Pepper snorted. "He doesn't deserve your sympathy. He's a bully and a loudmouth."

Not as demure as first impressions might indicate. "We saw you speaking with him before he rang the dinner bell." I didn't mention she'd been clutching a knife. "I'm surprised you haven't been approached to help, Pepper."

"I offered. But I'm not needed. He knows I'm a better chef than he is." She sniffed, clearly offended. "He'll change his mind. He's already in the weeds with this service. He won't get out of it without some help."

Betty leaned across the table, turning her attention on her newest friendly target. "Tell us all the dirt. Cookie here interrupted him and that blue-haired chef arguing. It was vicious. Yelling. Cursing. Slamming of pots and pans. Do you think he could have killed her?"

Good grief. A gross exaggeration. If this

was how she talked to the other guests, no wonder they thought I was involved in Addison's death.

Mr. TV regarded me with a raised brow. He knew Betty well enough to know her account of the events was embellished. At the same time, he had to be curious to know what was fact and what was exaggeration.

Silence settled across the table as we all turned to Pepper. Her eyes were as wide as fry pans. "How would I know?" she squeaked.

We'd never get Hudson's secret out of her if she remained defensive. I attempted to redirect the dinner conversation. "So, Asher, you never finished your story. What happened between you and Addison?"

"It was an unfortunate misunderstanding, really. We had a disagreement about some missing cufflinks. I was certain I'd left them in the kitchen during a cooking lesson. I asked her about them a few days later, and she blew up. Accused me of calling her a thief."

Betty gasped. I knew exactly where she was headed. I rested my hand on her arm and squeezed gently.

"Were you? Calling her a thief?" I asked.

"I was simply asking her a question."

"Was that recent?"

"A few weeks ago."

"Did you find them?"

He rubbed Eddie behind the ears. "Unfortunately, no."

Well, that was interesting. Was Addison a blackmailer and a jewel thief? Was she killed over stolen cufflinks?

Did she have my Grandma Tillie's brooch *and* my mother's letters?

Excited chatter rippled through the diners, cutting the tension at our table. Black-tie servers marched down the lighted pathway, carrying our dinner on large silver platters. I smiled as I saw a pile of lamb kabobs on half of the trays.

Immediately, there was concerned talk about whether or not it was safe to have wooden skewers because of the dogs. The concern wasn't needed. The canine version of lamb kabobs was actually a meat patty served in a crystal sherbet glass, which was placed in front of each canine.

"What's in this?" Asher asked the young woman attending our table.

"Lamb, lentils, and spinach," she recited.

"I've never heard of feeding my dog spinach." Betty sniffed at Eddie's lamb patty.

"Leafy greens are a wonderful source of iron, fiber, and calcium. Addison taught me that." Asher broke up the patty with his fingers then set the glass before Harry. "Wait." Asher licked his finger. "Not bad. Nicely seasoned. Okay, you can eat."

The pooch sniffed the food, then immediately dug in. "He's a discriminating eater," Asher said. "Red did a good job."

Pepper huffed and mumbled something indistinguishable. Using her fork, she broke up Dim Sum's patty. Once she finished, she set her dog on the table. MacAvoy's eyes grew large, but he kept quiet. I immediately noticed the dog's paws were dirty. A dark brownish-red matted the white fur. Could it be dried blood? Was Dim Sum responsible for the bloody paw prints around Addison? If so, why wouldn't Pepper have noticed and bathed her dog?

Like Eddie, Dim Sum made quick work of his meal.

I picked up my fork and slid the lamb cubes, cherry tomatoes, mushrooms, and onions to my plate. "You were right to not take the bet." I winked at Betty.

"I knew you were up to no good." She piled her food on one side of her plate. "This isn't going to work at all. We need to pay that chef a visit. Raider will starve on these baby portions. I'll need a dozen doggie bags."

"I'm sure they'd never give a larger dog the same portion size as a small dog. Raider won't starve."

Conversations turned to how delicious the meal was and if the pet recipes would be made available to the campers.

"This is the best mint-cucumber sauce. I could drink it." I ran a piece of perfectly cooked lamb across the plate, soaking up the sauce. "I'm curious, does anyone know who'd want to hurt Addison?"

Asher pulled the last chunk of meat from his skewer. "I didn't spend a lot of time with her other than those few lessons. She struck me as someone who had a lot of secrets."

"Why's that?" I asked.

"She didn't share details about her life. She always had a new scheme on how to get what she wanted."

"You have no idea," Pepper muttered.

"Did you know her?" MacAvoy had been unusually quiet until now.

"Not as well as her." She pointed her empty skewer toward me.

Great. Obviously, she wasn't ready to let the whole job thing go yet. "I didn't know her as well as you might think."

Pepper fed her pooch a small piece of meat from her plate. "No one knew her. She liked being mysterious. I wasn't impressed with her. She was too competitive. Wanting to get the upper hand when there wasn't one to get. She liked to threaten people who got in her way."

Sounded like Pepper might have also had firsthand experience. "In what way?" I asked.

"She —" Pepper started, then quickly clammed up. "The typical hotheaded chef stuff."

I wasn't buying it. She was going to say something more specific. I wondered why she'd changed her mind at the last minute. Was it because it would paint Pepper in a bad light? Or was it because she'd killed her?

"When did you see her last?" I continued to look at my plate in hopes that my lack of eye contact would make it easier for Pepper to continue talking.

"I saw her slinking off to the spa. You could tell she was meeting someone there in secret by the way she kept looking over her shoulder."

"Do you know who she was meeting?" MacAvoy asked.

Pepper's hand froze. "No. No. I have no idea."

Oh, she was lying. My adrenaline kicked in. "Did she see you?"

"No. She never noticed me."

Did she mean ever or just at that minute? "Do you remember what time that would have been?"

"Right after the game. Around one-thirty."

I squeezed my fork. She had never planned on meeting me. When had I become such a sucker? "You might have been the last person to see her alive. Have you talked to the police?"

"I have. They asked me if I'd seen you." She smirked.

Of course, everyone looked at me. "I wasn't there."

She shrugged. "I couldn't say if you were or weren't. I just told the truth. I only saw Addison."

Only, that wasn't the truth. Pepper knew who Addison was meeting. Or maybe Pepper followed Addison inside and . . . and what? Exactly how was Addison murdered? "Does anyone know how she died?"

"Stabbed." That was Pepper.

"Choked." That was Asher.

"I take that back. I heard the program director say she was smothered," Pepper tossed out one more rumor.

Once again, campfire gossip spread like a southern California wildfire. Even Hudson was involved. Last I knew, he didn't have

145

any idea how Addison had died. I looked at MacAvoy. "Your turn. What do you know?"

"The cops are playing this one close to the vest. Betty's the one who found her. How'd she die?"

"Do I look like I know how to perform an autopsy? She was lying on the massage table with a white sheet over her body and a dinner fork sticking out of her neck."

"Was she dressed under the sheet?" MacAvoy probed.

Darn, that was a good question. I wish I'd have thought of it.

"I don't know, Hot Shot. I didn't lift up the sheet. I was busy screaming."

I held back a chuckle. I could see her, hands on either side of her face, screaming like the kid in *Home Alone.* "Take a minute and think back. You walked inside and then what?" I asked.

She closed her eyes and concentrated. "I was thinking about how long a massage I could talk you into paying for. I was annoyed because there wasn't anyone there to help me."

I rolled my eyes. "What did you see?"

"It was very pretty, peaceful. There were two massage tables. She was lying on the table on the right." Her eyes popped open. "The sheet wasn't laying flat. I saw her

146

black shoes. I think she was dressed." Her voice shot out with excitement.

So it was possible she was there for a secret meeting. Was she blackmailing someone else? Was she there to meet Hudson for a clandestine meeting? Addison was busier than I'd thought.

"Where is everyone?" A loud husky voice rumbled through the dining area, hanging on the evening air.

One by one, everyone turned to watch a stylishly dressed petite-sized woman plod toward the tables. Her sheer black top, tight leather pants, and four-inch-heeled, black fashion boots were out of place. She was definitely a newcomer.

"Hell-ooo. Can someone direct me to Hudson Jones?" She pushed a wisp of shockingly white bangs from her eyes. Her pixie haircut emphasized her strong facial features.

Hudson had been sitting at table three. He quickly made his way to the woman and engaged her in conversation.

"Who in the world is that?" Betty asked in a stage whisper.

"Bad news." Pepper grabbed her glass of wine and gulped it down, keeping her back to the stranger.

"You know her?" MacAvoy was practically

147

salivating at the prospect of a juicy story.

Pepper swept her pooch off the table and onto her lap. "That's Sunday Hill. Addison's agent for the cookbook." The panic in her hushed tone was unmistakable.

Hudson had mentioned Sunday was coming to collect Addison's personal belongings. He'd been expecting her hours ago. I watched as he guided the young woman back up the pathway, the same way she'd just come from.

"You don't like her?" I asked Pepper.

She shook her head frantically. "I'm terrified of her. She destroyed one chef's career because he went against her advice. A client was approached to be a contestant on a reality cooking show. He wanted to do it. She didn't want him to. He did it anyway. She got production to sabotage every meal he cooked. He looked like an idiot on national television. He had a meltdown and ended up in a mental hospital for three days. He's never worked as a chef again."

That sounded extreme, but it didn't explain why Pepper was afraid. What was their history? "You know this is true because . . . ?"

Pepper nodded. "I was his sous-chef for two years prior to his breakdown. I can't let her see me."

"I don't think you have to worry about that. Hudson just left with her."

That didn't seem to matter to Pepper. She scooped Dim Sum into her arms and stood. "I have to go." She dashed off toward the campfire ring.

"That was odd," Asher murmured.

MacAvoy's eyebrows pulled together. "Do you believe her?"

"She seemed truly afraid."

Sunday didn't look as ruthless as Pepper was making her out to be. Although there was also the side comment Hudson had made when we were at Addison's tent. He was also nervous about the agent's arrival. "I wonder if Sunday Hill knows who might want to hurt Addison."

"There's only one way to find out." Mac-Avoy stood.

"Where are you going?" I asked.

"Exactly where you think I am. To find out what Sunday Hill knows about Addison. Are you coming?"

Betty looked torn, not wanting to miss out. "Can I get a doggie bag first?"

CHAPTER TWELVE

Asher offered to grab as many leftovers for Raider as Red would give him. Betty proclaimed her gratitude and promised to return the favor. I inwardly cringed, thinking about how she might interpret the appropriate way to return the favor.

MacAvoy, Betty, and I followed Hudson and Sunday to the headquarters tent. I was disturbed that Mr. TV and I had somehow teamed up. I didn't trust him. But as Grandma Tillie used to say, keep your friends close, but your enemies closer. Not that I considered Mr. TV an enemy, but he wasn't a friend either.

"I heard about you and Grey." MacAvoy glanced at me. "I never trusted the guy. I tried to warn you about him."

"You're not a very good judge of character. I trust Grey Donovan with my life. You, on the other hand, I trust less than a courtroom full of crooked lawyers. Keep your nose out of my personal life." My Texas accent made a brief appearance. It did that when I lost my temper. I quickened my pace. Why in God's green earth, did he think he, of all people, should discuss my relationship with my ex-fiancé?

Betty cackled. "That's my spunky Cookie. We need to keep the handsome reporter around. He makes you ornery."

"He makes me disagreeable."

MacAvoy stopped talking to me, which helped my temper cool off by the time we caught up with Hudson and Sunday. The heavy canvas door was propped open. We could see them standing at Hudson's desk, talking. I stopped abruptly at the doorway. Betty let out an "oof" as she stumbled into my back. Would it be rude if we just walked inside? They were obviously having a private conversation. Not normally the one to second-guess myself, I didn't like the feeling of self-doubt.

"What'd you stop for? I can't hear them from here," Betty grumbled.

"Stop jabbering and maybe you'd be able to." My stomach tightened. The last time I'd been inside, I was questioned by Detective Finn. Thankfully, she wasn't around. I pushed aside the angst and concentrated on our mission — gathering info on Addison.

151

Mr. TV patted his back pocket. "Damn, I don't have my notepad."

"I thought you were working on a story? What kind of reporter doesn't have his notebook with him at all times?" Betty taunted.

At the moment, I felt less apologetic about crashing their meeting. "I guess everything's off the record then. You wouldn't want to report inaccurate facts."

I entered the tent, Betty and Mr. TV hot on my heels. The crime scene equipment that had been laid out earlier in the day was gone, as were the uniformed officers. The extra tables and chairs that had been set up as makeshift desks were still shoved up against the canvas walls.

I was about to announce our arrival, when Sunday's irritated voice ripped through the tent. "What do you mean, you don't have her personal effects ready? You've been expecting me. This is a nightmare!"

Ouch. I slowed down. Okay, so maybe she was as scary as Pepper insinuated. "Knock, knock," I called out.

Hudson whipped around. His look of irritation transformed into relief. "Mel. Come in. I was just explaining to Sunday that the police haven't released Addison's belongings yet."

"Who are you?" Sunday's large green eyes narrowed on my face. "You look familiar."

I blinked, surprised. She might look young at first glance, but she had the disposition of a hardened New Yorker. "We've never met. I'm Melinda Langston. This is Betty Foxx —"

She snapped her long fingers at me. Her perfectly red manicured nails were marred by a chipped index fingernail tip. "That's it. Addison showed me a photo of you. You're the non-celebrity writing the foreword to her cookbook. Where is it? She said you'd have that to her a week ago."

"She did?" Addison had a photo of me? Why had she shown it to her agent? What other games had the conniving pet chef been playing?

She gave me the once-over. I wasn't sure if I met with her approval, or if I fell short. A hard, cold-eyed smile stretched her thin lips. "Tell me, why did she pick you? I've never understood that pointless idea. But she insisted. You're not a chef or a celebrity." She sniffed. "Did she owe you some type of favor? Did you have something on her?"

I almost choked. "Hardly. I'm sure you can find someone much more qualified than me for that foreword. If the cookbook is still a go, that is."

153

"Why wouldn't it be?"

"Because Addison's dead," Betty piped up, wedging herself between me and Mac-Avoy. "Isn't that why you're here?"

Sunday crossed her skinny arms across her chest. "The plan was, I would join Addison during the day. I'm a day-tripper." Her tone was challenging, as if she were daring us to disagree with her.

Disagreeing wasn't going to be a problem. I'd read Betty's event invitation. There was no "day-tripper" category.

Hudson's eyes widened in surprise. "I wasn't aware of that. Addison never mentioned it to me. As the head chef, her days are . . . were . . . going to be busy with activities and food prep." He reached for a clipboard laying on his desk. "I don't recall seeing your name on the attendance list."

"It wasn't. Callum MacAvoy, Channel 5 News." Mr. TV stepped around Betty as he introduced himself, ensuring he was in Sunday's direct line of vision. He was also in the direct line of fire for her next verbal assault. *Knock yourself out.* "I was doing a story on Addison's celebrity rise in our community. I'm sorry for your loss."

Gag. He was manipulating the facts to suit the present situation. Until Addison's death, he hadn't even been sure if there'd be a story on her.

Sunday inhaled deeply, her high cheek-bones practically cutting through her skin. "Thank you."

"I'd like to talk to you about Addison. I have a cameraman with me. Maybe tomorrow afternoon?"

She pulled a business card from the outside pocket of her handbag. "Email me the questions. I'll approve the ones I want to answer, and we'll go from there." She turned her attention to Hudson, effectively dismissing MacAvoy. "I'll take Addison's sleeping area. That is if the *police* are finished with it."

Hudson set the clipboard on the desk. "I believe so. Gosh, are you sure you want to stay in the tent?"

It sounded like he didn't want her around. I couldn't blame him.

"Why wouldn't I? She wasn't murdered there."

No one spoke. What was there to say? As brash as her comment was, it was true. Hudson excused himself to call Detective Finn and make sure the tent was clear to use.

Sunday fished around in her bag, then pulled out her cell phone. She bent her head and concentrated on her email, acting as if

155

we didn't exist.

"Do you know anyone who may have wanted to hurt Addison?" MacAvoy asked.

She peered up through her bangs. "Is this part of your story?"

"It is now."

She raised her face. "I'm surprised you want to talk about this off camera."

"We can cover it again tomorrow. Think of it as a pre-interview."

"I haven't agreed to anything yet. But to answer your question, Addison did not have any true enemies. The chef community may be cutthroat, but it's still a family. I can't imagine anyone who would want to hurt her, much less kill her." Her low voice turned chilly and exact.

Her answer didn't make any sense. Addison wasn't killed at a chef convention. Or during a reality cooking show. Unless she was talking about Redmond and Pepper. "What about someone outside that community?"

She arched a heavily penciled eyebrow. "You mean like someone here?"

Duh. That was where she died. Was she really this obtuse or just testing us? "Yes."

Her lips twisted. "Since I just got here, I'm not in a position to answer that. You tell me. Did one of you hate her so much that you killed her?" She shifted her attention to me. "What about you? Addison confided to me you two had some childhood secret that you were worried she would expose."

I felt the blood drain from my face. My heart pounded so hard, my chest hurt. We didn't exactly have a childhood secret. What else had Addison shared? I refused to look at Betty or MacAvoy. I'd deal with their barrage of questions later.

"We're not killers," Betty spat out. She jammed her hands on her hips. "We ferret out the bad guys and then turn them over to the coppers."

Sunday narrowed her haughty eyes. "You're a funny lady. Who are you, again?"

"I'm a crime fighter." She snickered.

Sunday stared at Betty, trying to figure her out. I inwardly wished her luck. I was still trying to understand her. "Where's your cape?"

"I'm having it dry-cleaned," Betty shot back.

Sunday rolled her eyes so hard I thought they'd get lost in the back of her head. She brushed Betty off with the wave of her hand. "You're ridiculous. You, on the other hand, I don't trust." She glared at me. "Are you denying you had anything to do with Addison's death?"

What the heck? Why didn't she trust me? She didn't even know me. "Of course I am. I didn't kill her."

"Do you have the foreword you promised to write?"

"No," I lied. There was no point. Addison was gone, and I'd never wanted to write the blasted thing in the first place. "I told her to find someone more qualified. I assumed she had."

"On that, we agree." She glanced at her Rolex and frowned. "How much longer do you think he'll be? I'm famished. You don't suppose Redmond has leftovers, do you? He's not always accurate with the amount of food needed for large events."

"It's possible." I found it peculiar she called him by his full name and wondered about her relationship with him. "How well do you know Red?"

She shrugged a stiff shoulder. For the first time during the conversation, she seemed on the defense. "I was his agent. Years ago." She shoved her phone back in her handbag.

Could that have been another reason why there was so much tension between Red and Addison — the shared agent? Was one getting the prime gigs? Were there bad feelings between Red and Sunday?

"Did you part on good terms?" MacAvoy

asked. He must have been on the same line of thinking as I was.

"Of course," she answered a little too quickly.

Sunday Hill was lying through her pearly white teeth. Now we were getting somewhere. "Did Red have an anger management problem back in the day?"

"Are you saying he has one now?"

Darn. She was good. Deflecting our questions with questions of her own. It wasn't going to be easy to get information out of her that she didn't want to cough up.

Hudson reappeared. "It's settled. You can stay in Addison's quarters. If you have luggage, I can help you carry it to the tent."

She pulled her car keys from her handbag and held them out to Hudson. "Just take my luggage to the tent. I'm going to grab some dinner first." She slipped her arm through MacAvoy's. "You don't mind accompanying me to the dining area, do you?"

"Not at all." Mr. TV shot me a cocky grin over Sunday's head.

I wondered which story he'd concentrate on. The supposed childhood secret between Addison and me, or Addison's relationship with her agent?

He pulled his arm close to his side, bringing Sunday right up against him. "So tell

159

me, how did Addison become your client?" he asked, as they walked away into the sunset.

"I'll see you back at the rig. I've got to grab Raider's dinner before She-Devil steals his share." As she gave me a quick hug, she whispered, "You can fill me in on that secret she was talking about tonight." With a wave good-bye to Hudson, she raced after them. "Hey, wait for me," she shouted.

I didn't see myself telling Betty anything. She was a wild card when it came to keeping a secret. I turned to Hudson. He, on the other hand, seemed to be pretty good at keeping his lips sealed.

I smiled. "I think we're alone now."

It was time to pry some of that closely held information loose.

CHAPTER THIRTEEN

Hudson pocketed Sunday's key. "Sorry to drag you into that mess with Ms. Hill. What did you need?"

Answers. I had a page of follow-up questions about the secret Pepper had threatened to expose. I was ninety-eighty percent certain Hudson and Addison were having an affair. Hudson was obviously skittish about the topic. I had to ease my way into it.

I leaned against the desk. "You don't believe that 'day-tripper' story, do you? I mean, if she was only spending the day, why does she have luggage?"

Hudson's dark eyes filled with curiosity. "I hadn't thought of that." I could see he was working through something in his head.

I straightened. "Do you want some help with her bags? I can't imagine she brought only one. Or that what she did bring is light."

"No, that's fine." He pulled off his fedora and ran his hand through his hair. "She's exactly like Addison had described — abrasive, shrewd, and scary as hell."

Yes! Keep talking. I slowly maneuvered us toward the door. "Don't let Sunday manipulate you. Do you know which car belongs to her?"

He patted his pocket. "The key fob says Range Rover. She's parked in the day-use parking lot. I'll hit the alarm button and find it soon enough."

The sun had set and it was cooling down. It would be dark soon. Sounds of laughter carried to us in waves. Campfire smoke hung in the air. My stomach growled, hungry for roasted hot dogs even though we'd just eaten. What can I say, I have a fast metabolism.

We fell into step with each other as we headed toward the parking lot. "Wasn't Sunday supposed to be here hours ago?" I asked.

"She said she got held up on a conference call with New York. I was hoping I'd get Addison's personal effects from the police before she arrived, but they're still going through them. As you heard, Sunday's not happy about it."

That was the understatement of the evening. "She seems like someone who's used to getting her way. What I don't get is if she's staying for a few days, why would it matter if she got Addison's belongings today or in two days? Is there something specific she wanted?"

He shook his head. "I don't believe many people have ever told her no. I've dealt with enough people like her over the years. They want what they want, when they want it."

I laughed lightly. "You've just described about a third of my clientele. But, the police aren't just any 'people.' Do you really want to get on Detective Finn's bad side?"

"Gosh, I don't suppose I do."

We were halfway to the parking lot when Ranger Elliott drove by in his official park truck. The men exchanged a wave.

"I haven't figured him out. He seems good-humored, yet he doesn't seem very happy to have all the pets here."

"He worries about the delicate balance of the ecosystem here at the park."

"Where's he going?" I asked.

"He drives through the park a few times each day, spot-checking that the guests are following the rules and not endangering their lives or the lives of others. Looking for signs of wild animals."

I shuddered. "Mountain lions?"

It was getting darker, and I couldn't see Hudson's face clearly, but I think he nodded. Great. Just keep those big cats away from camp.

Hudson shoved his hands in the front pockets of his khakis. He glanced at me sideways again. I could tell he was working up the courage to ask me a question. "I was surprised to see you with the reporter. I didn't think you two got along."

"Not as surprised as I was," I said wryly. "Trust me, we're not chummy. We were both curious about Sunday. He didn't want me to get to her before he did, and I didn't trust what he might imply to her. Did you ever give him that interview?"

He shook his head. "No. After talking with the police, I declined."

Speaking of the police . . . "Sorry I ditched you earlier. Finn and I don't exactly see eye to eye."

"After you left, she asked me a lot of questions about you."

My stomach dropped. I wondered what he'd told her and how she'd reacted. I didn't like being the focal point of a police investigation. "Like what?"

"Gosh, let me think for a second. Well, she wanted to know what you'd taken from Addison's tent. What was the nature of your relationship with Addison? Why would you help Addison get a job here if you didn't like her? Had I ever heard you two argue? Did I think you had anything to do with Addison's death?"

I swallowed hard. Those were some serious questions. Questions the police would ask if they were trying to establish motive for murder. "What did you say?"

"I told the truth, of course. Addison didn't talk about you to me so I couldn't answer those questions. But my gut says you aren't involved with the murder."

Telling the truth seemed to be the theme of the evening. First Pepper, and now Hudson. In my experience, the truth was based upon that person's perception of the facts. As we all knew, everyone has something to hide.

"Thanks," I said.

He pushed his fedora back. "Don't get your hopes up. She still thinks you're involved. Heck, most people around here think you're involved one way or another."

I sighed. Of course. "I don't understand why they think that. There are other people with stronger motives to kill Addison than me."

He didn't say anything. Probably because he knew he was one of them.

"Did the police figure out who trashed Addison's place?" I asked.

"They're not sure. After you left, Detective Lark showed up. He mentioned it was possible Addison did that herself."

At the time, I would have thought that highly unlikely. But knowing now that Mama's letters weren't in their envelopes, I wasn't ruling out any possibility. Had Addison misplaced the letters? Had she hidden them too well and forgotten where she'd stashed them? Then, in the process of searching for them, ended up tossing her own room?

"What do you think?"

He shook his head. "She was messy, but an organized messy. She knew where everything was. That, that was . . . a disaster. She didn't do it."

We were missing something. I didn't know what it was, what it related to, or who held the key to figuring it out, but I knew in my gut there was a large piece of information that we weren't privy to. Yet.

Hudson pulled a flashlight from his belt. The bright beam lit up the pathway. It got dark quickly in the wilderness.

"You're like a Boy Scout. What time is it?"

"Just after eight. S'mores and pupcakes at the campfire in thirty minutes."

My mouth watered. I needed to get back to the RV and grab Missy. She'd enjoy the campfire and pupcakes. I'd enjoy the s'mores. We reached the parking lot. There were only four vehicles, one of which was a white Range Rover parked under the street lamp. We walked toward it.

"Hud, can I ask you a question?" I hoped I'd built enough trust between us that he'd speak freely.

"Sure."

I chose my words carefully so I didn't come across as accusatory. "I know you keep saying you and Addison had a working relationship. But from what you've said, she seemed to confide in you. It's been said that you two were more than co-workers."

He jerked his head around to face me, pointing the flashlight in my direction to see me clearly. "Who's saying that?"

I could tell he was worried. I debated if I should tell or not. I decided to tell him what I knew. "Pepper. She told MacAvoy that if she didn't get her job back, she'd go to the press and tell your secret. Is that the secret? You and Addison were lovers?"

He immediately swung the flashlight away from me, but I caught a glimpse of his face. I wasn't sure what emotion he was feeling, but tension radiated from his body.

He pressed the key fob, unlocking the luxury SUV. "Did she really say that?"

"Yes. Look, I'm the last person to judge anyone. I've made my share of bad decisions. But you have to admit, you two were closer than just co-workers. Heck, she talked to you about her agent enough that you said she'd described her perfectly. Plus, anytime we talk about her death, you become melancholy, withdrawn. That's not how someone with only a working relationship acts."

"We weren't as close as I'd thought. She didn't tell me her agent was coming." There was an edge of indignation in his voice.

"I haven't decided if Sunday is telling the truth or not about that." I had a feeling both women were liars. It was a matter of filtering out the falsehoods to find the facts.

"Do you think I killed Addison?" he asked, out of the blue.

"No," I said automatically. "But you may know who the killer is, and don't even realize it."

He thought about that for a minute then yanked open the passenger door on the driver's side. "Pepper has her own secrets she'd like to keep buried."

"Like what?"

He dragged two Louis Vuitton bags — one large, overstuffed rolling suitcase, the other a duffle bag — from the SUV. "She hasn't always been the renowned chef she professes to be."

I closed the car door and held out my hand for the duffle bag. Instead of handing it to me, he plopped it on top of the rolling bag and started back to camp. I rushed to keep up with him. When he got mad, he walked a lot faster.

"In what way?" I asked.

"She'd buy prepackaged food or hire a caterer and pass off the meal as her own creation, serving the entrees in her dinnerware." It was too dark to see his face, but judging by his tone, he sounded outraged.

Could Pepper be that conniving? I could see a single woman in her twenties, who wanted to impress her date, trying to pass off take-out as a home-cooked meal. But a supposed chef resorting to that level of trickery? I was almost speechless. Of course, I had more questions.

"How do you know this?"

"Addison told me." He was really worked up now. "She had proof too. That's why I fired Pepper."

Well, I wasn't the only one whose secret was being held in Addison's corrupt hand.

"But you gave her the other job. The dog show."

"It was safer. She doesn't have to cook in front of a crowd like she would here. She couldn't run out to Whole Foods and bring back a gallon of gourmet potato salad and think that would fly this week. The dog show is basically a catering gig." He lugged the suitcase over a curb. Suddenly, one of the wheels popped off.

"Dang!"

"I got it." I ran after the wheel, barely able to see it in the dark. I scooped it up and brought it back to where Hudson stood, flashlight pointing at the busted luggage.

"Omigosh. What happened?" The rolling suitcase had somehow exploded.

Hudson stood frozen at the side of the roadway, expensive women's clothes scattered around his feet. He pulled his fedora off his head and slapped it against his leg. "Why do you women insist on overstuffing your luggage?"

I shrugged and handed him the broken wheel. "We like choices." I bent down and immediately started to gather her apparel. "Check this out? I bet you didn't expect to see a Yankees ball cap in Sunday Hill's luggage."

"She is from New York. You didn't expect

170

a Dodger's cap, did you?"

Guys could be so clueless. "I wasn't referring to her team choice. She doesn't come across as someone who wears ball caps."

He crammed his fedora on his head. "None of that matters. How are we going to get all this back inside there?"

"We have bigger issues to worry about. Who's going to tell Sunday her three-thousand-dollar piece of luggage is broken?"

He gulped.

"How good are you at rock, paper, scissors?" I asked.

CHAPTER FOURTEEN

Luckily for us, Ranger Elliott finished his rotation early. I guess we were all behaving.

He took one look at our luggage malfunction and promised he had exactly what we needed. Hudson and I stuffed what felt like a department store worth of clothes back into Sunday's suitcase, and Ranger Elliott loaned us a bungee cord to anchor it shut. Perfect. Just like he promised.

The guys dropped off the bags at Addison's, er, Sunday's tent. I returned to the RV. Betty had left a note that said she and Raider were off to the campfire and she promised to save me a seat.

Missy greeted me, drooling and wagging her tail. I was equally excited to see her. After a few minutes of a loving rubdown, puppy kisses, and a good scratch behind the ears, Missy expected a treat. I rummaged through the cupboards and found Betty's stash of dried apple rings.

While Missy devoured her treat, I grabbed a hoodie from my duffle bag. It had gotten a little chilly after the sun went down. I checked to see if I needed to charge my cell phone. I still had forty percent of my battery left. Plenty for photos.

As I slipped my cell in my back pocket, I realized I still hadn't called my mama back yet. It wouldn't matter that it was already after ten o'clock in Texas. Her feelings were going to be hurt, she'd think I was ignoring her, and she'd be certain I was punishing her for some fabricated misdeed.

The conversation with my mama would be emotionally draining. I was already tired. I sighed. I'd call her first thing in the morning. Tonight, I wanted to enjoy s'mores.

I grabbed the leash and called Missy. "Are you ready to go, girlfriend?"

She snorted and spun in a circle. I snapped the lead onto her collar and we tumbled out of the RV. The campground was aglow by the light of the full moon. A soft hue of shining lanterns cast a dim orange and red light across the lawn, while the white canvas tents seemed to be illuminated from within, creating the illusion of extra-large nightlights. It was beautiful.

I flicked on the flashlight, looking for anything that slithered as I took Missy on a short walk to do her business before joining the others. Not that I really needed additional light to see where I was going, but I wanted the extra reassurance. So far, no one had reported seeing any snakes or mountain lions. I sure didn't want to be the first.

Missy's nose led the way. Wouldn't you know it, she headed straight for MacAvoy's RV. After some hemming and hawing, she chose a spot next to the back tires. I know. I'm awful.

Once she was finished, we followed the faint sound of affable chatter coming from the campfire. To get to the firepit, we had to pass the spa where Betty had discovered Addison's body. The tent was no longer guarded by the police or barred with yellow crime scene tape. Over dinner, someone had mentioned the spa would reopen tomorrow. Would anyone actually show up for a massage or mani-pedi?

I wanted one quick peek inside. Since we were alone, it was the perfect time to check it out. I guided Missy toward the entrance past the enormous planter of orange snapdragons. I reached for the canvas door when my cell phone rang. I jumped twenty feet. Missy barked.

"Good grief." I checked the caller ID. I'd managed to catch my breath, only to have my heart explode out of my body for a completely different reason.

"Grey," I whispered.

Hearing his name, Missy barked excitedly, spinning in circles, tangling her legs in the leash.

Why was he calling? We hadn't talked in weeks. We'd made a clean break. Or, at least as close to a clean break as we got.

Something had to be wrong. My pulse echoed in my ears. I took a deep breath and answered. "Hey, is everything okay?"

Well, not the best greeting, but it's all I had at the moment. I waited, listening for anything familiar that I could grab hold of that would reassure me.

"You tell me. Is everything okay?" At first blush, he sounded even-toned. Neutral. But I knew him as well as I knew myself. I heard the underlying tension he was working to hide.

I walked away from the spa, following the lighted pathway created by the hanging Moroccan lanterns. There was plenty of light, so I turned off my flashlight.

"I'm fine. I'm with Betty at the ARL event."

"I know. That's why I'm calling. It's all over the news about what's going on up there."

Apprehension. I recognized it immediately.

I punched up the volume on the phone. "You're talking about Addison's murder."

"Yes. Why didn't you call?" His frustration was clear.

My heart broke all over again. Even when I wasn't around, I aggravated him. *Hold on a second.* If he was annoyed, didn't that mean he still cared? I closed my eyes for a moment, willing myself to show a smidge of vulnerability. "I-I started to. I wasn't sure you wanted to hear from me. We didn't exactly part on the best of terms after our last conversation."

"Mel," he said on a sigh. I could see him in my head, rubbing his eyes in exasperation.

A reluctant grin tugged at the side of my mouth. "You can't blame me."

"I . . ."

I waited for him to finish whatever he was about to say, but he didn't. "I'm still mad at you about the brooch. I can't believe you gave it to Caro." Crapola. Me and my big mouth. Why, why, why did I bring that up?

"It was the right thing to do."

"Well, now it's lost."

"What are you talking about? I gave it to Caro myself."

I pivoted on my heel and walked toward the spa again. "Betty fat-fingered it from Caro's. She brought it here to give to me in some grand gesture, and somehow lost it within hours of our arrival."

"Caro's going to kill you."

"Me?" I picked up my pace. "First of all, I'm not the one who lost it. Second, if you hadn't given it back to Caro out of some misguided sense of fairness, none of this would have happened."

"I didn't call to argue," he ground out.

I stopped behind the spa tent. I had a knot in my stomach. "I didn't answer the phone to have a fight." Lord knew we did enough of that the last few weeks we were together. Missy dropped to the grass, panting. I turned on the flashlight to quickly sweep the area for creepy, crawling, and slithering animals before I sat next to her. I reached down and stroked her back. "Let's change the subject."

"Did you see the evening news?" he asked.

"No, I've been a little busy. Why? What has MacAvoy done now?"

"He reported live from Laguna Hills Regional Park campground an hour ago. Why aren't you aware of this? I find it hard to believe Callum MacAvoy hasn't been sniffing around you and Betty since this happened. I have no doubt the two of you are inconveniently in the middle of every-thing."

Lordy, wasn't that the truth? The last thing I wanted was to admit I was sticking my nose into a murder investigation. Or that I was a suspect in said murder investiga-tion. Or that I was looking for my mother's letters to her lover. Not that he wouldn't have been sympathetic about the latter, because he would.

"Oh, he's been following us around, but there are plenty of other distractions. Betty and Raider won the Toss Across game, I helped the program director gather the contents of a busted suitcase, and there's a campfire tonight. So, what did Mr. Nosey TV Reporter say?"

"Not much, which I found unusual. There was a promo promising an exclusive inter-view tomorrow with Addison's agent and close friend."

"That's Sunday Hill. Trust me, she's not Addison's close friend. I met her earlier today." I laughed lightly. "MacAvoy might be a little presumptuous on the outcome of that interview. Sunday was very clear she'd only answer questions she approved. After spending less than ten minutes with her, I

imagine that's going to be one short interview."

He chuckled softly. My grip tightened. His
laughter was like a kick in the stomach. I
lay on my back and gazed into the night
sky. I imaged Grey lounging on his back
deck starring at the same stars.

Man, I missed him. I wasn't ready to end
the call yet. It felt so bittersweet to hear his
voice. "What time is this interview?"

"Six o'clock news."

Prime time. MacAvoy had to be ecstatic.

"You and Betty are okay?"

"I promise. We're fine. Betty has worked
her magic and made friends with just about
everyone here."

"Men *and* women? You'll need to keep a
close eye on her, or you'll end up hosting a
dance party tonight."

"Tell me about it." I laughed. "Believe it
or not, she's narrowed her potential love
interests to a fellow guest and MacAvoy.
Oh, you'll love this. Betty insisted we come
up with some kind of signal so I'd know to
stay away from the RV if she had a man
inside." Missy started to snore, loudly.

"Is that Missy?" Grey laughed. "Is she
right by the phone?"

"Yeah. She misses you," I said softly. I
wanted to tell him I missed him, but I had

179

the feeling he already knew by the longing in my voice.

"I miss her, too." He cleared the huskiness from his voice. "What signal did you and Betty come up with?"

"Nothing. She is not going to get busy with anyone this week."

An awkward silence weighed on us. "So, I take it you're in town," I said.

"For now. I just finished a case."

It was strange. My usual curiosity to get every detail about his cases was absent. I wondered what that was about. "So you'll be in town for a while then?"

"Yes."

If he was going to be in town for a while it was probably better to hear from me than the media that I was a suspect in Addison's death.

"I should probably tell you —"

"Hey, Mel," Veronica shouted across the grassy area. She was coming from the direction of the campfire. "Are you going to have s'mores? Betty's been worried you might have found a dead body without her." Veronica laughed.

"Grey, hold on a second." I sat up and covered the phone with my palm. "I'll be there in a few minutes," I yelled to her. I waved good-bye then returned my attention to Grey. "I'm back. There's a campfire tonight . . . Betty's waiting . . ."

He cleared his throat. "I'll let you go. I'm glad to know you're okay. I know you don't want to hear this, but stay out of it. You're not dealing with Malone."

He had no idea how right he was. "I gotta go. I'll talk to you later." I hung up before the words "I love you" fell out of my mouth.

Here's the funny thing about my conversation with Grey. A part of me wanted me to skip the whole event, race home to tell him I was sorry, and convince him to try again. Yet there was a small part of me that was relieved he wasn't here. I was either protecting my heart, or I was a coward.

I guess only time would tell.

I started to stand when a large brown rabbit raced out from the back of the tent. Missy jumped up, barking, ready to give chase. I held tight to her leash, commanding her to stay. She stopped tugging on the lead, but continued to bark.

"Enough. Stop. Stay." I caught my breath. "Where'd he come from?"

Assured Missy wasn't going to run off, I investigated where the bunny had come from.

I shined the flashlight at the spa tent and noticed the edge was unfastened, allowing just enough space for a dog or smallish-sized person to fit through. How long had that opening been there? What did it mean, if anything?

I got on my hands and knees and tried to shove my body into the tent through the opening. It took some effort, but I was able to squeeze inside. Missy scampered in behind me.

I stood, brushing off my jeans. I pointed the light around. Two massage tables draped with white sheets were situated side by side on one side of the tent. On the other side sat a couple of chairs, foot tubs, and tables for mani-pedis. I moved across the tent, the wooden floor sturdy under my feet. Missy sniffed around the massage tables.

The tent was supplied with lavish hand-made soaps, fluffy towels, white robes, and a basket of slippers. It smelled like cloves and cinnamon. I could see why Betty wanted to get a massage.

The inside was smaller than I thought it would be. Intimate. This wasn't a place you'd go to meet someone you barely knew. My gut told me Addison had to have known her killer fairly well. Someone she'd have trusted.

Big mistake.

CHAPTER FIFTEEN

After my conversation with Grey, I was feeling happier than I had in weeks. I know, I know. It didn't mean anything. One phone call, showing concern because I happened to be camping at the same park as a deranged killer, didn't mean he still loved me. But it could.

The s'more feast was well underway by the time Missy and I arrived. Even Mac-Avoy was there with his cameraman. They were acting suspicious, not really engaging in conversation, their gazes roaming the crowd. I'd need to keep an eye on those two. No telling when they'd decide to film "b-roll," which in reality would be a ploy to capture any drama on film.

The servers were back, dressed as butlers, minus the white gloves. They bustled around the bonfire, loading guests' roasting sticks with gourmet marshmallows: mint chocolate chip, red velvet, toasted coconut, espresso bean, and my favorite — chai tea. A table had been set up behind the chairs with a spread of hazelnut, orange, dark, and milk chocolate candy bars, homemade graham crackers, and a medley of red wine. A small section of pupcakes for the canines were regulated to a back corner of the table. This meal was all about the humans.

I pulled out my cell phone and snapped a handful of candid photos. I thought it might be fun to print them off and hang them up at the boutique. I spotted the Swansons drinking red wine and chatting with Pepper. Apparently, Pepper was no longer in hiding. I took a couple of more pictures. Their pooches were stretched out under their respective owners' chairs, snacking on pup-cakes.

Missy and I scooted around the fire pit and toward the table. I grabbed a couple of treats for her and an orange-flavored, dark-chocolate bar for me. I inhaled deeply. I loved campfires. Rich yellow and orange flickering flames. The smell of woodsy smoke. The crackling, sizzling hisses.

Campfires reminded me of my childhood, sitting around the fire listening to music, telling ghost stories, finding my favorite sweatshirt under my bed in late November, and it still smelling like that last campfire of the fall. Yup, there was nothing better than a campfire.

Betty waved me over. She was sitting in a director's chair, nestled next to Asher, with Raider at her side, slobber dripping from his jowls. Poor guy was the largest dog of the group. He looked so sad, as if none of the other humans wanted him to play with their pooches. Then again, he was a Saint Bernard; sometimes their resting face was just sad. I raised my cell phone to capture Betty with Asher, but missed the shot. Asher lowered his head to talk to the man next to him. Betty looked up and quickly posed with Raider. I took a couple of pictures of them.

Missy and I joined Betty. The heat of the fire immediately warmed my face. I pulled the chair back for more distance from the flames. I didn't want to overheat Missy. I picked her up, then set her down in my lap. Missy tried to get comfortable. She wasn't real quick about finding the perfect spot on my legs. She was killing me.

"Did you uncover any new clues?" Betty asked.

"Not really. How'd Raider like his dinner?" Missy settled in and licked my hand.

"He loved it." She patted his head. "I had a little taste. To make sure it was as good as

185

what Red fed us." She smacked her lips together. "Cookie, it was delicious. Missy was begging for some, so I gave her one, too. She woofed it down in no time. Don't you feed her?"

"Every day," I drawled.

Raider must have realized we weren't going anywhere. After a heavy sigh, he lay next to Betty's chair, resting his chin on his big fluffy paws.

"Asher scored me six meals, and I have two more for Raider's midnight snack. He's a growing boy, you know." She leaned closer, and spoke quietly. "I got to tell you. Marsha Thompson told Veronica that Asher's a widower."

"That's fascinating," I whispered back. "Why do we care that Asher's wife is dead?"

"Cookie, he's available." She wiggled her raspberry lipstick eyebrows.

I shook my head. "No. Not this week, he's not. You are not to be alone with him. Do you understand what I'm telling you?"

"But he likes me. He gives me a groovy vibe." She shimmied in her chair, bumping into Asher. He stopped talking to the gentleman on his other side and asked Betty if she needed anything.

I'd tell him what she needed. She needed to eject from Never-Never Land and return to earth.

Betty asked for a hot chocolate. He asked if I wanted him to bring me back anything. I declined, but thanked him for offering. Asher excused himself and promised to return quickly.

I grabbed Betty's sleeve and tugged her to me. "I don't care what kind of vibe he's giving you. No hanky panky in the RV. Got it?"

She pulled away. "Just because you're not getting any, I don't see why I can't. You really need to loosen up, Cookie."

I sighed. "If I were any more loose, my arms would fall off. What happened with MacAvoy? How'd he get Sunday to give him an interview?"

She slapped her knee. "That woman is a real piece of work. She'd give your mama a run for her money. On the short walk to the kitchen, she had that handsome reporter tripping all over himself begging for an interview. She agreed to five minutes."

"Were you around for his live update?"

"Nah. I saw Asher with all those doggie bags and raced to take them off his hands. How'd you see it?"

I looked into the fire as I stroked Missy's back. "I didn't. Grey called to check on us."

Betty waved Chase, the butler, over. He

187

loaded a toasted coconut marshmallow on her roasting stick. "Did you tell him we can take care of ourselves?"

"I assured him we were fine."

She stuck her marshmallow directly into the flame. "Did you tell him the police think you're a prime suspect?"

"I'm not a prime suspect."

She pulled her scorched marshmallow out of the fire. "Fine, fine. You're just a suspect. Either way, the police think you're capable of murder."

I scowled. "Can you say that a little louder? I'm not sure everyone heard you."

She carefully picked off the burnt crust, revealing a warm gooey mess. "I'm not trying to hurt your feelings, Cookie. But you gotta wake up and smell the coffee. You're in some trouble."

I was speechless. If I was in trouble, it was only because Betty was pushing me square into it with her loose lips.

Veronica strolled over to join us, carrying a folded sports chair. She moved Asher's empty one aside, making room for her and Harry. "Glad you finally made it," she said to me. "Betty wouldn't admit it, but she was worried about you."

More like she was worried I'd find a clue to Addison's killer without her.

"Did you find your phone?" Betty asked her around a mouthful of sweetness.

Veronica plopped down on her chair. "Sure did. Right where Pepper said I'd find it."

Rewind. I was missing the beginning of this conversation. "You lost your phone?" I asked.

"I was worried about Pepper; she seemed so scared. After dinner, I went to check on her. I must have set it on the table and forgot all about it when I left the tent. Did you know she's writing a cookbook?"

What was with the sudden rash of chefs writing cookbooks?

"I had no idea. Is this for people or dogs?" If what Hudson had said was true, I wondered what type of cookbook she could be writing. How to make take-out look like a homemade meal? I might actually buy that.

"I'm pretty sure they're pet recipes. I didn't look too closely, I was there to get my phone, not snoop through her private papers. But what was in plain view looked like reviews of recipes on her table. Betty, did you find your granny's brooch yet?"

I squinted at Betty. "*Your* granny's brooch?"

She licked sticky, melted sugar off her fingers. "You know, Cookie. The awful pin

189

she left me."

"Oh, I know exactly the one you're talking about." Her cover story was the brooch belonged to her? Give her an inch . . .

"Veronica was helping me look for it. She suggested I talk to Ranger Elliott."

"That's not a bad idea." Heck, if anyone had turned it in, that was the guy they'd give it to. Or Hudson. Hmmm. I should talk to him, too.

Betty shook her head. "I don't like him. He's got small eyes."

I sighed. "Enough about the small eyes."

"Betty," Veronica interjected, "he takes his job seriously."

"He's hiding something," Betty insisted.

"No, he's not," I said. "He's . . . single-minded."

Veronica's cheeks brightened in the glow of the roaring fire. "Actually, before you two arrived, there was a little scuffle. I'm surprised you haven't heard about it yet."

"See. I told ya. He's sketchy," Betty argued.

I shushed Betty and encouraged Veronica to continue.

"Well, he showed up at the campground all worked up, demanding to know who'd parked in the daytime parking lot. When he found out it was Addison, he got really mad.

Apparently, he'd already told her the day before she couldn't park there. He told her to move her car or he'd have it towed."

That didn't sound odd to me. Especially after what Hudson had explained about his routine checkup around the park. "Isn't that his job?"

She nodded. "Addison blew up and they got into a yelling match. Ranger Elliott had her car towed right then and there. He called it in over his radio."

I wish I could have seen that for pure entertainment value. "That still doesn't sound like he did anything wrong."

"Oh, I'm sure that was all aboveboard. He told her where she could pick up her car and how much it would cost her to get it out of storage. She said if he didn't drop the whole situation, she'd report him to his superiors, and he knew why. He handed her his cell phone and told her to go ahead. He even told her what number to call. He said she wouldn't threaten him the way she had everyone else. He wasn't afraid of her, and told her to back down or she'd pay."

Holy crapola. Pay how? With her life? Over a car parked in the wrong lot? Or over whatever she'd threatened to spill? Addison had been a very busy girl. Whatever could she have been holding over Ranger Elliott,

AKA Dudley Do-Right?

I was wrong, and Betty was right. Those were words I never thought I'd utter. But it sounded like Ranger Elliott *was* hiding something.

Hell's bells. If only Malone was here, I'd encourage Veronica to tell him her story and he could check it out. I wondered if I should tell her to talk to Lark or Finn. I'm sure at some point they'd be back like a bad computer virus.

CHAPTER SIXTEEN

After batting around lame ideas of what Addison could have been holding over Ranger Elliott with Betty and Veronica, I was ready to call it a night. It had been a long day, and I was exhausted. At some point, Missy had jumped off my lap and was now asleep under my chair. Asher had returned with Betty's drink and a beer for himself.

I was about to turn in, when Betty squeaked as if she'd been stepped on. Raider lifted his head and let out a deep bark.

"Are you okay?" I asked Betty.

"What are they doing here?" she muttered.

I looked in the direction she was starring. My stomach dropped. "Well, they're the cops, investigating a murder, so they're probably not here for the roasted marshmallows and chocolate bars."

She frowned. "They're a real drag."

My thoughts exactly. I grabbed Missy's leash and stood, hoping they weren't here to talk to me in front of an audience.

Detective Finn and her sidekick Detective Lark headed toward us. A quick glance around the campfire confirmed my fear. Everyone had stopped talking and was now focused on me. MacAvoy's cameraman immediately started filming. Wonderful. Forget background footage; I was providing the prime time broadcast for Mr. TV. He was probably praying I'd be arrested right there in front of everyone so he could interrupt the eleven o'clock news with a breaking eyewitness update.

"Ms. Langston." If it was possible, Detective Lark looked even more rumpled than the last time I'd seen him.

"Detectives." With a loud snort, Missy laid next to my feet. It was as if she knew what was about to happen. "I was just calling it a night. But you're still in time for roasted marshmallows."

"We'll pass," Lark said. "We had a few follow-up questions."

I firmly believed they had planned this. To take me away in front of everyone for further questioning, planting doubt in my fellow campers' minds, so if they had any information, they'd tell the police. Lark might look like a bumbling cop, but he was wily.

I pointed to the camera behind me. "You're on TV."

Finn marched over to MacAvoy and his cameraman. "Turn it off, or I'll take it away."

MacAvoy stepped in front of the camera. "Hudson Jones, the program director, gave us permission to film during the campfire."

Finn stepped closer to him and pushed her face into his. Her blond ponytail was pulled back so tightly her face looked more fierce than it had this afternoon. "Since I have the gun and handcuffs, I trump a silly program director."

MacAvoy's Adam's apple bobbed up and down. He reluctantly waved off the cameraman.

I felt a small sense of pleasure as he shut down the equipment.

Satisfied, Finn rejoined Lark.

She studied me as her partner asked, "When was the last time you saw Miss Rae?"

Betty stood and planted her hands on her hips. "We're a having a party here. Can't this wait until tomorrow?"

"You're not helping." I gave her a hug,

and told her to stay and enjoy herself. "Can we do this on the way back to camp?" I asked Finn. I wasn't going to help them publicly convict me of a crime I didn't commit in front of MacAvoy and the others.

"Lead the way." Lark motioned with his hand for me to start walking.

"I'm coming, too." Betty grabbed Raider's leash. She said her good-byes, then followed us.

I pulled out my flashlight and shined it on the pathway. "What do you want to know?"

"When was the last time you saw Ms. Rae?" Lark asked, operating his own flashlight.

I glanced at him. "You've already asked me that. My answer isn't going to change."

Lark pulled out his notebook and flipped through the pages. "Yeah, well, my notes are a little messy. Why don't you tell us one more time?"

He was lying. He wanted to catch me in an inconsistency. But why? What new information did they have that pointed them in my direction?

I focused on the path. "I talked to her in the kitchen. She was arguing with Redmond about the dinner menu."

"Wait," Finn barked.

Everyone froze. My pulse sped up. Finn

flipped through her notepad. "You didn't mention they were arguing."

"Are you sure? I thought I did." Okay, maybe I didn't. Now I was confused as to what I'd said or hadn't said. There was too much information for me to keep track of.

I wished my best friend Darby was here for moral support. Or Grey. I could use his sound advice about now. Heck, at this point I'd take Detective Malone.

Finn closed her notebook. "What about the phone call from the victim?" she asked, unable to hide the irritation from her voice.

"What phone call?"

"According to her cell, her last call was to you."

I shook my head, confused. "I didn't get a call from her."

"You won't mind letting us check your cell phone then."

So they had recovered Addison's cell phone. Poor Hudson. I wouldn't be surprised if he'd be the next target of a police investigation. I reached for my back pocket, and my fingers brushed against my cell. If all they wanted was to look at my call history in order to clear my name, I had no problem.

I caught a gleam of victory in Finn's eye. What was I doing? I had enough experience to know that this was most likely a ploy to get my phone and access to everything on it. Who knew if I'd even get it back?

I shoved my hand in my back pocket. "Do you have a warrant?"

The detectives exchanged a frustrated look.

"We can get one." Lark pushed his man lips together. He didn't look threatening, he looked tired. Well, so was I.

"Let me know when you do. I'll be happy to turn it over."

Finn nailed me with a hard look. "We'll be back. And next time, we'll make sure to take you for a drive to the station."

Great. I'd just been threatened with jail. Some things just didn't change. It didn't take a brain surgeon to figure out I was their main person of interest. I had to redirect their investigation.

"I heard an interesting story tonight. The park ranger and Addison had a heated argument yesterday. By the end of it, he threatened to make her pay. Maybe you should concentrate on him for a while."

Finn raised an eyebrow, shooting me a glassy stare. "I think you should worry about yourself and let us handle the investigation." After that last pronouncement, the two detectives walked away into the darkness.

Betty and I watched Lark and Finn stalk off. Once they were out of earshot, she grabbed the flashlight from me and pointed it at my face.

"Are you going to call Grey? I bet he can get you a really good lawyer."

I yanked the flashlight away from her. "Chill out, sassy pants. I can't think straight when you're shining that in my eyes."

I hated that Betty was probably right. Somehow, I'd managed to make myself a target. I needed to find a way to get that bull's-eye off me and onto the real killer.

If only I knew who that was.

Back at our RV, I made up the pullout bed in the dining area while Betty showered. Missy jumped up on the bed and made herself at home. I slipped into a pair of sleeping shorts and a Dallas Cowboys T-shirt before brushing my teeth and washing my face at the kitchen sink.

All the way back to camp, Betty had kept asking me about the secret between Addison and me. It didn't matter how many times I said Addison had lied, Betty didn't believe me. I knew the minute she finished with her shower, she'd start pestering me all over again.

Ready to turn in for the night, I flipped off the lights. I eased between the cool sheets, careful not to disturb Missy who was already sawing logs with gusto. Aah. It felt so good to stretch and clear my mind of all the craziness of the last twelve hours. I rolled over and lightly stroked Missy's back. In a perfect world, I'd fall asleep before Betty finished her bedtime routine.

With my eyes closed, I concentrated on breathing. Instead of counting sheep, or even Missy's snores, I ended up counting suspects. So much for clearing my mind. Red, Hudson, Pepper, and possibly Ranger Elliott had made my mental list. I didn't see the park ranger killing Addison over a car parked in the wrong lot, but I kept him on my list. It sounded like he had a secret and Addison knew about it. I wondered how I could find out what that might be.

Since it didn't seem like I'd be falling asleep anytime soon, I moved on to my mama's letters. If they weren't in the envelopes, where could they be? Scattered in Addison's belongings, maybe? I scoffed. There was no way Sunday Hill would grant me permission to look through Addison's things. And even if by some miracle she did,

I couldn't imagine under what circumstance she'd just hand those letters over to me.

There was a small part of me that wanted to just leave the whole mess alone. At this point, what did it matter? Addison was dead. The letters weren't in their envelopes, so how would anyone know they belonged to my mama? They were simply addressed to *Barbara.* Not many people would recognize who Barbara was. Maybe I needed to just walk away from that whole situation. It would make my life a lot easier.

I heard the water shut off. Betty would be back, ready to pick up where she'd left off with her endless interrogation. I flipped to my other side, keeping my back to the bedroom door.

A distorted shadow on the window shade reminded me of a frumpy Lark silhouette. He obviously didn't like me and thought I was involved with Addison's death. Perhaps Betty had a point — it was time to call Grey and get a lawyer.

The bedroom door swung open. I held my breath.

"I know you're not sleeping," Betty said into the darkness.

I remained quiet. Missy lifted her head for a second. With a sigh, she snuggled into the blankets and fell back asleep.

Betty shuffled to the bed and sat on the edge. "Are you ready to tell me about the secret you and Addison had?"

"There is no secret," I ground out. "She was lying. I just met her a couple of months ago."

"Why would she lie?"

"I don't know. Why did she want me to write her foreword? Why did she lie to Hudson about her agent being here? She did things I can't explain, let alone understand myself." I yawned. "Please, go to bed."

"Are you going to call Grey?" she pressed.

"I'm going to go to sleep."

"Do you want to compare notes on suspects?"

"No."

"Do you want to tell ghost stories?"

"No."

She bounced on the bed, jostling Missy and me. "I imagined this trip being more like a slumber party. Staying up late. Gossiping. Making a plan to find your brooch."

Missy grumbled, and jumped off the bed. The sound of her nails clicking on the marble floor echoed in the quiet as she made her way to the recliner. I wished I could escape as easily.

"I promise I'll find your granny's pin. Don't you worry about it. I got a plan." Apparently, Betty refused to stop talking until I engaged in conversation for a few minutes.

I surrendered and sat up. "You know, Veronica had a good idea. If you're not going to talk to Ranger Elliott tomorrow, I will. I'd like to find out a little more about his relationship with Addison anyway."

"You're barking up the wrong tree. No one turned in the brooch. It was stolen. I think Addison did it. We need to find a way to get the police to let us look through her stuff."

My eye started to twitch. I was either overtired or stressed out. I didn't know how to get Betty off the jewel thief track. "Sunday has her belongings now. If we have to beg anyone, it's her. Good luck with that, you'd get further with the police."

"Tomorrow, we'll poke around the other RVs and tents. Bet we find a clue. Oh, I know. We can sneak into Sunday's tent and look through the pet chef's belongings while she's giving that interview with Mac."

Whoa. "You call him Mac? When did that start?"

"He told me to. Cookie, you gotta admit, he's hot stuff." She wiggled her freshly applied Pretty in Pink lipstick eyebrows. She was going to get makeup all over the pillow case.

I punched the middle of my pillow, then fluffed up the edges. This conversation was over. "You be careful. Like my Grandma Tillie used to say about the losers I brought home from college, 'Even rust will shine if you scrub it long enough.' "

CHAPTER SEVENTEEN

The next morning, I woke up with dog paws in my face, and no clear direction about the letters. There was no dream, no epiphany, no grand idea on what my next move should be. It was a rather disappointing moment, but not unexpected.

I rolled out of bed, pulled my hair into a ponytail, and tugged on a pair of sweatpants with a T-shirt. I took Missy out for a quick potty break. The morning sun filtered through a small cluster of sycamore trees, bathing the lawn in a golden glow. Weather wise, it was going to be a beautiful day. I waved to my fellow campers who were also out with their pooches. They waved back with a quick good morning shout. Maybe the whole situation was looking up. It seemed like I was off the camper pariah list, which was surprising after the late night visit from the Dynamic Duo.

Once Missy finished, we returned to the

RV to find a chai tea latte waiting for me. Hanging out with Betty had its perks. She tried to talk me into wearing matching outfits again. I'm not gonna lie, it scared me a little to think she might have bought animal print silk pajamas for me. Next, she'd want to paint my eyebrows with Vengeful Red lipstick.

We had an hour until we were supposed to meet at Asher's RV to start our snooping tour. I grabbed the mug of tea and hurried to shower. I was determined to find a way to turn the investigation off me and onto the real killer. I needed a Hail Mary. I needed a miracle.

Betty, Raider, Missy, and I rolled up to Asher's RV at exactly nine o'clock. Betty wore a bright pink ensemble, with the glittery words, "KISS ME" on her shirt. Discretion wasn't her middle name. To think, I could have had one too, if only I would've agreed.

Betty adjusted her handbag to rest in the crook of her arm, then rapped on the side of the RV. After fluffing her hair, she licked her lips.

"Stop," I said. "It's too early in the morning for your crazy."

Betty pursed her lips, looking me over with an assessing gaze. "You could use a little crazy."

Call me a stick in the mud, but I preferred to camp with no makeup, jeans, and my graphic T-shirt, which read, "Bulldogs are a girl's best friend."

My stomach growled. "What do you think we'll have for breakfast? I'm starving."

"I'm looking forward to some flapjacks and bacon."

Asher swung open the door. "Good morning, ladies." He greeted us with a wide smile, his white teeth a sharp contrast against his creamy mocha skin. "You look lovely this morning. Come in. Come in." His accent seemed less British this morning.

He jumped out and held the door open for us. The man was handsome. Betty wasn't exaggerating about how sexy Asher was. This morning, he wore a gray beanie cap, long-sleeved white cotton tee, and black jeans. But his charisma was a little too rehearsed. Almost as if he was raised to be charming, not sincere.

And I just had to say it. Why was a man in his forties showing interest in a woman twice his age? Was he just being nice? Or did he have an ulterior motive?

"Eddie's in the bedroom. Once you're all inside, I'll bring him out. There shouldn't be a problem, but I didn't want to over-whelm him."

"Thanks again for letting us check out your coach," I said as we climbed the entry steps.

He closed the door. "You're welcome. Pepper isn't here yet. I made coffee, if you'd like some."

I hadn't thought it was possible, but Asher's RV was even more posh than ours, with two-toned leather couches and recliners, a dropdown TV, and cherry wood cabinetry. Plus, he had a pop-out balcony.

Betty ooed and ahed, running her fingers over the railing. "Cookie, you gotta buy a rig with a balcony."

She was so believable, I was half convinced I was in the market for an RV. "How many people does it sleep?" I asked.

"Eight."

It was definitely roomy. Three adults, a Saint Bernard and two mid-sized dogs, walking around the middle of the coach, and I didn't feel like we were all on top of each other.

"The tile floors are heated from the front of the coach to the back." Asher pressed a button on a touch screen panel. The re-cessed LED ceiling light blinked on. I looked up and blinked in surprise. Mirrored ceiling tiles. I'm sure someone thought it was tasteful. Maybe Betty and Asher were more suited for each other than I realized.

Betty moved to the galley, pointing out the wine chiller. She began opening and closing drawers. "I bet you're a good cook."

He shook his head. "Not really. I bet you are, though. What's your signature dish?"

My phone rang, saving me from whatever dance those two were performing. I pulled the phone out of my pocket and saw Mama's number. I sighed. I couldn't keep putting it off. I needed to take the call.

I handed Betty Missy's leash and promised I'd be as quick as I could.

I exited as I answered, immediately taking an offensive approach to direct the conversation. "Hey, Mama. It's pretty early for you to be calling. Did you see Daddy off on a business trip?"

"Good morning to you too, Melinda Sue. I watched the news last night on that celebrity network channel. Your daddy told me not to call, but I couldn't sleep. Aren't you camping in Laguna Hills?"

I rubbed my face. News of murder traveled fast. Apparently all the way to Dallas. She had to be upset if she was calling me at six-thirty, Texas time. The worry in her voice was real. But its direction was unclear. Was she concerned for me or because I was once again smack dab in the middle of a scandal? As if she had room to talk.

"Yes, Betty and I are glamping in the hills." I headed toward the RV for some privacy.

"The same campground where that pet chef was mur-dered?" Her voice rose, breaking on the word "murdered."

"Yes." I debated if I should mention the letters. Or that Addison was the daughter of a former Miss America judge she'd slept with all those years ago. I felt myself getting prickly.

"Did you know her?" she asked cautiously. If we were together, she'd be pouring a tall glass of sweet tea to deflect the importance of the question. I was on to her manipulations.

"Not as well as people thought. Why do you ask? Does her name sound familiar?" I baited her.

Suddenly, a memory of Mama and James Rae, giggling over dinner, popped into my head. They gently touched each other's hands as they discussed who would pay for the check. I felt sick. How had I not picked up on their relationship at the time? I shook my head to erase the image.

"Whatever do you mean?" Mama cried.

"Why would a California pet chef's name sound familiar to me? You're not making any sense lately. I thought we had gotten closer after my last visit. I'm just heartbroken that you've pulled away from me."

I sighed. Suddenly, it was all about her. A familiar tactic, making it difficult to determine if she was playing me by diverting the topic, or just being herself. "I've done no such thing."

"Yes, you have. The last few weeks, you've been distant and stopped confiding in me."

I reached our RV just as my mama said, "Are you upset that I called Grey? I was just trying to help bring you two back together."

Adrenaline raced through my body. "You did what? When?"

"Uh-oh." She sounded like a little girl who'd gotten caught in a lie. "He didn't mention that to you?"

I grabbed the door to the RV and swung it open. "No, he did not. Mama, why in the world would you do that?" I continued on, not letting her explain. "Why can't you stop interfering in my life? Lord knows, you have your own problems; stay out of mine." I slammed the door, then stomped up the entry stairs.

Silence on the other end. Not so much as

a breath filtered across the airwaves.

I sighed. She was waiting for me to apologize for losing my temper. And maybe I should. But I wasn't going to. I just couldn't do it, not now that I knew for a fact she'd cheated on my daddy. How dared she stick her nose into my personal life?

"You've never talked to me like that before," she said softly.

I opened the blinds, keeping an eye out for Betty and the dogs. "Maybe I should have."

"You think you know something about me." The iron in her voice was back. She wasn't one to be walked over, not even by her own flesh and blood.

I matched her grit. "I do. Addison Rae is the daughter of your former lover, James Rae —. Olympic athlete, and former Miss America judge."

Mama gasped. I waited for her to deny it. To rattle off some lame excuse. Instead, she hung up.

"Really?" I shouted into the phone. "You just hang up?"

I'd never pegged my mama for a coward. Raw emotions boiled inside me. I wasn't sure what I was feeling at the moment, but none of it was positive. A sob of anger caught in the back of my throat. Damn her.

I looked out the dining area window for a sign of Betty and the dogs. I'd been gone longer than I'd expected. Who knew what she was doing?

My phone rang. Mama was back. I sucked in a fortifying breath. I didn't even get in a greeting; she was already talking fifty words a second.

"I was in the bedroom with your daddy. Do you want him to know we're talking about this? Are you trying to break his heart all over again? We've moved past that whole sordid business years ago. Whatever she said to you, it's a lie. I cannot believe you would throw this in my face, Melinda Sue Langston. We do *not* talk about *The Incident.*"

I'd never heard or seen her lose control. She was the original perfectly composed, iron-fisted lady. I couldn't begin to picture what she looked like right now.

"Lord have mercy, Mama. You need to calm down. You're talking so fast I can barely understand you."

I could hear her sniffling on the other end. I dropped to the recliner ashamed, and buried my face in the palm of my hand. I'd made my mama cry. And for a brief moment, I'd actually experienced a spark of satisfaction about it. "Are you going to let me talk?" I asked softly.

"I don't know that I want to hear what you have to say."

There was no easy way to tell her. "Addison had your letters to her father."

She gasped. "Hell's bells."

The beginning of a smile played at the corner of my mouth. "Exactly. He passed away recently, and Addison found them. Up until then, she had no idea about the two of you. She was consumed with seeking some form of revenge, and threatened to send them to Daddy if I didn't help her establish herself in town."

"That can't happen —"

"It won't," I interrupted. "She's dead."

"Oh. Yes. Well, that's unfortunate." She regained her composure. "Are you okay?"

I was slightly taken aback at the question. My knee-jerk response was I was fine. But was I? Heck, I wasn't even sure what she was asking me. Okay about the affair? Okay that Addison was dead? She didn't even know I was a suspect. "I'm getting there."

"Melinda, she was blackmailing you."

"I know."

"And now she's dead." She was starting to piece it all together.

"That's right." I paced the length of the galley. "There's more."

"I don't know how much more I can take.

I have never had a case of the vapors in my life, but if I was ever going to, this would be the time. Okay, I'm sitting down. Tell me everything."

I explained all the things Addison had wanted me to do in order to get the letters back. How I'd upheld my end of the agreement, but Addison always found a way to drag it on for just a little longer.

"That's because you're honest. You may be as hardheaded as a mule, but you're as honest as the day is long."

"Thank you." Even though it was backhanded, it was probably the best compliment she'd ever given me. "The day Addison died, I was supposed to meet her to finally get the letters."

"Do you have them?" She wasn't able to keep the hope out of her voice. "Your Daddy can't see those. I don't remember what I wrote, but I can imagine."

I preferred not to imagine. "She never made it. I've looked for them, but I've come up empty-handed. I have the envelopes, but that's it. She must have hidden the actual letters."

I was momentarily distracted by Pepper scurrying around the RVs with a white trash bag. Why was she acting so sneaky? And why wasn't she with Betty and Asher?

Mama's voice brought me back to our conversation. "Do I need to come out there and help you? Those letters and photos need to be destroyed."

"No." The word came out harsher than I intended. I softened my tone. "Please. Stay home. No one knows Addison was blackmailing me. Not Betty. Not Grey. Not the police. I need to keep it that way. The homicide detectives have already questioned me because someone overheard Addison and me argue. I'm trying to cooperate, but keep a low profile."

"I can be there in just a few hours."

I rubbed my temple. "Mama, think about it. What are you going to tell Daddy? You were just here. Besides, you and Betty have one thing in common. Neither of you know how to fly under the radar. I got to go. Love ya."

Heck, I wasn't even sure I wanted to find those letters anymore. What was that going to accomplish?

"But you have to make me a promise," she begged.

"What?"

"When you find those letters, you burn them. Don't read them. Please."

If I found the letters, I promised I wouldn't read them.

CHAPTER EIGHTEEN

"Sorry that took so long. Did I miss Pepper?"

I'd just returned to Asher's RV. From the looks of the patio table, Betty and Asher had shared coffee and pastries while I was away. My stomach growled. I hoped Betty wasn't thinking about skipping breakfast because she'd shared a bear claw with dreamboat Asher.

Asher carried the mugs to the sink to load the dishwasher. Betty was nowhere to be found. "Pepper never showed."

Really? I wondered why. I'd just seen her dumping her trash. I'd assumed she was preparing for our visit. Had she gotten caught up in cleaning and lost track of time? No way. Last night, she'd wanted to spend time with Asher on a more personal level. She liked the idea of becoming his new pet chef. So what could have happened that she blew off the opportunity to cozy up to a potential new client?

"She probably overslept. The fresh air does that to some people."

He offered me a cup of coffee. I passed, explaining I was more of a tea person.

"Where'd Betty disappear to?" I asked.

He nodded toward the back. "She's in the little girl's room."

Ah. Betty code for snooping. I think this was the point where I was supposed to keep him occupied. "Are you still planning on checking out Pepper's tent?"

His smile seemed a little uncertain, which I found totally out of character. "I'm not sure that's a good idea."

"Why's that?"

Betty darted out of the bedroom, her straw handbag swinging from her arm. "Cookie, what took you so long?"

"I was talking to my mama."

She rolled her eyes. "Yeah, you're normally much quicker to get her off the phone. She must have been on a real tear." She patted Asher's forearm. "Handsome, you don't mind if I show Mel the bedroom, do you? I want to her to see your cedar-lined wardrobes."

He checked his watch. "I agreed to meet someone at ten."

"You're not meeting another woman, are

you?" Betty batted her eyes.

He smiled. "I thought you were in a hurry to get to breakfast?"

"Don't worry. We'll be lickety-split," Betty promised.

I followed her to the main bath, which was in the bedroom at the rear of the rig.

"Check this out," she whispered.

After placing her handbag on the counter, she opened the wardrobe, then pulled out a drawer. Shoved in the very back was a square mahogany box.

"This bedroom is much better. Oh, double sinks," I spoke loudly so Asher wouldn't wonder what we were doing.

Betty followed my lead. "Look at the shower."

I dropped my voice to a low whisper. "Forget the box. We're looking for my brooch, remember?"

"It's an urn. There's someone in it."

My mouth dropped open. "For real? How do you know?"

"Well, duh. I looked. There's a bag of ashes inside. What if his wife didn't die from an accident and he had her cremated to hide the evidence?"

I looked over my shoulder. "That's a huge leap from an urn to murder. You've got to stop this madness. And if he did kill his wife, why in the world would he bring her ashes on a glamping trip with his dog?"

"People do strange things all the time."

"Not that strange." I pointed to the white box shoved behind the urn. "What's in there? Is that my brooch?" I asked, excitedly.

Betty palmed the small box and quickly flipped the lid open.

I caught my breath. Diamond cufflinks and diamond earrings. Just like the cufflinks Asher had claimed he was missing. The ones he insinuated that Addison had stolen from him. I looked behind me again, making sure we were still alone.

Had he lost the cufflinks? He specifically said he'd never found them. Why would he lie about it? I rubbed my face. There was so much going on, I wasn't sure what was important to remember and what was a random situation.

"Put it away," I whispered.

Betty quickly shoved the box back inside the drawer.

"Look how much storage room there is?" I practically shouted. I pushed past Betty and walked right into Asher's six pack. Oomph. "Hey. Betty's right, your rig is so much better than what we have." My heart raced as I worried what he'd seen.

His six-feet-two frame blocked the only exit. "What are you doing in here?" All charm had vanished. In its place resided suspicious ire.

Betty snagged her handbag and slipped around me. "Sorry, big boy. You might as well know the truth. I like to snoop in medicine cabinets. By the way, you seem to have an awful lot of Prozac and Spiderman Band-Aids for a guy in his forties."

He wasn't smiling. "Those are for Eddie."

"The Band-Aids or the pills?" I asked. I know, I know. But I couldn't help myself.

He crossed his arms. "He's got a bad case of OCD."

My stomach growled, interrupting the silent who-will-blink-first standoff. "Can we go eat breakfast now? I missed my morning *treat.*" I spoke loud enough for Raider and Missy to hear. Predictably, both dogs came racing toward us at the "T" word.

Raider pushed his head around Asher, shoving him aside. Betty pulled a dried apple ring from her pocket and tossed it to him. He snatched it up immediately, begging for more. Missy, on the other hand, sat next to him waiting patiently for her turn, a drool puddle at her front paws.

"Well?" I motioned with my hand for Betty to give my girl one, too. Betty handed me a treat. I bent down and held it out. Missy snapped it up. I patted her head and told her she was a good girl.

"Thanks again for the tour. You've got a great setup." I grabbed Betty's sleeve and dragged her with me. "We gotta go. I don't want to miss breakfast. And you have your appointment, after all." The dogs charged after us, dragging their leashes. Once we were at the front of the coach, we grabbed our pooch's leads.

"I'll see you at the obstacle course later, big guy," Betty called out. She blew him a kiss good-bye.

We scrambled out the door. "Seriously? You're making a date with the guy who just caught us snooping in his bathroom? And I might add, who you think may have killed his wife."

"Absolutely. He digs me." She wagged her eyebrows.

"Really?"

She shrugged. "I guess he could have been pretending he was digging it. But it doesn't matter. *I* was digging it."

I would never understand how her mind worked.

At eighty-something, Betty wasn't one to pass up a possible date with a single man.

I'm not one to pass up a free meal.

After escaping Asher's RV by the skin of our teeth, we made our way to the kitchen and stuffed ourselves with scrambled eggs, waffles, bacon, strawberries, and fresh-squeezed orange juice. For the canine camper, a tasty sweet potato hash, rice pudding, and a bowl of "tail" mix was laid out in abundance.

I'm not a proponent for the all-American breakfast buffet. The food tends to be dry and overcooked, the eggs rubbery. But I had to admit, everything I ate was perfectly prepared, fresh, and delicious. Red might be an angry soul, but he could cook.

He remained busy between ordering his staff around, cooking, and talking to diners. I caught him giving me the evil eye a few times. I really didn't understand what he had against me. He watched Betty taste the sweet potato hash before giving it to Raider. He frowned, muttering a string of incoherent words as he walked away.

As we finished our meal, I looked around for Hudson. The man was MIA. I asked if anyone had seen him, but no one had. It wasn't surprising, really. He was probably hiding somewhere, licking his wounds from the tongue-lashing Sunday had given him last night about her broken luggage. Or he could be doing his job, preparing for the day's events.

I swallowed the last of my orange juice. "Any sign of my brooch while you were tossing Asher's RV?" I asked Betty.

She dropped a waffle at Raider's front paws. "Nada. I saw diamond earrings and a gold band."

"I think we need to find Hudson and see if anyone has turned it in to the lost and found. In fact, we should have done that immediately."

Betty licked a dollop of syrup off her finger. "I guess we can trust him."

I wasn't sure what trusting Hudson had to do with finding my brooch. "Speaking of trust, what's going on with you and Asher?"

"I'm just getting started with him, Cookie. He liked my shirt." She pointed to the glittery lips on her top.

"Please tell me he didn't kiss you."

"Not yet. Soon. But if he's a bad guy, I've got to drop him like a hot potato."

She probably needed to drop him regardless.

"About the urn." I lowered my voice. "You can't go around accusing him of killing his wife just because he travels with an urn full of ashes. You're making assumptions that could negatively affect his life." And hers.

"I'm not so sure." She held up a finger and ticked off her points, one by one. "We know his wife is dead. We know he lied about the cufflinks. We know he thinks you were involved with offing Addison."

I narrowed my eyes. "I'm not so sure about that last part. Does he really?" She made valid points, which confused me as to why she'd even consider him a potential love interest.

She shrugged. "He did. Maybe he changed his mind."

"But none of that points to him being a wife-killer. Maybe he loved his wife so much, he can't stand to be apart from her, even in death."

Betty scoffed. "Don't forget, Cookie. I'm a widow. I know all about losing a spouse. There's something off about a person who travels with a dead body. Even if that body is ashes."

"If there's even the slightest possibility he could be dangerous, you need to stop trying to get . . ." I made circles with my hands, not sure how to say it, ". . . get him to make a move on you."

Betty sighed. "You're a real killjoy."

"I'm thinking clearly for the both of us. You're walking around in a fog of lust."

I tapped my fork against my plate. He had

lied about not having the cufflinks. Was it possible he set up Addison to take the fall? Why would he do that? I wondered if he'd filed an insurance report. Lying about missing jewelry didn't make anyone a murderer. Why didn't he want to tour Pepper's tent? Who was he meeting with?

Missy, who was chilling under my chair, grumbled. I tossed half of a piece of bacon to her.

"What time was MacAvoy going to interview Sunday?" I asked.

"They agreed on eleven o'clock. She had a conference call with New York early this morning."

She seemed to have a lot of conference calls. "Did you hear where the interview was being conducted?"

"Nope."

I gathered our dishes and placed them in a plastic tub while Betty snagged a napkin full of tail mix and stored it in her purse for later. We left the kitchen and walked along the stone pathway toward headquarters.

"Who was that guy Asher was talking to last night? I don't remember seeing him before," I asked Betty.

"Craig Sutton. He belongs to that really cute Lhasa Poo, Codi. He thinks they'll clean up on the obstacle course."

"Why's that?"

"Codi's very intelligent and quick to obey."

I nodded. "That's half the battle right there. I've been meaning to ask, what prizes did you donate on behalf of the boutique?"

"Don't you worry about it. I shipped the normal donations: flying discs, balls, and collapsible water bowls."

"Back to Asher. Who do you think he was meeting at ten? He was being a little secretive about that."

"As long as it's not a woman, I don't care."

I glanced at Betty. She'd heard what she wanted to hear. He'd never confirmed or denied if he was meeting a man or a woman. He'd avoided answering that question altogether.

I continued to process what we knew about the brooch, the letters, and Addison's murder. The brooch was lost and those people who we'd talked to hadn't seen it. We needed to speak to Hudson.

The letters were missing from their envelopes. Had someone tossed her tent and, in the process, nabbed the letters? If so, who could have done that? What if she'd never brought the letters and they were back at her house in Laguna Beach? I hadn't thought of that possibility until now. How would I get my hands on them?

As for Addison's murder, there was no clear suspect. There seemed to be a number of people who had motive, but no one stood out from the rest. It was possible Sunday had information that could help uncover the killer. I wanted to hear what MacAvoy was asking her.

I stopped walking and turned to Betty. "I want to crash the interview."

Betty beamed at me like I'd just invited her to a ten grand shopping spree. "Let's do it."

We agreed that, as the one in charge, Hudson would know where the interview was being held, so we made our way to the headquarters tent. Unlike the previous day, the door was closed. Apprehension settled in my gut. I pulled back the heavy canvas and stepped inside.

"Hello. Hudson?"

Empty. No Hudson. No MacAvoy. No Sunday.

Betty and Raider crammed inside behind me. "Where is everyone?"

Good question. Until today, headquarters had always been open. Why not now? Where was Hudson? Missy and Raider headed straight to the water bowls. They were empty. Hudson hadn't been in yet.

If I were MacAvoy, where would I want to conduct the interview? What would make the best TV? I thought about it for a second. Either the scene of the crime or Addison/ Sunday's tent.

"Let's go to Sunday's tent and then the spa. If MacAvoy could arrange the interview at either of those locations, it would make great TV. And we all know he's about getting the story and bringing in the viewers."

"Good thinking."

We skedaddled to Addison's old tent, which was on the far end of the campground. Site number five, where there was the most privacy. Betty and Raider took the lead. We walked quickly, making good time. Within a couple of minutes, we could see the tent.

In the distance, a tall masculine figure skittered along the backside of Addison/ Sunday's tent. Raider immediately went on high alert, barking and lunging. Betty jerked forward, struggling to keep control of the large pup.

"Heel," she yelled. "Heel."

He continued to bark, dragging her as he charged toward the stranger.

Missy and I raced to catch up, Missy snorting and panting the whole way. I grabbed Raider's leash from Betty, tugging

229

him backward. "Sit," I shouted.

He turned his head to look at me as he continued to run.

"Sit."

He finally stopped running in front of Sunday's tent. He sat, with a dopey dog smile, waiting to be rewarded for obeying.

Betty caught up to us. She bent over, hands on her thighs, sucking in a couple of deep breaths. "Th— thanks. He got spooked."

Raider waited expectedly for his reward. I wasn't so sure he deserved one, but Betty opened her purse and pulled out a dried apple ring. I doubt Caro would have thought that was a good idea.

"Did you see who that was?" I asked.

"I sure did. Red. He's a sneaky snake. What was he doing?"

I pushed my lips together, deep in thought. Didn't we just leave Red at the kitchen? What could have been so important that he'd leave his mealtime responsibilities to snoop around Addison's tent? What could he be looking for?

"Sunday said he was a client years ago. Maybe he's trying to get back in her good graces."

Betty scrunched up her face and looked in the direction Red had run off to. "By creeping around her personal space? We need to keep an eye on him."

Agreed. "Whatever he was doing in there, he wasn't sticking around long enough to chat about it."

What did he think he would find in Addison's tent? And why was he looking for it?

CHAPTER NINETEEN

We were still set on crashing MacAvoy's interview with Sunday. Although, after Raider's shenanigans, including the dogs wasn't ideal. Bringing him to an event like this might have been premature. Don't get me wrong, Raider wasn't a bad dog. He's a one-hundred-and-thirty-pound Saint Bernard puppy, full of energy, but lacking discipline.

Since Betty had rescued him, I'd been concerned that if she didn't learn how to control him, she could be seriously injured. She was barely five feet, and couldn't weigh more than a hundred pounds.

With some careful wording, I convinced her that leaving Missy and Raider in the RV until the obstacle course competition at two o'clock was best for both the dogs. They'd be well rested and compete better.

Since Sunday's tent was a bust, we hurried to the spa. Believe it or not, there was a line. Apparently, a little murder didn't detract people from pedicures and massages. There was no interview happening there.

"Now what?" Betty tapped her foot in the grass.

I should have known better. Hudson didn't trust MacAvoy any more than I did. Hud wouldn't have agreed to allow the interview at the spa. There was only one place left — MacAvoy's RV.

"Come on." Luckily, we knew exactly where to go since Mr. TV's campsite was right next to ours.

As in a typical campground, a handful of campers and their pets played on the grass, while others sat in their lawn chairs in their campsite, shooting the breeze, getting to know each other.

Almost everyone called out hello to Betty. They wanted to chat. I dragged her away, solidifying the perception I was an awful person. Sure, we could have stayed behind to mingle with her friends, but I didn't have that luxury right now. I was a murder suspect. My objective had to be clearing my name. And the only way to do that was to either be a star witness or get the goods on the real killer. Since I had been nowhere near the crime scene, I couldn't play the role of star witness. That left finding evidence on who was letting me take the rap for their crime.

It was almost eleven. If the interview was going down here, it was about to happen at any moment. We were a few yards from Mr. TV's RV.

"Hold up." I grabbed Betty's arm and slowed her down.

"I thought we were in a hurry?" she complained.

"We are. But let's not draw any more attention to ourselves than we already have."

"Oh. Oh! Are we in stealth mode? Maybe we should be wearing all black," Betty whispered.

I shot her a questioning look. "What are you talking about?"

"Aren't we spying? In the movies, spies always wear black."

I pointed to the group of campers tossing a dog disc on the grass. "We're surrounded by people. There's no chance of spying. We're going to eavesdrop. There's a difference."

Okay, there really wasn't, but this was one of those times I mentioned earlier where redirecting Betty was easier than stopping her. In Betty's mind, spying required a disguise. Eavesdropping was what she did on daily basis.

We nonchalantly approached the coach, acting as if we belonged there. I noticed all the blinds were pulled shut. Because he was gone, or because he wanted privacy? Either option was a possibility.

Betty shoved her ear against the side of the coach.

"What do you hear?" I asked.

"Quiet as a church mouse. I don't think they're in there."

"I'm going to ring the bell. Back away so he doesn't hit you with the door if he answers."

Betty stepped back just as the door swung open, almost knocking her in the head.

"Are you trying to kill me?" she cried out, glowering at MacAvoy.

He looked me straight in the face, his green eyes narrowed. "You shouldn't be snooping."

"We're not," Betty denied.

"How'd you know we were here?" I asked.

He leaned out the door and pointed to a small black circle on the side of the RV. "The security camera. I've been watching you." He smiled casually, and I wanted nothing more than to wipe that self-satisfied grin off his face.

I'm sure we looked ridiculous sneaking

around, acting like he was expecting us. I wondered how long he'd been watching.

"How'd the interview go with Sunday?" I asked.

"She hasn't arrived yet." His gaze flitted around the area; he was obviously looking for her.

I couldn't help smiling myself. "She stood you up?"

Frustration flashed across his face. "Not at all. What do you want? Have you finally realized you need my help?"

Lordy, he sounded like a broken record. "I can't imagine what type of assistance you could even offer me."

"You'd be surprised. I have connections you'd find helpful."

I had no idea what he was referring to. Nor did I want to know. If I needed some type of favor, asking MacAvoy would be an option so far down the totem pole, it'd be underground.

"Aren't you part of the RV tour? Asher let us peek inside his rig earlier; now it's your turn." Betty tried to walk inside.

MacAvoy held out his hand, effectively stopping her. "Hold up there. This isn't a good time."

"Oh. Do you have a lady friend in there? Don't you worry, I'm not jealous. We're very discreet. Our lips are sealed." She tried to push her way inside again.

His eyebrows shot up. "Even I know you don't keep quiet."

"So you do have someone in there?" I asked, surprised.

"There you are," MacAvoy called out over Betty's head, relief coloring the cheerfulness in his tone.

I spun around to see Sunday stomping across the lawn, teetering side-to-side as her heels sank into the grass. "You're the media, you need to do a report on this. It's ridiculous," she shrieked.

MacAvoy stepped out of the RV. Betty and I parted like the Red Sea for Moses, eager to watch, but not wanting to get caught up in the middle of whatever meltdown was about to happen.

Sunday barged past us, stopping inches from MacAvoy. Her face was pale and puffy, her eyes red-rimmed and swollen. From crying? Hardly. She didn't seem to be the type. Maybe allergies. Pollen? Grass? Dogs?

"I don't have time for their red tape." Her voice rose with each word. "I have business to conduct."

MacAvoy looked like he was about to tell her to calm down. He'd better rethink that fast. Sunday didn't come across as a woman who appreciated being told to "calm down."

He cleared his throat. "Come in. Let's talk. What seems to be the problem?" he asked, holding the door open for her.

She didn't move. Could be because her high heels had sunk into the ground, rooting her in place like an oak tree. Most likely because she wasn't finished being angry.

"The police still have not released Addison's personal belongings. I'm on a deadline. I need her stuff now."

MacAvoy nodded his understanding. "Of course. I'm not sure what I can do. The police have their own timetable. Have you talked to them?"

So much for his claim that he had "connections."

She huffed. "Of course, dimwit." She turned in my direction. She looked like she was channeling the devil with her red-rimmed eyes. "Who has leverage with the police around here?"

I held up my hands. "Don't look at me."

"You won't get the coppers to cough up that pet chef's stuff until they're good and ready," Betty said.

"Why are you here?" Sunday asked Betty. "Are you giving an interview too?"

"Not me. Cookie doesn't want me talking to Handsome." She squinted. "You sure you

238

want to go on camera looking like that?"

Sunday touched her face. "Like what?"

"Like you've been crying all night. You need some ice. Mac, get her something for her face." Betty pointed to MacAvoy. He didn't move. He looked to Sunday for direction.

She tensed. "It's allergies. I took a pill twenty minutes ago. I'll be fine in five."

"Grass?" I asked.

"Cats."

Betty's gray eyes widened in fear. "The only cats around here are mountain lions. Let me inside." Betty charged up the steps, pushing MacAvoy out of the way.

"You can't go in there," he sputtered.

Sunday quickly followed Betty. I was right behind. No way I was going to miss the show.

MacAvoy's RV was modest compared to the other RVs we'd toured. That's not to say it wasn't luxurious, because it was. Maybe there were only high-end RV manufacturers.

His coach was shorter than ours, and instead of a dining booth, he had wooden chairs for two. The floor was tile and not marble, but it was still beautiful. I was a little disappointed. Mr. TV didn't have a woman inside. Instead, he had a scruffy cameraman who wore cargo shorts, a Channel 5 polo shirt, and unruly curly red hair, preparing for the interview.

"You know, I've seen you a lot lately. I think it's time I called you by something other than the cameraman. I'm Mel."

He looked at me suspiciously. "Ben."

MacAvoy handed an icepack to Sunday. She eyed him skeptically before gently placing the pack against her face.

"Now that you've made introductions, Melinda, it's time for you to leave." MacAvoy pointed toward the door.

"We just got here," Betty whined.

"Excuse me, this is my interview." Sunday took control of the conversation. "There's been a change in plans, Callum. We're going to talk about the police and how they're botching this investigation."

For a second, I wasn't sure who she was talking to. Had I not just learned the cameraman's name was Ben, I'd have thought she was talking to him. I don't recall hearing anyone refer to MacAvoy by his first name. It sounded odd.

"I'd rather we talk about Addison." *Callum* shot her a pointed look.

Unfazed, she glared right back at him. "Do you want this interview or not?"

He swallowed hard. "Have a seat. Ladies,

if you wouldn't mind waiting outside?"

Betty claimed the driver's seat, which was facing the back of the RV. "Oh, no. I wouldn't miss this for anything."

"Look, we'll see it eventually. What does it matter that we see you film it? Unless you plan on spinning it in an unflattering way?" I said.

Sunday plopped down in the chair. Once Ben had her hooked up with a microphone, he handed her eye drops, and she shoved the icepack in his hand.

She took a few seconds to freshen up her makeup. "I told you five minutes; the timer has started. If you want to keep wasting time arguing with those two who don't matter, that's up to you. Just know, you're now down to four minutes, thirty seconds." She looked at Betty. "How's my makeup?"

"You look great," she reassured her.

The camera was set up, ready to shoot them sitting in the recliners. Sunday was looking stylish in a crochet-lace top, linen tie-belt shorts, and nightclub heels. Mac-Avoy was dressed in his boring khakis and Channel 5 polo shirt, just like Ben.

Sunday perched herself on the edge of her seat, her legs extended toward MacAvoy. It was almost as if she were blocking him from escaping. Or maybe she was trying to com-

241

municate she wasn't intimidated by him. Whatever she was trying to convey, she was used to being in control.

I made myself comfortable on the passenger seat. I found the release lever and swung the chair around to face the show.

"Wish I had some popcorn," Betty whispered.

"Shh." Ben glared at us.

I mouthed "Sorry."

Ben motioned to MacAvoy that he was recording. Once MacAvoy introduced Sunday, he quickly started with the questions. "Tell me about Addison Rae. She was the head chef for the ARL fundraiser this week."

Sunday looked bored. "She'd been cooking for her dogs back in Atlanta for years, but wasn't finding the fame she longed for."

Wow. She couldn't sound any more bored if she was reciting the names of the U.S. Presidents.

"Her father recently passed away. On his deathbed, she'd promised him she would move to southern California to fulfill her dream to be a pet chef to the stars. That led her here." Sunday tossed out facts about Addison's life like a careless gesture. All that was missing was an eye roll. I wondered how that would translate on camera.

"Was she finding that fame? I know she

had some help from a few friends."

My stomach knotted.

She shrugged. "Addison told me she had someone who promised to help her. To introduce her to people who could give her a boost up. I tried to tell her she couldn't count on that. She had to do the work herself. But Addison liked to take short-cuts. She didn't always know when to keep her mouth shut."

Sunday's lips flattened. Was she upset that Addison hadn't listened to her? According to Pepper, Sunday didn't take to kindly to her clients going against her wishes.

"What type of short-cuts?" MacAvoy asked.

She shifted in her chair. "I want to talk about the incompetency of the local police department. I was promised Addison's personal property yesterday. As of this morning, I have not received her belongings, nor have they contacted me with a timeline as to when I will receive them. I'm not even sure if they are taking this investigation seriously. They aren't talking to me." She stared straight into the camera as if speaking directly to Detective Finn and Lark. "If the police are watching, you need to call me with an update."

Yowsa. That could blow up in her face.

They might do more than just update her; they might toss her high-maintenance fanny in jail.

Ben held up two fingers.

Mr. TV nodded in acknowledgment. "Do you have any idea who might have wanted to kill Addison?"

She looked directly at me. "I've heard rumors."

He leaned forward as if inviting her to trust him with her secret. Him and a hundred thousand viewers. "Rumors?"

My stomach dropped. I sucked in a breath waiting for her answer. Certainly Addison hadn't confided to her agent that she was blackmailing me.

"Someone was blackmailing her."

I thought MacAvoy's eyes were going to fall out of his head. Whatever he thought she was going to say, that wasn't it. He didn't have a believable poker face.

He'd moved to the edge of his seat. "Who?"

"Her." She pointed her nasty, lying finger at me.

Ben swung the camera around and aimed it in my direction. I flinched.

Well, hell's bells.

CHAPTER TWENTY

I was trapped and everyone in the RV knew it.

MacAvoy's green eyes were huge. I could tell he was torn between wanting to jump up and down for an amazing story dropping in his lap, and disbelief that I would blackmail someone. Euphoria was winning.

For the first time since I'd met her, Betty was speechless. She clenched her hands together. It was obvious by the strained look on her face, she was worried.

"That's a lie," I ground out. "I barely knew her." I know. I should have kept my mouth shut.

I'd just given MacAvoy exactly what he wanted. Judging by the satisfied smile on Sunday's face, I'd played right into her plan as well.

Dang. Dang. Dang.

Ben turned the camera back to MacAvoy and gave him the wrap-up signal. I didn't wait to hear what he had to say; I busted out of the RV before I further damaged my character. Betty quietly followed.

Outside, I paced the length of the RV, waiting for Sunday to emerge. She had to explain why she'd lied.

"We need to talk, Cookie." Betty's matter-of-fact tone was final. She wanted answers. I didn't blame her.

"I know. Later." The second Sunday stepped out of the RV, I planted myself in front of her. "Why would you lie? You know I wasn't blackmailing Addison."

She raised a blond eyebrow. "Do I?"

I sensed MacAvoy watching from the RV doorway. "What would I get from holding anything over her? She had nothing I wanted." I cringed inwardly at the lie. She did have my mama's letters. *But Addison was blackmailing me.* Which was a stronger motive to kill someone.

I pushed the hair from my face, frustration pouring from my body. "Was Addison really being blackmailed?"

She folded her arms across her chest. "Yes."

"And she said it was me?" My voice quivered. I hated the betrayal of my body.

She shrugged. "She never said who. You were convenient." Her gaze darted toward

Betty. I almost missed it. "I've heard stories about the two of you fighting."

Was she implying Betty was telling stories about Addison and me? I didn't believe it. Why was she implicating Betty now?

I took a step back as I struggled to get my emotions under control. "I'm also a suspect, and you just gave the police a major reason to look at me. And it was a lie."

I rubbed my temple. "How many times do I have to say I didn't kill Addison until people start to believe me?"

Sunday rolled her eyes. "Don't be so dramatic. The more you protest, the more people think you have something to hide. If the police suspect you, they must have a good reason."

"Seriously? A good reason? Like the lie you just told? As her agent, and someone who supposedly cared about her, I'd think you'd want the police to arrest the right person."

"The police will follow the evidence. Or so they assure me."

I wanted to scream. Those were the same words Detective Malone had said to me repeatedly. The difference was, when he said them, I felt a semblance of comfort that he'd analyze all the evidence and would know what was real and what was fabri-

cated. With Sunday, I felt nothing but un-
ease.

The big fat liar turned to sashay away.
Probably back to the pit of darkness she'd
clawed her way out of. Good riddance. I
spun around to tell Betty I was ready to
leave when I noticed MacAvoy staring at
me from the steps of the RV. For someone
who'd just gotten the story break he'd been
begging for, he didn't look as elated as I'd
imagined he would.

"Melinda," Sunday hollered. I spun
around. "Where's Hudson? He owes me
new a new Louis Vuitton bag."

"I haven't seen him," I ground out.

"When he turns up, inform him I'll need
replacement luggage by the end of the
week." She stalked off toward her tent.

"Do I look like a receptionist?"

"No, you look like someone with something to hide," MacAvoy chirped from his
RV perch.

Irritation raked through me. "She just
admitted she lied. If you air that entire
piece, you're nothing better than one of
those trashy TV tabloid reporters. What's
next? Hacking my phone? Completely fabri-
cating a story just to look good?"

"Come back and tell your side of the

story." He motioned inside the RV.

"When hell freezes over."

Betty and I retired to our RV for some damage control and a drink.

I was hanging on by a thread. I poured us each a glass of iced tea. "I can't believe he thought I'd sit down with him for an interview. What a snake. He better not air that ending."

Betty's questioning gray eyes met mine as she accepted the glass. "Why does Sunday dislike you?"

I shook my head. "I don't know. I just met her, but she obviously has no problem making me look guilty." If it was a fight Sunday wanted, I'd give her one.

I took a sip of my tea, then set it on the counter. I couldn't sit. I was too antsy.

Betty carried her glass to the dining table and sat down. "Why did Addison hate you?"

I sighed as I began to pace. "I don't think it was me she hated. I can't go into detail, but just know, I wasn't blackmailing Addison. I had no reason to."

"I believe you, Cookie, but whatever you're hiding is making you look bad."

I stopped pacing in front of the table. I pulled the hair tie from my ponytail and quickly put my hair back into a messy bun.

"Yeah, well, the truth will only make it look worse."

"The truth will set you free."

I looked up at her. "Really? The truth will set me free? That's all you've got? A Bible quote?"

She shrugged. "You got a better source?"

"No."

"Is it working?"

"Not at all."

Betty pushed her glass to the side and clasped her hands together in front of her. "I know you. You only act like this when you're protecting someone. I'm not in the middle of this one. Darby's visiting her dad in Idaho —"

"Nebraska," I corrected with a grin.

"Sure, sure. You and Grey are Splitsville. You and Carol aren't talking. So that leaves your crazy mother or saintly daddy. Which one is it?"

"What?" I ignored her incorrect reference to Caro. Did she really know me that well? Was I that predictable?

"You're not that difficult to figure out. You're as loyal as a Golden Retriever. You protect those you love, and you only love a handful of people." Her gray eyes softened, even though there was an edge to her tone.

I blinked. "You've got to understand, I

want to tell you, but you're not the best at keeping secrets."

Betty looked crushed. But it must have dawned on her what I said. She slipped out from behind the table and gleefully grabbed my arms. "So you *are* keeping a secret. I knew it. Tell me."

I shrugged off her grasp. "What did I just say? It's better for both of us if I don't tell you. You have deniability that way."

"You're in some serious trouble if you're worried about what I know. You need to call that sexy detective."

"Malone? I thought you wanted me to call Grey."

She shook her head. "I think this is over his head. He's good-looking and smart, for an art dealer. But just because he likes watching cop shows doesn't make him a match for Fark and Lameo. You need to call in the professionals."

I smiled, laughter edging its way out of my mouth. I loved the names she'd given Finn and Lark. But she had no idea what she was talking about regarding Grey. You couldn't get any more "professional" than undercover FBI agent Grey Donovan.

I patted her wrinkled hand. "I adore you."

She shrugged a thin shoulder. "I know. So, are you going to call him?"

I shook my head. "Not yet."

I grabbed my tea from the counter and took a drink. I was beginning to feel calmer and less anxious.

"You didn't want to compare notes on suspects last night. Are you game now?" Betty asked.

"Sure." I settled into one of the recliners. Missy bumbled over and lay next to me.

Excited, Betty grabbed a notepad and pen from the drawer. She returned to the table. "Where do we start?"

"Let's start with Pepper."

She jotted Pepper's name on the pad of paper. As we rattled off what we knew, she made a list of facts. By the time we finished with all the suspects, we had a couple of pages of information.

Betty swiped the pad off the table and move to the couch next to Raider and recapped. "You heard Red argue with Addison and Pepper. He overheard you and Addison argue. He rejected Pepper's offer to help."

"And he's been gossiping about me." A minor point, but still important.

"Got it." Betty made a quick note. "Hudson fired Pepper so he could shack up with his lover, Addison. Do we know when they started hitting the sheets?"

I choked back a laugh. I didn't want to encourage her. "No."

She tapped the pen against the pad. "He knew you and Addison were meeting, but kept quiet about it. Addison told him Pepper's secrets, but she didn't tell him Sunday was hanging out with us this week."

"I wonder why she kept that from him? It seems like she told him everything else. It really bothers him that she didn't mention her agent's visit. He could have outted Pepper, but he gave her a different job instead. So he's not heartless."

Betty scoffed. "He was covering his tracks."

"That's possible. He knew Addison really well. He was worried there was some type of evidence about their affair in Addison's tent."

Betty huffed. "I can't believe you snooped without me."

I smiled apologetically. "What can I say? The opportunity presented itself. Let's get back to the list."

"Yeah, yeah. Pepper got fired because of Addison. She hates Red. You think Dim Sum had bloody paws. Pepper buys her food pre-made." Betty looked up from her notes and wrinkled her nose. "What a sneak. She saw Addison at the spa, meeting someone, but won't tell us who. She's a scaredy cat when it comes to Sunday, but threatened to expose Hudson's secret. Oh, and she's suddenly writing a pet cookbook."

"And she has a big knife."

She rolled her eyes. "All chefs have big knives."

"And she wears the most sensible shoes I've ever seen."

Betty tilted her head. "You really want me to write that down?"

I laughed. "No."

Missy started to snore. "I'm glad she sleeps with you," Betty grumbled.

"You get used to it. It's my white noise now. It helps me sleep."

Betty rubbed her hands together. "Now, for our new favorite suspect. Sunday knows Addison was being blackmailed, but not by who. She goes on a revenge spree when clients go against her advice, and dummy Addison did exactly that by asking you to write the foreword for her cookbook. When are you going to explain that to me?"

"Soon." I leaned forward. "She also said Addison didn't have enemies in the chef community. All we have to do is look at that list and we know that's a lie. Sunday also said she was Red's agent years ago and that's why she calls him Redmond. For all we know, she's lying about it all."

"We can't believe anything that comes out of her mouth, Cookie."

I nodded. "Agreed. We've got to add Asher. Addison was his private pet chef until he fired her. Either he lied about Addison stealing the diamond cufflinks or he killed Addison and took them back."

Betty *tsked.* "Such a shame a man that sexy could be a killer."

I just realized he could have been the one who tossed Addison's tent looking for the cufflinks. "You have to stop hanging out with him. Either way, he's dangerous."

"What about Dudley Do-Right?"

I looked at her questioningly. "Who?"

"That mean ol' Ranger Elliott. He argued with Addison about her car parked in the day use area and then he got all bossy and towed it. That's when Addison threatened to report him to his superiors for a reason only they knew about."

I wondered what Addison could have had on Ranger Elliott. That he didn't like dogs? That he had a fetish for towing guests' cars? The whole thing was odd.

I stood up, ready to get moving again. There were things to do.

"We need to talk to Hudson about the brooch." I guzzled the rest of my iced tea before placing the glass in the dishwasher.

Betty jumped up. "If he doesn't have it, are we gonna talk to Dudley Do-Right?" She snickered.

I sighed. I never called him that in front of her. "You know you can't say that to his face."

She held up her right hand. "I swear on a stack of Bibles, I'll never say that to his face."

I laughed. I loved how she repeated exactly what I'd said. "Let's take the dogs for a quick walk to relieve themselves before we leave to talk to Hudson and Ranger Elliott. We'll come back and get them for lunch."

Betty's face lit up at the mention of food. "I wonder what's on the menu today."

"Whatever it is, I bet it's delicious."

I was guessing Red made one killer sandwich.

CHAPTER TWENTY-ONE

The rest of the morning passed quickly. We still hadn't seen Hudson. I don't know why, but I was a touch worried that no one had seen him since last night. It didn't feel right.

We hiked up to the park entrance and found Ranger Elliott in his plain green uniform, sitting in his shack watching the Dodgers game on a small TV.

I knocked on the sliding window.

Ranger Elliott looked up. He made his way to window and slid it open. "How can I help ya ladies?" There it was again, that hint of laughter in his tone.

I pulled off my sunglasses. "I hate to interrupt, but I was wondering if anyone has turned in a fruit basket brooch."

He blinked in obvious confusion. "Say that again."

Betty pulled off her white sunglasses placed them in her handbag, then pushed me aside. "We're looking for a brooch. You know, a pin, like your grandma wore." She pointed at her chest. "It's a gold basket filled with colored gems in the shape of fruit. It's gawdawful ugly, but it has a lot of sentimental value."

He shook his head. "No one has turned in a brooch."

I blew out a long breath of disappointment. My heart dropped. I didn't want think about the possibility of never finding the brooch again. Or how I would ever explain this whole mess to Caro. I rested my glasses on the top of my head.

"If someone does turn it in, will you call me?" I gave him my cell number.

He pushed his hat back. "Where do you think you lost it?"

I looked at Betty for an answer.

She immediately got defensive. "Don't look at me like that. I didn't mean to lose it. It fell out of my pocket. I don't know where. I didn't know it was gone until I was looking for it."

He nodded. "O-kay. If someone turns it in, I'll give you a call."

He asked me to describe it in detail, one more time. I spared no details. By the time I was through, Ranger Elliot had drawn an exact replica of the brooch.

He looked up, perplexed. "You want that

back?"

I tried not to take offense. I knew it was ugly. But it was mine.

Betty pushed her lips together. "I told you. It has sentimental value. Her granny left it to her. Or her granny could have left it to her sassy cousin, Carol. Either way, possession is nine-tenths of the law, and right now it's in Cookie's possession, so it belongs to her."

I frowned. "Actually, it's not in my possession, that's why we're here."

Betty waved me off. "Details. Details."

Ranger Elliott glanced at the ballgame on the TV. He was finished listening to us bicker, and ready to get back to the Dodgers.

"One last thing," I said. "I was wondering if you've seen Hudson this morning. I've been looking for him for a while and haven't seen him yet."

He shook his head. "I haven't."

"Isn't that odd? That he hasn't been out making rounds with you?"

"Not really. If he has a busy day scheduled, I won't see him until it's time for me to make my evening rounds, verifying the daytime guests have left for the evening."

Betty rammed her pocketbook into my side. I cut a side glance at her. "That was unnecessary," I said under my breath.

"It was an accident." The twinkle in her eye told me otherwise.

I shifted my weight away from Betty and returned my attention to Ranger Elliott. "Like Sunday Hill and Addison Rae?" I leaned in as if we were about to exchange office gossip around the water cooler. "We heard that Addison was parked in the day parking lot and refused to move."

He adjusted his hat nervously. "Unfortunately, that's not uncommon. It happens."

"I also heard you two argued when she refused to park in the overnight lot."

His dark eyes narrowed. "There was no argument. I had her Range Rover towed," he snapped.

Wow. That was an expensive car for an up-and-coming chef. "No wonder she wasn't happy about it. How did she get it back?"

He shrugged, a vindictive gleam in his eye. "I don't think she did."

"Is that why she threatened to report you to your superiors?"

"That was an empty threat. There was nothing to report. She insisted I take her to pick up her vehicle. It's not my responsibility to provide her transportation to the storage facility. She could have had someone pick it up for her, if they were willing to pay the fine."

Let's just say he wasn't someone to go out of his way for you if he thought you were abusing the system. And from what I knew about Addison, that was her motto. Who would she have asked for help? Hudson? Sunday? "Do you record license plate numbers?"

"Only when I call for a tow."

"By any chance, can I get her plate info?"

Ranger Elliott shook his head. "No. Good day, ladies." He slid the window shut and returned to his game.

Betty blinked. "That went well. Especially that last part, when he shut the window in our faces."

CHAPTER TWENTY-TWO

As we power-walked back to camp, I shared my theory that Addison's vehicle was either still in storage or Sunday had picked it up as a favor for Addison. That would explain why Hudson didn't know Sunday would be here for the week. It was a spur-of-the-moment decision.

Betty pumped her arms energetically, her purse swinging like a birthday piñata as we walked down the side of the paved road. "Nice try, but that doesn't explain the luggage," she huffed.

"Unless at the last minute, Sunday took that opportunity to keep an eye on Addison. We know she doesn't like it when her clients go rogue and ignore her career advice."

A red Chevy Cruz slowly passed us. Betty waved at the driver. He smiled absently and gave a half wave in return. He looked like a nice man. A much more reasonable potential love interest for Betty than Asher,

Malone, or MacAvoy.

"Who's that? He looks familiar."

She looked at me, her sunglasses engulfing her small face. "Craig Sutton. You asked me about him last night. You need to work on your memory. Do you need to borrow my Sudoku puzzle book? A puzzle a day can help your faulty memory."

I lifted my glasses to make a face at her. "I was preoccupied thinking about my lost brooch."

"Ha! You're a terrible liar. If you would have been listening at the campfire last night, you would have heard Craig say his Lhasa Poo had an appointment with Jade at Divine Spa. Lhasa Poos can be high-maintenance on hair care. If their hair gets too long, it mats."

That seemed to be a constant theme for pooches with double-coated hair. I wondered why his dog didn't get a cut from the groomer at camp. Unless Jade considered that "cheating." Knowing her demand for excellence, that was a definite possibility.

I shot a sly smile at Betty. "Are you going to ask him out?"

She made an ugly face. "He's happily married. I'm not that kinda girl."

Sweat trickled down the middle of my back. I lifted my ponytail, wishing for a breeze of any kind. It had to be in the mid-eighties already and it was only noon. It wasn't normally this warm in June. This was more like August type of weather.

I sighed. "I could really go for another iced tea right now."

"I'd rather have a beer."

I chuckled. A tipsy Betty would be entertaining, but more than any of us could handle.

The walk back to camp had worked up our appetites. We headed straight for the round kitchen yurt, hoping to get in lunch before the obstacle course competition started in a couple of hours.

There were a half a dozen tables set up inside the yurt, the rest set up outside in the sun. We noticed Veronica and Harry were there eating lunch with Pepper and Dim Sum inside.

"Girls, over here." Veronica waved us over to the table. "I've been looking for you two."

I settled my sunglasses on the top of my head, giving my eyes a minute to adjust to the light inside the tent. Pepper looked up from her plate of BBQ chicken and spinach salad without acknowledging us. Ever since Betty and I had created our suspect list, I was looking at people in a more critical light. And the pet chef in sensible shoes seemed to have the strongest motive to kill Addison.

We sat next to Veronica. Betty placed her sunglasses and handbag on the table. She patted her thigh for Harry to join her. He jumped from Veronica's lap into Betty's. She loved him up, telling him what a handsome boy he was.

I reached across the table to let Dim Sum sniff my hand before petting him. I noticed immediately he'd been bathed and nails trimmed. Interesting.

"Pepper, we missed you this morning," I said.

She swallowed a mouthful of salad. "What are you talking about?"

Was she really that clueless? Or was she that cunning?

Betty sniffed, not buying the forgetful act. "Asher's RV. Where you invited yourself for a tour."

"Oh, that." She shrugged, unconcerned. "I overslept. I stayed up late working on a new project."

I wasn't buying that excuse for one minute. Did she dump her garbage while sleepwalking?

"Are you writing a cookbook?" Veronica's face brightened with excitement.

Pepper bristled, dropping her fork on her

plate. "How do you know about that?"

A blush crept into Veronica's face. "I'm sorry. I didn't mean to snoop. When I was in your tent, I saw a stack of recipes and foodie photos on the table next to my cell phone."

Pepper quickly regained her composure. "I don't remember leaving those out. I'm usually more careful."

"Do you worry that someone will steal your ideas?" I asked.

She shook her head. "It's difficult to copyright recipes. A recipe is just a list of ingredients and how to prepare them. Chefs duplicate each other's work all the time. It's the way a dish is plated, or the way it's described in a cookbook that can be copyrighted. That's when the claws come out."

I had always assumed when a chef published a cookbook, those were his or her recipes. Did the freedom to duplicate another chef's recipe make that world more or less cutthroat? Did Pepper have more or less of a motive to kill off Addison than the other suspects? I had all new questions.

A server brought Betty and me plates of BBQ chicken, grilled pineapple rings, and a spinach salad. I studied the plate, thinking about what Pepper had said. "So, if Red had a cookbook, and this was one of his dishes,

I could publish the same recipe as my own?"

"The ingredients and how to prepare them, yes. But not the words or way he explains how to put everything together. Certainly not the way he plates his dish." She sneered. "But why would you? He doesn't utilize negative space; the color is bland." She used her knife to push my stack of chicken over. "Why does the chicken have to be piled like a medieval castle tower? His plating lacks creativity."

Pepper's nondescript appearance hid a sharp understanding of the culinary world. She actually sounded like she knew what she was talking about. I studied her as she nudged the last few bites of food around her plate. Was it a case of being a better teacher than cook? Or had Addison lied to Hudson to make Pepper look bad?

"I liked breakfast better," Betty said, around a mouth full of pineapple.

She was right. The chicken was dry and sauce a little on the sweet side. It was hard to believe this was something Red had created.

I took a long drink of water, washing down the overcooked chicken. "Have you guys seen Hudson?"

Veronica shook her head. "No." She lowered her voice. "Did you know you're in the news?"

Man, I had been hoping MacAvoy would do the right thing. Thinking he would suddenly grow a conscience overnight was insanity on my part. I didn't want to know how MacAvoy had spun that last conversation with Sunday, but from Veronica's strained expression, it wasn't in my favor.

"Don't believe everything you hear," Betty said.

Veronica looked offended. "I know that. But you two need to see this blog." She whipped out her smartphone and pulled up the website in question. Once she found what she was looking for, she handed me the phone.

Holy cow. A "celebrity blogger" claimed Addison and I were childhood friends. According to a "close friend," I was jealous of Addison's success in the pampered pet world, and was now a prime suspect in her murder. With a link to MacAvoy's exclusive interview with Sunday as the blog's main source.

I broke out into a sweat. I handed the phone back to Veronica before it slipped from my grip.

I looked at Betty. I could feel my Texas indignation boiling to the brim. I was so mad, I could start a fight in an empty house. "He ran that whole interview. He's slicker than a jar of slop."

Veronica's gaze bounced between Betty and me. She vibrated with nervous energy. "There's more. I think this part is good news, though. Since Callum MacAvoy's interview aired, there's been pressure all over social media for the Laguna Hills police to turn over Addison's personal items to Sunday."

I pondered what she'd said for a second. I shoved my plate to the side and stood up. "We need to see what the police turned over to her."

Betty tossed her napkin on the table and jumped up ready to defend my honor. "And then we can take down the sexy reporter."

Pepper shot me an appraising look. "Sunday Hill doesn't like you. How are you going to convince her to let you look at Addison's things?"

I shrugged. "We'll cross that bridge when we come to it."

Betty grabbed her handbag and sunglasses. "You gotta start paying attention, Cookie. You blew up that bridge when you called her a liar."

CHAPTER TWENTY-THREE

Once we were finished eating, it was time for the obstacle course. We'd have to look for Sunday later. We grabbed the dogs and joined the others on the field. The empty field. There was no obstacle course set up. No one there to get the game started. That bad feeling I had earlier had morphed into a really awful feeling.

I was worried about Hudson. Something was wrong. He would never miss a camp-sponsored event. It was time to take action. I called the Laguna Hills police, but they weren't interested in filing a missing person's report since he had been missing for less than twenty-four hours.

I explained he was the program director and it wasn't like him to skip an event he had planned. I'd also reminded them there had been a murder here days earlier, but that didn't matter.

They had rules. Procedures to follow. It

gave me a headache listening to them. I hung up, frustrated. I looked round at the group of guests and fifteen canines waiting to be entertained for the next hour.

I needed advice. I needed someone to rattle the police's cage and take this seriously. Addison was already dead. Who knew what was going on with Hudson?

"I'm calling Malone."

Betty immediately began primping — fluffing her hair and pinching her checks.

I rolled my eyes at her. "You know he can't see you, right?"

Betty stuck out her tongue.

Nice.

On the fifth ring, he finally answered. "Malone."

I didn't waste words. "It's Mel. I need some advice."

"You sure do." His sharp voice bit through the air and into my ear. "I thought I already told you to call Grey? I saw that interview with MacAvoy and Sunday Hill. Somehow, you managed to find yourself smack in the middle of everything, including a murder investigation."

I turned my back to the group. "I'm not calling about that. The program director, Hudson Jones, is missing." I quickly filled him in on the details. "The last time he was seen was around eleven o'clock last night. I've called the police, but they won't act. He's missed all the meals, and the events he had planned for the day. That's not like him. He's hyper responsible. There's a problem."

"If you've already called the local police, what do you want me to do?"

I blew my bangs out of my face. "I don't know. Do what you do so well. Talk to someone. Have them start a search party. Make them do what cops are supposed to do when someone is missing."

Whatever Malone said was muffled by the phone. Or it could be that he'd turned his mouth away from the receiver as he cursed. "I'll make a call."

"Thank you." I was about to hang up when he suddenly felt the need to provide some unsolicited advice.

"I saw the news. You need to lay low. Keep your nose clean. Did you get yourself a good lawyer?"

I moved away from the crowd. "Not yet. Do you really think I need one?"

"As soon as we hang up, you should call an attorney."

My breath caught in my throat. "Is there any way you could come here and help out these two clueless cops?"

"No." I could hear the finality in his voice.

I had a clear picture of what his face looked like right now. A stern frown that usually went along with the words, "Stay out of my investigation or I'll toss you in jail."

I rubbed my forehead, pushing my hair out of my eyes. "Can you call and put in a good word with Lark and Finn?"

"Detective Finn?"

"Yes. Female, tall, blond, athletic, wears these ugly blue blazers, and has zero personality."

"You just described half of the female homicide detectives," he said wryly. "But yes, I know her." He didn't sound positive about recognizing who Finn was.

"I don't like the way you said that. Now I'm scared."

"You should be. Stop talking to MacAvoy and get a lawyer."

I hadn't realized I'd been walking as we talked. I found myself standing on the trail to the campfire ring, and somehow, Betty and the dogs were right behind me. I glared at her. She glared right back.

"How do I convince Finn to look for Hudson?"

"If you've already called to report him missing, that's about all you can do right now. Have you reported his alleged disappearance to the park ranger?"

I rolled my eyes at the word "alleged."

"I talked to Ranger Elliott earlier and mentioned we hadn't seen Hudson today. He didn't seem concerned. But that was before Hudson missed the obstacle course event. Do you think Hudson got lost or injured on a trail?" I looked at the vast mountainside.

"I don't rule out anything when dealing with a missing person."

With one last reminder to stop talking to MacAvoy, he hung up.

Betty planted herself in front of me. "Is he on his way?"

I shook my head. "No. We're on our own."

She eyed me. "What's the plan?"

"Let's go to headquarters and see if we can find a clue as to where he might be. Maybe there's a perfectly reasonable explanation for his absence."

I didn't believe that for a minute. And by the skeptical expression on Betty's face, she didn't either.

Ten minutes later, we were inside the empty headquarters tent looking for clues pointing toward Hudson's whereabouts. The air was hot and stale. The fan hadn't been turned on for the day. It was eerie to think about how quiet the tent was at the moment, when just days ago it was bustling with purposeful police, working Addison's homicide case.

Betty stood in front of Hudson's desk, her hands on her hips. "He's a neat freak. There's nothing out of place. No potato chips, no leaky ink pen."

I rummaged around the makeshift desks the police had created days earlier. Raider and Missy were curled up next to a couple of high-back chairs toward the rear of the tent, panting as they slept.

"Have you seen how to turn on the fan?" I asked.

Betty waved a blue piece of paper above her head. "I found a schedule for the week," she yelled.

I darted to her side. My stomach sank. "According to this, he planned on being here."

"It's not looking good, Cookie." She shook her head.

"Look for a revised version." I knew I was grasping at straws, but I couldn't shake the ominous feeling Hudson was in danger and it was up to us to save him. I had the sudden thought, if something happened to Hudson, who was in charge? Loni from the ARL?

I returned to the desk I was searching and stumbled across a blue folder with a large coffee stain on the front, hidden under a stack of papers attached to Hudson's clipboard. Judging by the coffee stain, the folder didn't belong to Hudson.

I flipped it open and leafed through the pages. I frowned in confusion. I flipped through the pages slower, reading instead of skimming this time. It looked like police notes pertaining to statements given by the guests. Including one from Ranger Elliott. There was also a preliminary cause of death — suffocation. To the side there was a handwritten note that read "pillow?"

Why did Hudson have this? Was it left behind on accident, or had Hudson taken it?

Suddenly, Sunday barged inside carrying a large cardboard box. "Where is he?" she shrieked.

I jumped, dropping the papers on the hardwood floor. The dogs leaped to their feet, barking at the unexpected visitor. I sighed in exasperation. It only took a couple of seconds to get them under control, but if Sunday had possessed common sense or consideration regarding the special circumstances of the glamping event, calming the pooches wouldn't be necessary.

"Oh, joy. It's you," Betty griped.

I scrambled to pick up the papers I'd

dropped. I was at my wits' end with Sunday. "You know, we're out here with dogs. When you enter a room shrieking at full volume, it upsets them. Can you tone it down?"

I thought I'd handled that rather calmly. Sunday's brittle smile shattered into a thousand pieces, making me think I wasn't as reasonable as I'd thought.

She glared down her condescendingly straight nose, sneering at Missy and Raider. "I can't wait to get out of here."

A sentiment we could all agree on. "What do you need to make that happen?"

She strutted through the middle of head-quarters, her dramatic entrance wasted on us. She stopped in front of Betty. With a patronizing look, she dropped the box, which landed on the scarred oak desk with a loud thud. "I want to talk to that inept program director. Where is he?"

"I don't know." I shook my head. "We're looking for him, too."

"Someone needs to find him now. I'm missing very important items."

Betty peeked inside the box. "That sounds more like your problem than his."

Sunday flipped her wispy blond bangs to the side of her face. "He helped the police gather Addison's belongings, and the most important things aren't there. The police insist this is everything. I know for a fact it's not." She crossed her arms, clearly conveying it was now our problem.

This was the box of Addison's personal effects? For once, good luck shined its face on me. I looked inside. My heart skipped a beat as I searched through the items.

My eyebrows knitted together in concern. No letters. No recipe cards. No USB drive. As much as I detested it, I had to agree — this wasn't all of it.

"And the police said this was everything?" I asked. "No backpack?"

"I wasn't given a backpack. Did she have one?"

"She could have. I thought I'd seen one," I lied. Heck, I not only knew she had one, I'd searched it myself.

"Addison's recipes are missing, and her photos."

Photos? I'd never seen any photos. "I don't understand. The way Addison talked, the cookbook was ready to go to press. Other than the foreword."

"She had made some . . . changes. She was going to give them to me here. I need those recipes. Especially the pictures."

"What pictures?"

"Plating shots. Dogs eating her food. Her childhood photos of her and her parents."

278

She waved her hand dismissively, pretending it wasn't important. She wasn't fooling me.

"Childhood photos?" It was difficult to swallow past the lump in my throat.

The corners of her mouth tightened. "That's right. We were doing a ten-page spread of candid shots. Addison and her parents. Addison's parents in their early years together. Her father was an Olympic athlete, you know. And a Miss America judge."

"Hey, Cookie's a reformed beauty queen. Maybe you —"

I cut Betty off with a look. She immediately looked hurt. I'd have to explain it to her later.

I turned to the drama queen from New York City. "As soon as we find Hudson, we'll let him know you need to talk to him. Until then, you can either take this back with you or leave it here. I'm sure whatever you don't want, Hudson will be happy to take care of."

"I have no use for any of this. Hudson can take care of it along with my new traveling bag. He can find me in my tent. I can't wait to leave this Godforsaken dirt bowl."

She clip-clopped out the door, leaving Addison's personal effects on Hudson's desk. After all the chaos she'd stirred up, the heartless battle-axe only cared about herself.

"Mission accomplished, Cookie. The hot mess express has left the building."

I wanted to die inside. Mama had mentioned photos, but I was distracted by Pepper dumping her garbage. Could there possibly be photos of my mama and Addison's father? Could Addison's recipes and photos be on the USB drive I'd seen in the missing backpack?

Good Lord, could this get any worse?

Chapter Twenty-Four

The rest of the day went by at warp speed. After we left headquarters, Betty and I made the rounds asking about the brooch. We came up empty-handed once again. At this point, I wasn't sure what more we could do. I was devastated. Eventually, I would have to break the news to Caro. Just the thought of how that conversation would go made me want to join the witness relocation program.

Once again, dinner was delicious. The salmon was moist, the garlic potatoes perfectly seasoned. I wasn't sure what had happened with lunch, but Red had made a full recovery.

Throughout the meal, the conversation centered on where Hudson might have disappeared to. One rumor floating around was that he'd been called back into town for a family emergency. By the end of the meal, the consensus was to cancel the s'more fest for the evening.

Mr. Swanson had whispered to Betty that Red had brushed off everyone's concern as busybody paranoia. Apparently, last night, Hudson had offered to pick up Red's grocery supplies this morning. Red claimed we'd all feel silly when Hudson waltzed into camp later tonight, upset that we weren't gathered around the campfire.

I would love to see that happen. But I wasn't holding my breath.

After a day like today, I would have preferred a soak in the tub and a glass of red wine. Instead, I got to hang with Betty watching reality TV. Thankfully, I still got the glass of wine.

Betty had bought us both adult onesie pajamas. I swore this would be the one and only time I'd wear them. So there we were, in our purple cotton onesies, feet up in the recliners, glasses of red wine in our hands, the dogs stretched out on the couch snoozing, as we watched two naked strangers volunteer to be dropped in the middle of the wilderness to "survive" for twenty-one days on TV.

"Good news. If we lose our shoes this week, I know how to make us palm frond footwear," I said during a commercial break.

Betty set her wine glass on the side table.

"I'd sign up for that show. I could do it."

I shook my head. "I couldn't watch you. Even if your body parts were pixilated."

Betty laughed for a second before turning serious. "I've been thinking. When Sunday mentioned Addison's daddy was a Miss America judge, you got antsy and changed the subject."

She watched me intently. Maybe she'd drop the topic of conversation if I went back to watching the show. "I wonder if there's a waiting list to be on this show."

Betty picked up the remote and with one click removed my only defense against her line of questioning. "Is that was this is all about? Your *Miss America* scandal? Are you protecting your mama and daddy?"

I jerked my head toward her. "How'd you know?"

"I know my way around the computer. A simple Google search can produce a lot of information. I've known since the day I started working for you."

I took a sip of wine, savoring the warmth of the full-bodied pinot noir. I set my glass next to Betty's on the side table between our recliners. There wasn't an easy way out of the conversation this time. "I'm sorry I cut you off earlier. Addison was blackmailing me."

Betty sprung up in her chair. "No way! You lead a very exciting life. You could be a reality show star."

"I have no desire. Look, you have to keep this quiet. I haven't told anyone. Well, that's not exactly true anymore. After our phone call, my mama knows. Addison found letters between her father and my mother, and I have no idea what she may or may not have told her agent."

Betty went bug-eyed. "That's why you were being so nice to her? Because your mama did the horizontal hokey-pokey with Addison's daddy?"

I closed my eyes and shook my head. "Please don't say that again. I do not need that visual. Addison promised if I got her this job, and introduced her around town, she'd give me the letters. But she never did. She reneged every time. And then came up with some new hoop she wanted me to jump through."

"She was a horrible person, Cookie."

I wasn't about to argue when I felt the same way. "When I was supposed to meet her on the day she died, we'd come to an agreement. I'd give her the foreword and she'd give me the letters."

"But she never showed," Betty filled in the rest.

I shook my head. "Someone killed her first."

Betty pushed up her onesie sleeves. "I got your back. We'll find your brooch and your mama's letters. You can count on me."

At sunrise, the dogs were begging for an outside trip. I'd slept better than I had in weeks. Betty was certain it was due to the adult-sized baby clothes she'd conned me into wearing. I was pretty sure it was because I was emotionally drained.

Even with awesome sleep, I wasn't a morning person. I dragged my body out of bed, tossed on a hoodie, then snapped Missy's leash onto her collar. I slipped on my sunglasses to hide my puffy eyes from too much wine in case we ran into anyone, which was a definite possibility.

Betty, on the other hand, was bright and cheery, looking like she'd been up for hours. Her puppy was just as annoyingly chipper.

The minute we exited the RV, the dogs were immediately nose deep in the dewy grass. Missy headed toward MacAvoy's RV. I showed some kindness to the RV's tires, and led her toward the pathway away from our neighbors.

Raider quickly took the lead.

He made me nervous. "Don't let him drag

you like that," I called out. The grass was slick from the dew; I was worried she'd lose her footing.

"He's anxious. He's gotta go."

How long was she going to make excuses for his bad behavior?

I picked up my pace, annoying Missy. She was already finished with her business and ready to eat. A morning walk, no matter how pleasant the weather, was not on her agenda. Across the road, I noticed a fuzzy brown bunny, nose twitching, watching us. I stop walking and quietly called to Betty to stop.

"Why?" She turned to look at me.

"Over there, next to the garbage, there's a rabbit. Lead Raider away from it."

She huffed. "I got this. He's not into chasing fluffy bunnies."

I didn't believe her. How many times had he already chased after shadows and strangers? I slowly walked toward Betty, Raider watching me.

"He's a dog. As soon as that rabbit moves, Raider is going to charge. Tighten your grip on the lead."

Sure enough, the rabbit twitched its head and Raider flinched to attention. The bunny sensed danger and frantically hopped away, zigzag style. Both dogs immediately began barking. I tightened my grip on Missy's leather leash, keeping her up against my leg. Raider still had plenty of slack and managed to charge toward the panicked bunny. He knocked over the garbage can in his way.

"Heel," I yelled.

Thankfully, I had long legs and was able to catch him before he dragged Betty into the wilderness. The big lug whined as he watched his furry prize get away.

I wrestled control of the fear that Betty could have been seriously injured. "He is not ready for this," I stated, emphatically.

Betty's eyes teared. "He's a good dog."

My heart broke for her. She loved Raider deeply and worried she'd have to give him up. "I know. But you need to keep working with Caro. And do what she says." I released a deep breath. "Let's clean up the mess."

The garbage can wasn't full and most of what was in the dark blue plastic container was in bags, and only slightly smelly. We made quick work of gathering the trash. Betty picked up a white plastic bag with red drawstrings and carried it over.

It looked familiar. "Hold up."

"You want to look through garbage?" she asked disgusted.

I grabbed the bag and held it up, the morning sun providing a natural spotlight on the unexpected treasure. I had sunk to new lows. I was about to rummage through someone else's trash.

"I think that's Pepper's. She lied earlier. She didn't oversleep. When I was on the phone with Mama, I saw Pepper carrying a white garbage bag in this direction."

"You think we'll find something important in there?"

I shrugged. "Anything is possible."

She shook her head, her white hair bouncing with the quick movement. "We must be desperate. We're digging through the garbage looking for clues."

Within minutes, we were back in the RV, washing our hands. The dogs sniffed the bag, but thankfully weren't eager to get inside. It made me think Pepper hadn't thrown away leftover food.

I tossed my sunglasses on the counter. "Are there any rubber gloves?"

Betty looked inside the cabinet and found one pair. She handed them to me. "It's your show, you do the digging."

"Let's take it outside. I don't think there's any food in here, but I'm not willing to take any chances."

"Wait." Betty opened the bottom drawer and pulled out an extra-large pair of BBQ tongs. "Ready."

We left the dogs inside and looked for a place to open the bag. Being the end campsite, there was little to no privacy. MacAvoy's shades were down, but I wouldn't put it past him to have found a sneaky way to watch us. We moved to the side of the RV farthest from MacAvoy's windows.

"Here we go." I pulled on the gloves and ripped the bag open.

There wasn't leftover food, but there sure were a number of empty plastic food containers. Curried chicken salad. Mozzarella pasta salad. Roasted red pepper hummus.

"Do you think she was eating this?" Betty jabbed the BBQ tongs inside the bag.

Hudson's words played in my head about Pepper passing off someone else's food as her own. I continued to pull out empty Whole Foods containers. Was she pretending to cook for someone, or was she on an eat-anything-you-want fad diet?

"I don't know. Maybe she thought Hudson would give her the head chef job after Addison died and she was preparing for it by stocking up on ready-made dishes."

Betty rummaged around at the bottom, and slowly pulled out a sheet of pale pink stationary. I recognized my mother's handwriting.

My heart raced; was it possible Pepper

had stolen my mama's letters?

"Don't read it." My voice caught.

"I got it." She pulled out two more. "That's it."

I released the breath I'd been unknowingly holding. We had to be sure there weren't more. I dumped the bag upside down, emptying the remaining contents onto the grass. The possibility of finding the letters overrode the need to be sanitary.

"There were seven envelopes. There should be four more." I spread the trash over the grass.

Betty's tongs tapped a stack of extra-large index cards. "What's that?"

I picked one up and read it. "Pawfect Chicken Salad. Didn't Sunday say she was looking for Addison's recipes?" I held it out. "I think we found them. When I looked in Addison's backpack, I saw these cards. There was also a USB drive."

"I bet she didn't throw that away." Betty said, her sarcasm unmistakable.

I bent down and started to gather the index cards. I could hear a car approaching behind us.

"Hurry, someone's coming. We've got to clean this up."

Betty stood with a hand on her hips and the tongs at her side. "We're fine. We look like we had a problem taking out our trash."

"Right. In purple onesies, rubber dish gloves, and BBQ tongs?"

Betty suddenly flashed me a toothy grin. "We're in disguise."

"Stop jabbering and get stuffing."

I jammed trash inside the bag. A vehicle slowed to a stop behind me. I kept working as quickly as I could. I said a short prayer that the driver would move along.

"Uh, Cookie. We've got company."

My heart raced. "Shhh. Don't look at them. They'll keep driving."

"I don't think he's leaving." Her voice sounded small.

"I'm almost finished." I heard a door shut behind me. Darn.

I looked up. Betty's eyes were huge. I had a bad feeling Ranger Elliott was standing behind me.

"Melinda." A deep male voice hit me from behind.

Grey. Crapola. Why did the world hate me?

Ranger Elliott would have been a blessing. This was the perfect time for a gang of flying monkeys to whisk me away to their fearless leader.

Betty eyed him with a fidgety smile. "Hey, Handsome. You've been gone too long."

Grey, dressed in relaxed jeans and a light

blue V-neck tee, strolled over to her. He bent down, and gently kissed her wrinkled cheek. "It's good to see you."

The rumble of his deep morning voice rolled over me, waking me from the shock of seeing him. I stood, clutching the letters in one hand, and the garbage bag in the other.

Grey's sharp blue eyes quickly assessed the situation. A spark of laughter flashed across his face. His cheek twitched, but he didn't laugh.

I smoothed my hair with the back of a rubber gloved hand, clenching my mama's letters. I smiled awkwardly.

"Hey. What brings you to our neck of the woods?"

Chapter Twenty-Five

I was a hot mess. This was not how I imagined our face-to-face reunion playing out. While Grey parked his SUV in the day parking area, Betty, I, and the dogs scrambled to the RV.

Betty barked out orders. Hide the letters. Take a shower. Put on something sexy. I was rattled enough I obeyed.

I stashed the letters in the overhead cabinet before showering as quickly as possible. I didn't bring anything sexy, so I settled for a pair of New Religion jeans and a graphic T-shirt — my favorite: "You Had Me at Woof." It seemed fitting.

As I dragged a brush through my wet hair, I could hear Betty and Grey's comfortable laughter. I smiled sadly. Betty had missed Grey. It was obvious by the way her face lit up when he kissed her. A breakup didn't just affect the two people who'd decided they were better apart than together. Regardless of what happened between Grey and I moving forward, he needed to spend more time with Betty.

I finished pulling my wet hair back into a loose braid, then tossed the brush in the drawer. I swiped on a hundred layers of mascara, applied clear lip gloss and pronounced my makeover complete.

I found Grey and Betty at the dining table. Betty had changed into a navy blue jumpsuit and sneakers. She'd even managed to find time to brush her hair and reapply her Envious Orange eyebrows. She had Grey trapped at the table. But judging by the relaxed smile on his face, he didn't mind.

"I know you're thinking we have a chance, you know, now that you and Cookie aren't an item. But I gotta turn you down." She squeezed his arm. "It's a girlfriend code."

Grey's expression turned serious, but his eyes sparkled with good humor. He nodded gravely. "I understand."

I walked toward them slowly, making a memory of how kind Grey was with Betty. He looked up, locking eyes with me. I felt my checks warm. With a rush of air leaving my body, I dropped onto the booth across from Grey and Betty.

He slid a plate full of food in front of me. "Eat."

Someone had made fluffy scrambled eggs with gooey cheddar cheese, and perfectly browned toast sprinkled with cinnamon sugar. I'd wager fifty dollars it was Grey. It was a meal I'd eaten with him for years.

"Thanks." I picked up a fork and took a bite. I sighed. Exactly as I remembered. I struggled to find a neutral topic. My emotions felt like a bundle of kindling, just waiting for the right, or wrong, type of spark to set them off. I wasn't sure what I wanted. To apologize and try to rebuild what we had. Or to accept it was over and learn to be around each other without wondering, "what if?"

Finally, I settled with the inane comment of, "You look good."

"I liked your matching pajamas." He grinned boyishly.

I rolled my eyes. "About that. Wipe that image from your mind and never speak of it again."

"He thought you looked sexy." Betty made kissing sounds.

Grey patted her hand. "You weren't supposed to tell her."

She poked his shoulder. "Yeah, well, since you broke her heart, she's been needing some cheering up."

I drummed my fingers on the table. "If

you don't want me to kick you, stop helping me."

Betty huffed. "Well, you're not helping yourself. Somebody's got to do the work." She gathered their empty plates and carried them in the sink.

While Betty banged dishes around, I ate my toast, waiting for Grey to explain why he was here. He seemed content to silently stare at me while I finished my breakfast. I cleared my throat, wishing I could clear the tension in the room as easily.

"You two are ridiculous." Betty stood in front of the table. She pointed a thin, accusatory finger me. "He saw MacAvoy's interview and got worried you were in trouble."

"Is that true?" My voice remained amazingly calm, considering my racing heart.

"MacAvoy didn't mention you by name, but he didn't have to. You're the only local pampered pet boutique owner in Laguna Beach. I knew you were in some sort of . . . situation."

I grimaced at his matter-of-fact assessment. "It could have been worse." I filled him in on Sunday pointing her finger at me as the blackmailer and Ben catching it on camera.

Grey's face tightened. "He couldn't show

you on camera without your consent."

"I hadn't thought of that." I placed my fork on the empty plate.

"That's only part of it," Betty supplied. "Cookie's in serious trouble and needs your help."

Grey tilted his head and pinned her with his interrogation stare. "Aren't you in trouble, too? I heard you lost the brooch? How are you going to explain that to Caro?"

Betty squirmed. "I'm taking care of that. I'm talking about something else. I'm going to take a walk. I'll be back in thirty minutes." She gave me the evil eye. "If you don't tell him, I will." She kissed Grey's cheek. Then held his face in her hands like a mother chastising her son. "Don't let her down. You got it?"

He blinked as if surprised by her stern tone. Heck, I was just as surprised.

"I understand," he said.

She studied him for a minute, then released his face. "Well, now. Raider and I are going to find your granny's brooch." Betty reached for his leash.

I stopped her. "Leave him here. He'll be fine. You'll get more done without him."

"Fine. Bossy pants." She grabbed her handbag, then stomped out the door. Muttering about how she wished she'd met

Carol first.

I stood and put my dishes in the sink. "You didn't need to come. I'm fine. Like it or not, this isn't the first time I've had to dig myself out of a bad situation."

"Your inability to let those who care about you help is what keeps getting you into these types of situations. You keep trying to do it by yourself and, in the process, dig yourself deeper into trouble."

I spun around, my expression tight, my tone tighter. "That's not fair. Keep in mind, trust is a two-way street. Maybe I don't ask for help because when I do, it comes with conditions."

Suddenly, all the anger and frustration about why we'd broken up came rushing back. I'd gone behind his back to get my Grandma Tillie's brooch from the FBI (long story). He'd lied about being in town, and had secretly used Betty and me to help him solve the case. I hadn't trusted him. He hadn't trusted me. Yet somehow, I was supposed to always blindly trust him. I wanted to scream in frustration.

His eyes shifted away from my face. I knew he was formulating a retort. I crossed my arms, bracing myself for whatever he was about to say. I'd had weeks to form my arguments. I was ready for a fight.

Without a word, he pushed back from the table. He walked to the sink and started rinsing dishes. I unclenched my jaw and exhaled. I didn't know what to do next. He was just giving up?

We loaded the dishwasher in strained silence. I wiped down the counters and stove with a paper towel. "I heard my mama called you. Do I want to know what she said?"

"No." He crossed his arms and watched me. "You're right."

I paused. "About?"

He rubbed the back of his neck. "I could have handled the case involving Hayden Stone and the Dachshund races better. I should have told you I was working on a case in town that you were entangled in."

I tossed the paper towel on the counter. With my arms crossed, and chin set at a stubborn angle, I faced him. "Innocently entangled in. Malone had asked me to keep Betty out of trouble. And then when I straight up asked you what was going on, you lied."

"And because you got your feelings hurt, you put the case, my life, and *your* life in danger." His words crackled with pent-up anger.

I opened my mouth to deny it, but I

couldn't. As much as I detested liars, here I was standing before him, lying by omission, knowing that I was keeping the fact that Addison had been blackmailing me to myself.

"We've both made mistakes." I pushed past the hurt and struggled to let my guard down in order to begin rebuilding the trust. "Where do we go from here?"

A sad smiled pulled at his mouth. "I don't know."

He shoved his hands in his front pockets. I couldn't remember another time when he looked so uncertain. To steal a line from Betty, I was kinda digging it.

He cocked his head to the side. "So do you want to talk about why Betty's pushing us together?"

I smoothed my braid nervously. "Not really. But we should."

"How bad is it?"

I made myself look him in the eye and forced the words past the lump in my throat. "I have motive for Addison's murder. Blackmail."

He blinked, leaning back onto the counter edge. "I don't understand. Blackmail how?"

I grabbed the paper towel and twisted it, needing to do something with my hands. "Addison's father was James Rae."

His eyebrows rose. "The Olympic athlete?"

"He was also the judge Mama is rumored to have slept with in order for me to make it into the Miss America finals."

He didn't say anything, but he didn't need to. His face showed his surprise, and then awareness. He moved closer, until we stood side by side, close enough that I could feel his body heat.

"So it's true." The sympathetic understanding was almost my undoing.

I cleared my throat. "It's worse than her just sleeping with someone as a way for me to win a contest. She had feelings for him. They were lovers, and Addison had letters."

"Between your mother and her father." His voice sounded so calm compared to mine.

I spilled my guts. It felt good to get the whole sordid affair off my chest.

"Are you going to read the letters?" he asked once I'd finished.

I wrapped my arms around my waist. "I thought I would. But now that I've seen them, I can't. I don't want to. I'm going to burn them, like I promised."

"And the police don't know about this?"

"I haven't told them."

"This isn't good, Mel."

"I know. You know how I feel about lying. And that's all I've done for the past month."

He stood quietly, processing the information. "You haven't found any photos?"

"Nothing. I think they might be on the USB drive I saw in Addison's backpack."

"Do the police still have her personal items?"

I scoffed. "No. The police finally released Addison's belonging to her agent, who dumped them off at the headquarters tent complaining the police didn't give her everything, and what they did give her she wasn't interested it. She's a real piece of work." I thought about the contents with a new perspective. "I want to look through that box now that I know what I'm looking for."

"That's a good idea." His sharp eyes studied me. "Can we set aside our issues and concentrate on getting you out of this mess?"

I nodded, my heart pounding against my chest. "I can do that. Since Betty's already over-shared, did she tell you there may be a jewel thief among us?"

"A murderer and a jewel thief?"

"Um, one more thing. The program director, Hudson Jones, has disappeared."

He ran his palm over his face. "Can't you

two ever go anywhere without some type of disaster happening?"

CHAPTER TWENTY-SIX

The sun glared down on us from the cloud-less blue sky. It was going to be another unseasonably hot one. Grey and I found Betty chatting with Craig Sutton and his black-and-white Lhasa Poo, Codi, near the snack shack. When we approached, Betty gave me the thumbs-up. I wasn't sure if she was telling me she'd found my brooch, or if she was asking if Grey and I were on again.

I introduced Grey to Craig and Codi. Codi's soft ears perked up on high alert, sussing out if we were friend or foe. She looked adorable with a bright red bow on her collar. I bent down and held out my hand.

"Hi, Codi. I love the gold bone hanging from your collar."

After a thorough palm inspection, she didn't reject me, but she wasn't one hundred percent sold on me either. I got one lick before she stepped back and watched, reserving judgment. Smart dog.

"She loves that bone," Craig said. "We picked it up in England last year."

"Do you travel often?" Grey asked.

He shook his head. A big smile spread across his friendly face. "Not as much as we'd like. Got to stay close to the grand-kids."

I straightened and took a step back. Codi relaxed and sat next to Craig's feet. "We saw you coming back from the groomer yesterday," I said.

His face reddened. He yanked off his Dodgers ball cap to run a hand through thick silver hair. "Ah, we were in a bit of a hurry to get back to the coach. Mrs. Sutton and Codi watch their favorite soap at one-thirty every afternoon without fail. They love their shows." He settled the hat back on his head.

Betty grabbed my arm. "Cookie, Craig hasn't seen your brooch. I gave him your cell number in case he finds it later so he can call you."

Really? She just passed out my number to random strangers? He looked harmless, but there was a killer on the loose. A little discretion would be a good course of action.

"I was just telling Betty that I've also lost

something this week. My watch. A Bremont MBII. The wife gave it to me for our thirtieth wedding anniversary."

I whistled softly. That watch ran about six grand. "Oh, no. When did you have it last?"

"I believe it was the night of the campfire." Bored, Codi climbed on Craig's leg, begging for attention. Or to continue their walk. Who knew how long Betty had been bending his ear? Craig bent down and patted Codi's head.

I turned to Grey and explained, "That was the night Addison died. The police showed up at the campfire to talk to me. It was rather chaotic."

Craig shook his head sadly. "It's too bad what happened to that little girl. It doesn't matter how many people didn't like her. She didn't deserve to die that way."

"What way is that?" Grey prodded.

"I heard she was stabbed." He rubbed his chin. "But that doesn't make sense, since there wasn't much blood at the scene."

I knew Addison hadn't been stabbed, but had been smothered, possibly with a pillow, because I had seen the police officer's notes. How did Craig know about the blood? Before I could ask, Grey had transformed into FBI mode.

He relaxed his shoulders, then shoved his

hands in his pockets. I watched as his facial muscles relaxed, presenting a nonthreatening appearance. "I didn't realize you were at the crime scene."

"Oh, we're parked in site eleven, across from the spa." He pointed behind him. "I could see inside the tent before it was quarantined off. The wife and I heard raised voices just before one-thirty. But it didn't last long. That's when their show is on, you know." He looked down at Codi. He pulled a treat from the pocket of his jeans and held it out for his pooch. "The wife turned up the volume. There was a great fight scene between Nikki and Victor, and she didn't want to miss a word."

"Are those two still at it?" Betty asked, bright-eyed.

Grey shot her a look to keep quiet.

"What? It's not like you're a cop. I just wanted to know about Victor and Nikki."

"Later," I mouthed. Betty sulked, but pressed her lips together.

"Could you tell if it was a man and a woman? Two women?" Grey continued to question him.

Craig thought about it before replying. "It sounded like two women, but I can't be certain. It could have been a man and a woman. It was hard to tell with Victor and

Nikki arguing at the same time. They've been at it for twenty years." He shared a conspiratorial smile with Betty.

I lifted my hand to shield the morning sun from my eyes. "So your RV faces the back of the spa tent, right?"

He nodded.

"The other night, I noticed the back of the tent was loose. There was a hole just big enough for someone to squeeze through." I pointed at Grey. "Don't ask me how I know that."

"I wouldn't dream of it." His sarcasm wasn't lost on me.

I worked to keep my tone light. "I was curious if you'd ever seen anyone sneaking in and out of the tent."

He shook his head. "I can't say that I have. Although, now that you mention it, after lunch, there was a young teen loitering around the back of the tent. Do you think he had something to do with Addison's death?"

"It's possible. Do you remember what he looked like?" I didn't recall seeing a teenager among the campers.

"I just saw him from behind. Smaller size for a guy, thin. Wore a ball cap."

I pushed the bangs off my forehead. I looked at Betty. "You've met everyone here.

Sound like anyone you've met?"

She shook her head. "Sorry, Cookie."

Craig redirected the conversation back to me. "I noticed you were taking pictures at the campfire. Did you happen to take one of the s'more layout? Our youngest daughter is getting married next year and the wife thought the gourmet s'mores were a good idea for the reception."

"Sure." I pulled out my cell phone and scrolled through my pictures. "Do you like this one?" I held the phone out for him to see.

He nodded, a wide smile on his face. "Yes. That would be very helpful. Thank you." He gave me his cell phone number and I texted him the photo.

Once he was assured he'd received the picture, he said goodbye with the promise we'd talk more in the afternoon. After *The Young and the Restless.*

Once Craig and Codi were out of earshot, Grey asked, "Can I see your pictures?"

I shrugged. "Sure." I handed him my phone.

He positioned me in front of him as a shield from the sun so he could see the screen better.

"Betty, I don't remember ever seeing a teenager. Have you?" I asked.

"Not one. Do you think he has bad eyes?"

"It's possible." I looked over my shoulder at Grey. "I thought it would be fun to have some snapshots of the event to display at the store," I explained.

"Um-hm," he responded absently as he looked at the photos.

"Cookie, did you get a picture of me and Asher?" Betty stood next to Grey so she could see, too. "He travels with his wife's ashes. I think he might have had something to do with her death."

Grey snapped to attention. "What did you say?" I recognized that tone. He was on alert.

I spun round. This wasn't going to end well. Betty had no idea who she was divulging information to.

"Cookie and I came up with a plan to find the brooch. We decided to convince everyone to give us a tour of their rig so we could snoop in their private stuff to see if they had the pin without looking suspicious."

Grey closed his eyes and took a deep breath. "Fast forward to the part about his dead wife."

"She doesn't know whose ashes he has. She's making assumptions," I interjected.

Grey shot Betty a stern look. "You need to listen to Melinda on this one."

"Oh, sure. Take her side." Betty pouted. "Are you going to let me finish my story or not?"

Grey lowered the phone, giving her his undivided attention. "Please, continue."

"Thank you. So, like I was saying, I was in charge of snooping and Cookie was in charge of keeping Asher occupied. I found an urn hidden in the back of a drawer. He admitted to Marsha Thompson his wife died a few years ago. But when Marsha asked how she died, he wouldn't tell her. We think he's hiding something."

"Have you shared this theory of yours with anyone else?"

"Just Cookie." Betty wiggled her orange eyebrows, which seemed to be melting off her face. It was hot. We needed to get out of the sun.

"Good. Don't." He returned to swiping through the photos again. "Mel's right. You have to be careful —" His body tensed. "Who's that?"

"That's him." Betty exclaimed.

I looked at the blurry photo of her and Asher. "Asher Knox. I don't think he killed his wife, but I'm not sure I trust him. We've caught him in a lie or two."

Grey's blue eyes pinned me with a look that conveyed we were going to talk about this later. In greater detail. "Trust your gut. Stay away from him."

He handed me the phone. I really wanted to ask more questions. The only reason I didn't was because Betty was standing next to him, all ears. I flipped through the pictures, wondering what Grey had been looking for. I hadn't realized I had taken some really bad photos. I'd done a poor job of framing some of the shots.

I found it interesting I wasn't ever able to get a clear shot of Asher. In one photo, I'd managed to get the back of Asher's head and Craig Sutton's arm. There was his watch, clear as day. He was right, he'd had the watch at the campfire.

"Look, Handsome. You don't get to be jealous of Asher." Betty pouted.

Grey sighed. "You need to trust me on this."

She glared at me through slitted eyes. "Do you trust him?"

I nodded without hesitation. "With my life." I crossed my heart, knowing that would seal the deal with her.

She groaned. "I don't like it, but I'll do it. You two are a real damper on my love life."

The next item on Grey's to-do list was to search through Addison's box of belongings. I was also hoping there would be word of Hudson's whereabouts. We headed to headquarters and found a young kid, about eighteen, frantically digging through Hudson's desk.

"Who are you?" I shouted. Could he have been the teenager Craig Sutton was talking about?

He about jumped out of his army green cargo shorts. He whipped around, brown eyes wide. "J-John Bradley."

Grey motioned for us to stay back. "What are you looking for?"

His gaze darted around the room, as if he were looking for a way out. "I'm Hudson's backup. He didn't check in with Loni at the ARL, so she sent me out here to find out what was going on. I can't find him. I was looking for a schedule of events in hopes of tracking him down." His voice quavered as he explained.

"Do you have ID?" Grey asked.

Betty looked impressed. "Yeah, how do we know Loni sent you?"

With trembling fingers, he pulled his wallet out of his back pocket. He showed Grey his driver's license. "Are you a cop?"

Grey ignored the question. "Why don't you use the phone at the desk over there and call Loni. Let her know Hudson's been missing for over twenty-four hours. She needs to call the police."

John swallowed hard. He nodded rapidly. "Okay," he said, his voice squeaking. He scampered to the desk Grey had pointed to and picked up the phone.

"Where are Addison's belongings?" Grey asked quietly.

I pointed to the box under Hudson's desk, exactly where we'd left it yesterday. The three of us wasted no time retrieving it. Grey dumped out the contents on the desk.

It hit me again that an entire life was reflected by the items spread across the desk. Hair brush, dirty aprons, wallet, makeup, pens, books, jewelry, etc.

Betty picked up a diamond butterfly bracelet. "Nice." She clipped it on her wrist. "So, what are we looking for?"

I removed the bracelet and returned it to the desk. "The USB drive," I explained quietly. But it wasn't there.

I was convinced that device was the key. Whatever was on the drive was the reason Addison had been killed. The person who knew that information would lead us to who had possession of the evidence. Had Pepper swiped the USB drive along with Addison's recipes and my mama's letters?

I looked at Grey. "Now what?"

With the swipe of his arm across the desk, Grey whisked the array of personal items back inside the box. I distracted Betty by asking her to find the blue folder I'd looked through yesterday. I wanted Grey to have the opportunity to look through it.

While she was gone, I asked Grey, "Is there anything you can do? I've already called the police about Hudson and they didn't do anything. The longer he's gone, the more I'm certain there's foul play involved."

"I'll make a call."

I gripped his arm. My faced warmed at the touch of his smooth skin against my palm. I jerked my hand back, embarrassed that I couldn't hide my reaction. I cleared my throat. "Thank you."

His face softened. "You're welcome."

"Bad news." Betty interrupted the moment. I wasn't sure if I was relieved or disappointed. "It's not here. Someone took it."

John hung up the phone. He looked at us, fear in his eyes. "Loni's calling the police. What do I do now?"

Heck if I knew. That was the question of the hour.

CHAPTER TWENTY-SEVEN

Grey had instructed John to wait in the headquarters tent for the police. The three of us hurried back toward the RV so Grey could make his phone call in private.

Betty sniffed the air. "I smell bacon."

"Didn't you just eat?" I asked.

"Sure. But I always got room for bacon." She patted her stomach.

As soon as we approached the kitchen, we noticed a small assembly of campers and their dogs congregating outside near the entrance. Mr. Swanson was there. He stroked his beard as he leaned in to the group and spoke. Whatever he'd said, it couldn't have been positive — people immediately began looking in our direction, whispering with scowls on their faces.

I slowed my stride. "I wonder what's going on."

"They heard Betty was coming for the bacon." Grey grinned.

316

Betty smacked his arm.

Detectives Finn and Lark emerged from the middle of the gathering. They were attired in their usual garb of dress pants, button-up shirts, blazers, and angry grimaces. Under my breath, I told Grey who they were.

Grey dropped his jovial demeanor. "Keep your answers short. Don't offer information." His tone broached no argument.

I nodded my understanding.

Betty glanced at Grey in admiration. "You sure sound like Malone."

"Thanks," he said, never taking his eyes off the detectives. "Betty, follow my lead. Got it?"

"Sure thing." She threw her shoulders back, and tightened her grip on her handbag, ready to rumble.

Finn pushed forward and blocked our pathway, which kept us separated from the others. I took a deep breath. I could tell from the smirk on her face, it was about to get serious.

"Well, well, well. Look who's here." She pushed the sides of her blazer back, flashing her gun and badge in her signature move; like a character from a bad cop show. "We've been looking for you."

"Are you here because of Hudson?" I asked.

Lark slithered up next to his partner, looking like an unmade bed. He eyeballed me critically. "You've been busy. Calling our station, then the Laguna Beach police department. You've got some impressive friends."

"If you're talking about Detective Malone, I doubt he'd call me a friend." I wasn't being humble, just honest. Malone considered me a pain in his backside.

Finn eyed me. "But you have a relationship with him."

I felt Grey stiffen next to me.

Betty leaned forward and batted her eyes. "Detective Hottie only has eyes for me."

Lark scowled back at her, unimpressed.

"I'm not sure what you're getting at," I said. "I've been *involved* with a couple of his cases." Much to his dismay. "But that's the extent of it. We don't have a 'relationship.' "

"Involved enough that you felt you could call in a favor?" he asked.

Oh, for heaven's sake. That was what this was all about? "So you're annoyed with me because you're being made to do your job?"

Detective Lark closed the space between us. "You seem confused, Miss Langston, so let me break it down for you." He looked cocky and confident. Like he knew something I didn't.

Grey suddenly stepped between me and the detective. "I don't believe we've met. I'm Grey Donovan." He didn't extend a hand, nor did his smile reach his sharp eyes. "I understand you've already questioned Miss Langston. So unless you have something new to talk to her about, you won't mind if we excuse ourselves."

He didn't wait for a response. He placed a steady hand on our backs and pushed Betty and me toward the RV, past Mr. and Mrs. Swanson.

Grey whispered, "Don't look back."

That phrase could sum up the story of my life. My blood pressure shot up, knowing they could haul me down to the station for questioning at any time. We didn't get very far when Finn's voice cut through the hot air.

"Hold up there, Mr. Donovan." Her icy tone blew over us like an arctic cold front.

We immediately froze. Grey had made her look bad in front of everyone, so now she was about to make an example of him. I almost felt bad for her. She had no idea who she was up against.

Grey turned to face her. With measured

steps, he met her halfway.

"Who are you?" she asked Grey. Her eyes burned with frustration.

He shrugged. "Like I already said, Grey Donovan." His calm tone only made her look more unrestrained.

She eyed him thoughtfully, regrouping, as if she sensed there was more to him than met the eye, but wasn't sure what. "I don't remember seeing you before. Are you the lawyer?"

He looked surprised. "Does she need a lawyer?"

I bit the inside of my lip. I was always amazed to see him in action, but why in the world was he antagonizing her? He knew I had something to hide. And provoking the police just didn't seem like a good defense.

Finn crossed her arms. "You tell us? Is she guilty?"

Grey raised an eyebrow. "That's your job to prove, not mine."

I couldn't take it anymore. They were having a word play competition at my expense. The police weren't going to look in another direction unless I pointed them there.

I strode toward them. "No. I'm not guilty. Instead of concentrating on me, why don't you look into Pepper Maddox? She had an ax to grind with Addison for taking over her job as head chef, which you're already fully aware of. Add to that, Dim Sum had dirty paws at dinner that night of the murder."

"Dim Sum?" Finn asked, confused.

Okay, I admit, out of context, that did sound rather odd.

"Her dog," Betty supplied, not about to be left out of the party.

"So we should consider her a suspect because her dog is dirty? Have you looked around this place? It's a dustbowl, other than this grassy area you entitled rich people had trucked in for your special event."

I sighed. They had a grudge against people with money? Or people with dogs? "It wasn't dirt on her paws. It was dried blood," I insisted. Why was I doing their job for them?

Finn and Lark exchanged a look as they mulled over what I'd said.

Knowing I had their attention, I continued, "I overheard your uniformed officers talking about bloody paw prints at the crime scene. There was a theory that the killer had a dog. And at dinner that night, Pepper admitted she'd seen Addison heading toward the spa, acting like she was meeting someone. Did she bother to tell you that when you questioned her?"

Neither of them responded.

Knowing I was on the right track, I continued. "That puts Pepper at the scene around the time of death. And it's probable it was her dog that walked through the blood."

Pepper burst through the crowd in her elastic-waist pants, cotton T-shirt, and black clogs. "Liar," she screeched. "That's not true."

I shook my head. "I'm sorry Pepper, but it is. There are three other people who can corroborate what I'm saying. I think you were the one meeting Addison. She knew you were passing off pre-made food as your own cooking. That's why Hudson wouldn't give you your job back. I also know you had Addison's recipes in your possession."

"It's your word against mine," she spat out.

"Once we find Hudson, he'll confirm everything I'm saying. Was she blackmailing you? Is that why you killed her?"

I heard Grey groan behind me.

Damn. I knew he had wanted me to keep my mouth shut. To not offer information. I just couldn't help myself. When pushed into a corner, my instinct was always to come out fighting. To protect myself and those I love.

Lark's eyebrows wrinkled together. "Is

that true?" he asked Pepper. "You were being blackmailed by the victim?"

"I don't have to answer your questions unless I'm under arrest." She clamped her lips together.

Once again, Lark and Finn exchanged a look I couldn't decipher. Out of the corner of my eye, I saw Red and Sunday peak out from the kitchen entrance. Red was wearing his chef uniform, and Sunday was finally in something practical — skinny jeans, crop top, and Burberry rain boots.

Lark stepped forward in Pepper's direction. I swear he was about to drag her into town for questioning or arrest her, when Ranger Elliott came racing toward us, his arms waving above his head.

Betty snickered. "Look out, Dudley Do-Right lost his horse."

I choked back my laughter. Dudley's, I mean, Ranger Elliott's, face was deathly white.

"Detectives," he yelled. "I found Hudson Jones. He's dead."

CHAPTER TWENTY-EIGHT

A large gasp rolled through the group. My head was spinning. I closed my eyes for a second, taking in what he'd just said. Hudson was dead. I shivered, despite the sunlight that engulfed us.

Finn and Lark closed in around Ranger Elliott as he caught his breath. His green uniform was covered with dirt, making his pants look more dingy than normal. Campers shouted questions over each other. *What happened? Was it an accident? Was he murdered? Where did you find him?*

Sunday and Red left their hiding place at the kitchen entrance, joining the group, but staying on the fringe. I wondered why they were so reluctant to get closer. Better yet, why were they together in the first place? Was Sunday trying to get him to come back as her client?

Lark yelled for everyone to be quiet so he could hear, setting off the group of pooches for a quick outburst of barking. Once the owners managed to quiet their canines, an expectant silence settled over the crowd. Ranger Elliott's voice quavered as he explained he'd just found Hudson's body at the bottom of a cliff on a trail not designated for us, and, judging by the condition of the body, he'd been there since last night.

"Suddenly, you're a medical examiner?" Lark rubbed his neck. "So we're to believe he was just lying dead on the trail, and no one saw him until this morning?"

Ranger Elliott adjusted his hat nervously, then scrubbed his jaw with his hand, leaving behind a large smear of dirt. "First of all, that area was off limits to the guests with dogs. Second, I didn't find him on the trail." He searched the anxious faces surrounding him. We were hanging on his every word. He cleared his throat. "He was, uh . . . *moved.*"

Lark sighed like the weight of world rested on his next question. "Moved how?"

"Judging by the tracks, I believe by a mountain lion. Hud was missing part of his leg."

"It's time to go." Betty tried to push past Grey. "Unplug the water hoses and electrical cords, Cookie, we gotta get outta here. I don't do mountain lions."

Grey grabbed Betty and pulled her next to him, keeping her from leaving. "Hang on."

Betty wasn't the only one freaking out. Chaos ensued and the group began to break up; panicked voices shot out, setting off the dogs again. People began to scatter to the safety of their campsites.

"No one is going anywhere," Lark shouted. He cupped his hands around his mouth. "Everyone stay where you are."

Finn immediately got on her two-way radio and called for backup. Fear remained on most faces as Lark tried to create order from the pandemonium. It took a few minutes, but one by one, everyone started to calm down.

Betty turned toward me, realization in her eyes. "That's why Sunday's face was fatter than the Stay Puft Marshmallow Man. We should have known a mountain lion was close by."

I'm not sure how we should have known anything, but it did explain her allergic reaction. All three of us looked in Sunday's direction. She'd drifted back to the kitchen threshold where she covertly watched Detectives Lark and Finn. I wondered how close the big cat had to have been for Sunday to have had a noticeable reaction.

"It's too much of a coincidence for Hudson's death to be an accident," I said softly. "He knew something about Addison."

"I agree." Grey matched my tone. "We need to let this play out and see what happens. Let them do their job."

They were no Detective Judd Malone. I didn't share Grey's confidence in the two detectives' abilities to get to the bottom of the situation any time soon. I started working through what I knew. Everyone seemed to like Hudson. From what he'd said, Addison had confided Pepper's secrets to him. Was it possible she'd confided other secrets too? I was unclear who'd seen Hudson last. Red? Or Sunday and Ranger Elliott? If Hudson had been found on the restricted trail, had someone lured him there or had he been followed?

Pepper had managed to tuck herself away in the far end of the area, between Mr. Swanson and a large planter. I wondered if she was looking to make a break for it, or hiding from the cops. I glanced over my shoulder at Sunday, who continued to watch the detectives. What if Hudson and Sunday had had words about Addison when he'd dropped off Sunday's luggage?

Red caught me looking in his direction. I was surprised at the skepticism fixed on his face. Was that directed at me or the police? Lips set in a grim line, he disappeared inside the kitchen. I assumed to finish preparing lunch.

I looked up at Grey. "On the positive side, I can't be a suspect in this death."

"Let's hope not." His tentative smile was not reassuring.

Lark and Finn stepped away to talk discreetly, occasionally looking over at all of us, concentrating on me and Pepper. What I wouldn't give to hear what they were saying. I wondered if they'd take over the headquarters tent again. Speaking of headquarters . . .

I grabbed Grey's arm. "We've got to tell them about John. He's probably scared to death, waiting at Hudson's desk for an update."

"I'll do it." He lobbed a firm look at Betty and me. "Stay here."

I wasn't sure where he thought we'd run off to with official babysitters who wore badges instead of braces monitoring us, but we agreed not to leave.

Grey's confident walk garnered everyone's attention as he approached Lark. All eyes were on the two men. Judging by the unyielding look on Lark's face, he wasn't very receptive.

As I watched from a distance, conversations flowed around me. I picked up bits and pieces. Most people were curious about what the new person was talking to the police about. A handful of others, including the Thompsons, were afraid, convinced they should have left after the first death. I was beginning to share their viewpoint. Sunday was lying low in the background, watching the activity unfold.

"I wonder when that handsome TV reporter is gonna show up? He better get here quick. He's got the scoop on a man-eating mountain lion. It could be bigger than that *Sharknado* movie."

"Oh, my gosh. Stop already," I said.

"But he's missing out on all the craziness." Betty looked toward MacAvoy's RV.

She had a point. Any other time there was a juicy story unfolding, MacAvoy was smack in the middle of it. Where was he?

Suddenly, Veronica appeared from the direction of the spa, her round face white with alarm.

"Did you hear?" she cried. "The park ranger found Hudson's body. It's just awful." She threw her arms around Betty and hugged her tightly.

"I can't breathe," Betty mumbled into Veronica's shoulder, Betty's handbag caught between them.

"Oh, I'm sorry."

Betty brushed herself off, her purse swinging from the crook of her arm. "We were here when the news broke. Where have you been?"

"Harry had an appointment at the spa." Veronica fanned herself. "It's all over camp about Hudson. I'm just a bundle of nerves. I think I'm going back to Dana Point today. This is too stressful. I'd rather face a jewelry thief than a murder."

I jerked to attention, turning my back to Grey and the detectives. Pieces of various conversations fell into place, for the first time creating a very clear picture. "What did you say?"

Veronica's eyes widened. "I said, I'm going home?"

I waved my hand in front me, dismissing her answer. "No, no. After that. You live in Dana Point?"

She nodded, confused as to what I was getting at. "Yes."

Judging by the wariness on Veronica's face, I was making her uncomfortable. I made myself slow down and soften my expression. "The other day, you said someone broke into your house and stole a butterfly bracelet last month."

"That's right. It was frightening, but not as scary as someone killing innocent people."

My adrenaline kicked up. I was about to crack the jewel thief case. "By any chance, was it a white gold bangle with a butterfly made from diamonds?"

She gasped. "Yes, it was. How did you know?"

Betty rubbed her hands together. "We've seen it," she exclaimed at the top of her voice.

Everyone looked in our direction. Including Sunday and Pepper.

"Shhh." I held my finger against my lips.

Betty didn't look one bit contrite at my reprimand. "We know where it is, don't we, Cookie?"

Yes, we did. I was ninety-nine percent certain Veronica's bracelet was in Addison's box of belongings. Now I understood why Grey had wanted Betty to stay away from Asher. Grey must have recognized Asher in that blurry photo.

It was all starting to make sense. Knowing what I did about Addison, I believed she had found out Asher's secret life as a jewel thief and had been blackmailing him. I bet she'd taken the cufflinks as insurance. In the meantime, he was starting subtle rumors around camp that she was the thief. I'd wager a year's salary Asher was the one who'd tossed her tent, looking for the missing jewelry. Unfortunately, I didn't have proof of any of it.

We hadn't seen Asher all morning. I wondered where he'd been hiding. Or if he was planning another heist. Craig Sutton had managed to "lose" his watch after spending an evening with sticky-fingered Asher Knox.

Grey needed to know what I'd pieced together. I spun around to wave him back over, but he was no longer talking to Lark. Where'd he go? All he was supposed to do was inform the detectives about John.

I turned full circle, looking for a glimpse of Grey. We needed to get back to the headquarters tent as soon as possible, and grab the box before the police seized the area for their command center. We also needed to find a way to turn the cops on to Asher before he got away with Craig Sutton's anniversary watch. The minute the detectives were finished with us, we needed to grab Addison's box of possessions.

Where the heck was Grey? "Betty, stay with Veronica. I'll be right back."

"You can't leave me here with her," I heard Betty say behind me.

I made my way toward Lark, who was on his cell phone having what looked like a very intense conversation. Finn hurried over and held out her hand, keeping me from getting close enough that I might overhear what was being said.

"What do you want?" Her blond hair was pulled back into a severe ponytail, making her appear tired and stern. Or maybe she always looked like that. With her non-sparkling personality, it was hard to tell.

"I'm looking for Grey. Have you seen him?"

She eyed me. "Yes."

I waited for her to elaborate, but she didn't. Good grief, I hated one-word answers. "He told you about John Bradley from the ARL? Hudson's backup. We left him in the headquarters tent. He's just a kid. He's got to be scared to death."

Her eyes bored into mine. "He told us."

"Do you know where Grey went?"

"No."

I managed to unlock my gaze from hers. Not waiting to hand her an opportunity to question me about my involvement with Addison's case, I turned to leave.

"Hold up."

Ugh. Grey's words echoed in my ears. *Keep my answers short and don't offer infor-*

mation. I faced Finn and nailed a fake smile on my face that I hoped passed for cooperative.

Finn folded her arms across her chest, not pretending to be anything other than unyielding. "How do you know Hudson Jones wouldn't give Pepper Maddox her job back as head chef?"

"He told me. He said Addison had confided in him about Pepper's scam with passing off someone else's cooking as her own."

"Why would Addison trust him enough to tell him that?"

Was she testing me? "They were having an affair. Which you know about because you have her cell phone. I'm guessing there are photos."

She continued to study me. I decided there had to be a mandatory cop course on the proper interrogation stare, because both Malone and Finn had it mastered. I shifted my weight from one foot to the other.

"How did you know about the affair?" Finn asked.

"I figured it out. Hudson wasn't very good at subterfuge. Pepper knew about it, too. In fact, she'd told Callum MacAvoy, the TV reporter, that if she didn't get her job back, she'd spill Hudson's secret. Somehow, Hudson managed to convince her that being head chef for the dog show was a more high-profile gig, so she dropped it so his affair with Addison wasn't exposed." I know, I know. I was offering information. What can I say? She was making me nervous.

She gave me a pointed look. "And you know this how?"

"Hudson. He knew Pepper wasn't making her own food. If she was the chef here, she'd have to prepare meals in front of the guests. The dog show is more of a catering gig. She could continue to do what she's been doing — hire someone else to cook."

She mulled on that for a minute. "When you were deflecting our questions earlier, you claimed Pepper had Addison's missing recipes. How do you know that? Did Hudson confide that in you too?"

I sighed. "I found them in her garbage."

She raised an eyebrow. "Do you dumpster-dive often?"

I explained about Raider knocking over the trash and how I'd seen Pepper carry out the bag the day before. I didn't mention I was looking for my mother's love letters.

I could tell by the look in her eye she knew I was holding back. "If I'm to believe what you're saying, Hudson seemed to have confided in you. Were you sleeping with him? Is that why you killed Addison? So you could have him to yourself?"

I stepped back. "Absolutely not. Pepper's your killer."

She uncrossed her arms. "Laguna Beach homicide may be fine with you sticking your nose in their cases, but I'm not. Stop playing cops and robbers or I'll drag you down to the station. Got it?"

"I got it."

Good grief. No matter where I went, I just couldn't escape the threat of jail.

CHAPTER TWENTY-NINE

Grey still hadn't returned. I wouldn't lie, I was concerned.

Finn moved everyone inside the kitchen. Something about not wanting us to get sunburned and sue their department for police brutality. Her concern for our welfare was underwhelming.

She separated us into small groups and ordered us to stay put until either she or Lark had spoken to us. Most people had found a table to sit at, while a handful of guests stood whispering. Red was allowed to continue to prep for our lunch with his sous-chef, Chase, the former butler.

Seeing everyone in close quarters, there were less than twenty of us. I recognized the Thompsons and the Swansons. I realized the only people who weren't at the party were Asher, the Suttons, and Mr. TV and his cameraman.

I peeked out the front opening of the

circular tent. MacAvoy couldn't be far away. Sure enough, I caught sight of him and Ben standing on the opposite side of the roadway, which separated us from them. Ben had his camera, Mr. TV had his microphone. The dynamic duo had been regulated to the nosebleed seats. I smiled to myself. It didn't matter that MacAvoy was here as a guest, he wasn't getting special treatment.

Detective Lark grabbed the Swansons and escorted them outside to begin the questioning. Mr. Thompson asked how much longer they could keep us. No one had an answer for him. Betty, Veronica, and I sat at a table facing the food prep area.

The aroma of bacon was deliciously overwhelming in the confined area. My stomach rumbled. Whatever Red was preparing, I was ready to eat.

Pepper had managed to weasel her way to stand next to Red at the butcher block table where he sliced sweet potatoes. He growled at her to get out of his workstation. Pepper shuffled back to the table and sat. Red swore under his breath, complaining about all the losers intruding in his workspace. I wondered if he meant Pepper specifically, or all of us in general.

This was the first time I'd seen Pepper and Sunday in the same room since Pepper had blabbed she was afraid of the agent. I wanted to witness their interaction, but sneaky Pepper was doing everything possible to make sure there wasn't any type of contact at all. She had perfected the act of keeping her head down.

Veronica was upset because she'd left Harry in the RV. I tried to comfort her, telling her we wouldn't be much longer and that he was safe. The more I reassured her, the more insistent she was about breaking camp at the first available moment. Betty wasn't helping matters. She was on the same bandwagon as her new friend, insisting we were going back to Laguna Beach the second we were free.

The yurt windows were uncovered, allowing a clear view of the activity around us. Or lack of activity. I walked over and gazed out, searching for any sign of Grey outside. He'd been gone for at least thirty minutes. I pulled out my cell, and set it to vibrate, not wanting to draw attention to the phone lest the police feel the urge to confiscate it. I texted Grey, *Where are you?*

I shoved the phone in my back pocket and paced along the row of windows watching for him. In the distance, I heard sirens. Backup had arrived. Maybe the questioning would move along faster. The sirens grew louder as they got closer. Everyone gathered around the windows and entrance, watching as three police cars, a fire truck, and an ambulance pulled up.

The emergency workers jumped out of their vehicles and met up with Lark and Finn for a debriefing.

"Cookie, your man's back." Betty pointed out the window facing the spa.

Grey strolled up to the tent, pausing for a second to watch what was happening across the street. He shoved his hands in his pockets, his face serious. He pivoted on his heel, then strolled inside the tent. After a furtive glance around the room, evaluating the situation, he made his way toward me.

"Where have you been?" I tried to keep my tone even, pushing down my anxiety.

His eyes shifted as he formulated an answer that was publicly appropriate. "I made a phone call."

I had a feeling I knew what call he'd made. I pulled him aside, for as much privacy as we could have in a circular tent, under the scrutiny of Betty, Veronica, and who knew who else was watching us.

"About Asher?" I asked quietly.

"Yes."

"I know you can't say much, but is he a suspected jewel thief?"

He regarded me for second then nodded once.

"I put it together after you left. We need to tell the police."

Finn and Lark strode inside, sucking out the air in the room. There were two uniformed police officers on their heels. Slowly, they scanned the crowd. My heart stopped when Finn's gaze rested on my face. Her brows drew together as she looked past, her gaze landing on Grey. It took all my self-control to not look at him. She moved on, scanning through the rest of the faces, until she finally settled on Pepper who was seated at a table in the back.

They side-stepped the Thompsons and walked directly toward Pepper. "Pepper Maddox, we'd like to ask you some questions. If you'd follow us?" Lark took the lead while the others looked on.

Pepper remained hunched over the table, rooted in place. "I didn't kill Addison. I don't care what Melinda says," she hissed.

Lark pulled out his notebook and read off his notes. "Did you attend the International Culinary Center in New York City?"

She blinked repeatedly, looking confused. I think the rest of us were equally taken aback. Why was he asking her about her education and not about her relationship with Addison? Or Hudson?

"Is your real name Julia Flowers?" he continued.

Pepper blanched. She shook her head vigorously. "No. My name is Pepper Maddox."

Lark pulled out his phone and held it up to her. "This is the real Pepper Maddox. Your college roommate. She's been living in France for the past five years. Do you recognize her?"

Her eyes darted around, looking for an escape. "You've got it all wrong. I can explain everything."

"I doubt it," Betty muttered.

I hoped Lark didn't drag Pepper off for questioning until she had confessed all in front of us.

"This is all a misunderstanding," she insisted. "I couldn't afford tuition and had to drop out. She was moving to France to work for Pierre Herman, a renowned pastry chef. I just needed her school credentials to get my foot in the door. I just borrowed her name for a while."

Good grief. That explained an awful lot. How long did she think she'd get away with impersonating her roommate? And once she was finished "borrowing" her name, then what? She'd just go back to Julia?

"I knew she was a hack," Red called out from the preparation area. He shoved his way closer. His anger made him seem bigger, scarier. At least he had the presence of mind to leave his knife on the chopping block. "You're a complete fraud. I've never seen you cook a single dish from start to finish by yourself." He turned to glare at Sunday. "What did I tell you? Whatever her name is, she doesn't know what the hell she's doing in the kitchen. Why would you ever consider representing her? You never listen to me."

Sunday wasn't the least bit intimidated by him. She pulled her tiny body to full height and glared back. "Shut. Up."

Fascinating. They obviously had a relationship. Betty slid me a sly grin and wagged her lipstick eyebrows. She was thinking the same thing.

Finn stepped in front of Red, keeping him from getting any closer to Pepper. "Sir, you need to stay out of this. Go back to your table."

Lark pulled out his handcuffs. "Julia Flowers, you're under arrest for falsely personating Pepper Maddox."

"You've got this all wrong," she cried, as the uniformed officers helped her stand.

"We're also taking you in for questioning

regarding the murder of Addison Rae," Finn added.

"No, no, no. I didn't kill her. She was blackmailing me. She was blackmailing everyone," she shrieked, as Detective Lark slapped handcuffs on her. Pepper looked over her shoulder at me, drilling a hate-filled look of desperation in my direction.

I took a step back, bumping into Grey. He planted his hand on my shoulder, steadying me.

"I can prove I wasn't her only victim," Pepper yelled as the detectives and uniformed policemen dragged her off. "I have proof."

CHAPTER THIRTY

It all happened in a white-hot second. Lark handcuffed Pepper, dragged her out of the circular tent, and toward one of the marked police cars. All the while Pepper insisted, at ear-piercing volume, she had proof in her tent that she wasn't Addison's only black-mail victim.

Two uniformed police officers manned the kitchen exit, making sure no one escaped before we were questioned. We all gathered in the shadows of the doorway, watching as the detectives grilled Pepper. I changed my mind. I didn't want to hear what Pepper had to say. I wanted the cops to shove her into the backseat of the cruiser and drive away.

I turned to Grey, unable to hide the fear gnawing inside of me. "Do you think she's spilling her guts?"

Grey faced me, dead serious. "Yes."

My stomach dropped. "You couldn't

sugarcoat that at least a little?" I whispered.

"They gotta get a search warrant," Betty claimed. "They can't just march into her tent. Even a dirty, rotten, scoundrel like Pepper has rights."

"Actually, they can," Mr. Thompson corrected her. "If she gives the police permission to search her quarters, they don't need a warrant. It's called a consent search." He adjusted his wire-rimmed glasses to balance on his square, aged face.

Betty studied him with a great deal of suspicion. "How do you know all this?"

He shrugged. "My son's a lawyer."

"You got his business card? Cookie might need a good lawyer in a few minutes."

Grey's cheek twitched. I shot him a don't-encourage-her look. It was times like this I really didn't want Betty's help.

Mr. Thompson looked like he was about to say something, when someone in the group said, "There they go."

Grey pointed at Lark and Finn who marched past us, heading directly for Pepper's tent. Unlike Lark, who grinned like he was about to tie up the case with a pretty bow, Finn's flat expression said she wasn't convinced. Yet.

"Oh, yeah. She spilled her guts like one of those hopped-up police snitches," Betty jeered. "They're on their way to collect their booty."

I felt like throwing up.

A police officer with salt-and-pepper hair approached the tent. Officer Murdock, his name tag said. Everyone stepped back, granting him entrance. He flipped open his notebook and called for the Thompsons, Veronica, and Betty. The questioning had finally begun.

"I'll meet you back at the RV," Betty said as she followed Officer Murdock.

He returned within five minutes, and called his next group of targets. It became apparent he wasn't the one conducting the questioning; he was just the runner. On and on it went. Until it was Grey and me left with Sunday and Red.

Grey and I sat in silence, watching Red and Sunday do their best to ignore each other. It didn't make sense. One minute they acted like complete strangers, the next Red was jumping down Sunday's throat like a spurned lover.

Murdock was back; he called for Red, Sunday, and Grey, leaving me alone. I had a bad feeling I was being saved for Finn or Lark.

Red wiped his hands on his apron, grumbling about lunch being late as he traipsed after Murdock.

"Let's get this over with. I have somewhere to be." Sunday sailed through the tent flaps.

Grey and I exchanged a look. He squeezed my hand and said quietly, "Remember, answer their questions, don't offer information."

I nodded my understanding. "Keep an eye on those two. There's something going on there," I whispered.

Grey's eyebrow lifted. "Yes, sir." After a quick wink, he followed the others outside to be grilled.

Now alone, I paced the tent. The longer I had to wait, the more anxious I became. I wondered what Red had been preparing other than bacon. I slipped over to the butcher block table for a look. Bacon, tomatoes, romaine lettuce, sweet potatoes, mashed cooked carrots, and wheat flour. Lordy, I hoped the carrots were for the dogs and the bacon was for the humans.

I noticed a small leather notebook on the wooden table. I picked it up and leafed through it. It was Red's. Recipes, plating layout sketches, recipe ideas, odd notes. Most pages were dated. I flipped to the most recent page, which was the day we arrived.

Need ice

Addison recipes?
Meet Sun at 2
Lamb? Add beef?

Apparently, he didn't like Addison's recipes, and he had a meeting the following Sunday. Nothing earth-shattering there. I flipped back a couple of pages, past a few drawings and supply lists.

Yam chips thicker
"Pawfect" Chicken Salad
"Doggone" Chicken Salad
Barking Good Chicken Salad

"Langston. Let's go," Detective Finn's strong voice reverberated throughout the tent.

Startled, I dropped the notebook. I looked toward the entrance where Detective Finn stood wide-legged. She pointed at me, motioning for me to make my way toward her. I swallowed hard and followed her outside.

Finn kept her back to the sun, casting a half shadow over me. She pulled what looked like pages of pale pink stationery from her inside blazer pocket. I recognized the paper immediately.

"Anything you want to tell me?" she asked.

I cursed silently. "Not really."

She unfolded a letter and started to read with almost a mocking enthusiasm, "My dearest James, there are certain people who touch your heart in unexpected ways. For me, you are that person. My love for you will always remain strong, especially through our sacrifices for each other. The request that I made to you last night at dinner regarding Melinda —"

"Stop!" I swallowed the sour taste in the back of my mouth. I shook my head. "I don't want to hear any more."

Finn folded the letter and tucked it back in her blazer pocket. She studied me relentlessly. "Do you want to explain now? If not, there's plenty of room in the squad car for two."

I struggled with where to start and how much to say. I could feel my heart pounding against my ribs. "Years ago, Addison's father and my mother had an affair." I motioned at the paper in her hand. "They penned love letters to each other. Addison threatened to send them to my daddy if I didn't introduce her to certain people in the community and help her launch her career as a pet chef."

"That's it? She threatened to show these to your *daddy*?"

I sighed. "Back in the day, I was a pageant girl."

She looked me over from head to toe, taking in my jeans and cotton T-shirt. "Really? The evening gown? Swimsuit? Tiara? Did you win anything?"

Here it came. "Yes. I was Miss Texas."

Finn wanted to roll her eyes. I could tell because she looked like she was primed for a seizure. I did my best to ignore her condescension and continued to explain, hoping that in the process I wasn't paving a way to jail.

"During the Miss America competition, my mother was accused of sleeping with a judge to ensure I placed in the top ten. Even though at the time there wasn't proof of improper conduct, I was disqualified from the competition."

She whistled.

"Yeah. It was awful. Those letters prove that the judge she slept with was James Rae, Addison's father. It wasn't until Addison had arrived in Laguna that I knew the full truth about the situation. I mean, I'd always suspected my mother just let me believe the worst about her because she likes to be the center of attention. Even negative attention."

She cocked her head to the side. "That's why you 'recommended' Addison for the job here."

"Yes." I wasn't sure if I should explain the

rest of what Addison wanted or just keep quiet, so I asked a question instead. "How did you know the letter referred to me?"

"Julia Flowers found them when she tossed Addison's tent. She read them, put two and two together. Was Addison blackmailing anyone else?"

"You mean besides Pepper and me?" I shrugged. "I didn't ask where I landed on the blackmail target list. But I have an idea."

She scoffed. "An idea? Is this when I'm supposed to ask for your help?"

I shook my head. "Not at all. You asked me a question. I answered."

"But that is the game you play with the Laguna Beach police, right? You just happen to have theories or ideas to share about the case."

"It's not a game. I'm not a cop, so people confide in me about things they won't tell you." I felt my face warm. Not just because of Detective Finn's questions, but because I could hear Grey's voice in the back of my mind telling me to stop talking.

She crossed her arms, skepticism clear on her face. "Okay, I'll play. Tell me your theory."

I hesitated long enough to find a way to share my theory without outing Grey. "I think Addison was also blackmailing Asher

Knox. The way he tells the story, Addison was his private pet chef, until they had an argument. He was missing a pair of cufflinks. He asked if she'd seen them. She accused him of calling her a thief, and they parted ways. But Betty and I saw the cufflinks he claimed were missing inside his RV."

She looked bored. "So what. He found them later. Not a crime."

I shook my head. "He told us didn't find them. He lied. Why? There was no reason. Unless he had something to hide. Like, those weren't his cufflinks and Addison had palmed the jewelry as a form of insurance. Here's the other thing. Craig Sutton's über expensive watch has suddenly disappeared. He's been spending time with Asher. Remember that night you and your partner showed up at the campfire? Asher and Craig were hanging out together, and Craig had his watch that night. The next day, poof, his watch is gone."

A flicker of interest flashed across her face. "Continue."

"Have you heard about the jewelry robberies in Dana Point?"

"Of course."

"Asher lives in Dana Point. So does Veronica Scutaro. Veronica told us her gold-bangle, butterfly bracelet was stolen last month. Guess where it is right now?"

I saw the spark of understanding in her eye. "You really do poke your nose into police business, don't you?"

"Like I said, I don't mean to. Do you know if Addison's car is still in storage?"

She sighed heavily, reminding me of Malone after I've worn him down and all he wanted was for me to stop talking. "Storage?"

"Ranger Elliott had it towed because Addison had parked in the wrong area. I asked him if she'd ever picked it up. He said he had no idea, it wasn't his problem."

She scribbled in her notebook.

"So now you think Asher killed Addison Rae?" she asked without looking up.

"No. I still think Pepper did it. I think Asher's a jewel thief. And one more thing. Have you noticed there's something odd about Red and Sunday? One second they act like they've never laid eyes on each other until this weekend, the next minute they're yelling at each other like a couple of exes. Which doesn't make sense. Sunday admitted she represented Red years ago. Maybe she's trying to get him back now that Addison's gone. But that doesn't explain why they act like they don't know each other."

"Sunday has an alibi. She didn't arrive until after Addison was killed," Finn countered.

"That's what she says to you. Hudson told me she was supposed to have arrived earlier in the day. She claimed to be held up by a conference call. She could have taken that anywhere. Who's to say she didn't take that call from right here?"

Finn pushed her lips together, her eyes narrowed on my face. "Speaking of alibis, where were you really when Addison was killed?"

I swallowed hard, knowing Grey was going to kill me, and I didn't blame him. I met her gaze head-on. "I was waiting for her on the trail. We were supposed to trade the foreword to her pet cookbook for those letters. Addison never showed."

"What time was that?"

"I was supposed to meet her at two o'clock. I left camp around one-thirty. I was anxious to get it over with."

She narrowed her sharp eyes. "You understand you told me this without a lawyer present and I can use this against you?"

A jumble of bright white, billowy clouds slowly covered the sun. Lordy, I hoped that wasn't an omen. "I do. I didn't do it. You have the letters. I have nothing left to hide."

"I can't give these to you. They're evidence."

I raised my hands. "I don't want them. I planned on burning them if I ever got hold of them. Feel free to do the same." Mama would be relieved to know Daddy would never see the letters.

In for a penny, in for a pound. No sense in stopping now. "About Hudson," I continued. "I don't think that was an accident. Addison confided in him. He must have known something about her murder. When I saw him last, he was with Ranger Elliott bringing Sunday her broken luggage. Red insisted he'd spoken to Hudson after that and had asked him to run to town yesterday to pick up supplies for him."

"But you don't believe him?"

I shook my head. "But I don't know what he would have had against Hudson. I guess if you find a grocery list on Hudson, then Red was telling the truth."

Finn begrudgingly made more notes in her little black book.

"One last thing," I said.

She looked up. "Do you promise?"

"Red has a temper. It's legendary. Sunday even mentioned it."

She patted her firearm. "Luckily for me, I have a gun."

She was the kind of person who wouldn't
be afraid to use it.

CHAPTER THIRTY-ONE

I'm happy to report, I was not arrested. Unfortunately, Detective Finn had more questions, but we were interrupted before she could ask them all. I left her at the kitchen, talking on her cell phone to her captain. I headed back to the RV to catch up with Betty and Grey.

Snatches of sunlight shone on the grass. The campground was eerily quiet. With Hudson gone, most people were packing it in. Unfortunately, the event was a bust.

"Melinda," MacAvoy called out from behind me. "Wait."

"No comment," I shouted, refusing to turn around. Mr. TV reporter was the last person I should be talking to.

He ran to catch up with me. "Cut me some slack, I'm just doing my job."

I clamped my lips together and continued to hotfoot it toward our campsite. He shoved his hands in his jeans pockets. "Can you at least confirm that Hudson was mauled by a mountain lion?"

I stopped and spun around. "Who told you that?"

His green eyes lit up. "So, it's not true?"

"He wasn't mauled. That's all I'll say. You should really be talking to Detective Finn or Lark."

He pressed on. "Do they have any suspects? Do they think Hudson's death is linked to Addison's murder?"

I sighed. "I have no idea. They ask me questions. They don't give me details about their case." I turned to leave.

"I've dug into Addison's life."

He was killing me. "That's your job."

"I'll trade you information."

I didn't bother replying. He was getting to me, though. I really wanted to know what he'd learned about Addison's life. Yet it wasn't my place to confirm or deny anything regarding Finn's investigation. My nosiness only went so far.

"I know about James Rae," he said.

Well, hell's bells. That stopped me in my tracks. I slowly pivoted on the heel of my hiking boot. "What did you say?"

He held up his hands. "Hang on. Let's go to my RV and we can talk." He looked around, nodding toward the other campers who were hanging out around their sites. "Privacy would be good, don't you think?"

I planted my hands on my hips and invaded his personal space. "No, I don't. If you have something to say, just say it."

He cleared his throat nervously. "Well, after Sunday's interview, I did a little digging. First, I never really believed you were blackmailing Addison. That's not your personality. But your reaction was so strong, I knew you were hiding something. From what I already knew about you and from what Sunday had said, I was able to piece together the facts about Addison's father and your mother."

He studied me. My heart raced. I waited to feel sick, for the nausea to rise from my belly to my throat. But it never happened. I realized that now that Finn knew, none of it mattered anymore. For the first time in months, I felt great. I smiled and gave him a half shrug. "So now you know what Addison knew. Were you planning on holding that over my head, too?"

He blinked. "No. Not at all."

I nodded as if considering what he was saying. "So why bring it up? What have you accomplished other than ticking me off?"

He rubbed the back of his neck. "I admit, I totally handled this wrong. All right. I'm going to lay all my cards on the table."

I coughed out a constrained laugh. "I doubt that, but I'll pretend along with you."

He sighed. "I was telling you this to build trust. I know your secret. I'm not going to tell anyone. You know, you're a hard person to get close to."

I shook my head. "Not really. All it takes is sincerity and no ulterior agenda. I haven't seen anything remotely like that from you."

"Fair enough. I'm a reporter. My agenda will always be to get the story."

"That's too bad. I can't help you with that." I walked away.

I arrived at the RV and neither Betty nor Grey was there. The dogs were ecstatic to see me. I took them outside for a quick potty break — one at a time. As I walked Raider around for him to find a place to do his business, I noticed Betty had already disconnected the water hose and sewer. She wasn't kidding about leaving.

I didn't mind going home, but I didn't want to make Finn mad. Once both dogs had relieved themselves, I scribbled a quick note to Betty and Grey, informing them I went to the headquarters tent to make sure I could leave. I felt like I was finally off Finn's main suspect list. I didn't want to do anything that put me back on it.

I hustled to the tent, hoping they followed the same protocol as when Addison had been killed. The grassy area was still absent of guests and dogs. Instead, a group of uniformed police officers stood in a loose huddle, talking. It was a shame really that what had started out so promising had turned into a nightmare.

The fire truck, ambulance, and a police car were still parked on the roadway. I wasn't exactly sure why the fire truck had arrived, unless the firefighters were needed to recover Hudson's body. I shuddered, thinking how awful Hudson's last moments must have been.

I rushed up the stone pathway for what I hoped was the last time. I zipped inside, only to find it empty. No homicide detective. No crime scene techs. I wondered where everyone was. Could they be on the trail at the actual crime scene?

I was about to leave when a man wearing a ball cap suddenly stood up. It looked like he'd been under Hudson's desk. I watched him set the box of Addison's belongings on the desk and search through them.

"Hey, get out of there." I charged across the tent, intent on stopping him.

The man spun around. It was Red. He

had ditched his black apron for a Yankees ball cap. I recognized the hat from Sunday's luggage explosion. Did this mean Sunday and Red were an item?

Red slid the box away from me. "You keep popping up where you don't belong. Why aren't you leaving like everyone else?" His eyes flashed with anger.

I blinked in surprise at his hostility. He was making me nervous. "Where's Detective Finn?"

"Don't know, don't care." He picked up the box and started to walk off with it.

I grabbed his arm to stop him. "You can't take that. It doesn't belong to you."

With more force than needed, he pushed me away. I stumbled against Hudson's desk.

He must have realized his mistake. "I don't like to be touched." He tightened his grip on the box. "This belongs to Sunday. She won't care if I look through it. I loaned Addison some items. I've come to claim them."

Like what? Her makeup? What was in the box that he could want so badly? I ran through the items one last time: brush, apron, jewelry, wallet, books. There wasn't anything in there that belonged to him. What was he up to?

"How do I know that's true?" I didn't

want to call him a liar outright.

"It doesn't matter. Learn something from Addison's death. Keep your mouth shut before someone shuts it for you." He started digging through the box again.

Holy Shih Tzu. All the breath left my body. The police hadn't ever released the cause of death of — probable suffocation. I tried to step away toward the exit, keeping my eyes on him.

"Where is it?" he yelled.

"I don't know what you're looking for." I tried to keep my voice calm, even though my heart was bursting out of my chest. Unfortunately, this wasn't the first time I'd been in the presence of a killer.

He focused his crazy eyes on me. "The USB drive. It's not here. What'd you do with it?"

I slowly shook my head. "I haven't seen a USB drive," I lied.

Why would Red want Addison's flash drive? One by one, I started to fit the pieces together. Pepper's explanation about not being able to copyright recipes, only the wording and the art of plating. The recipe cards we found in Pepper's trash for "Pawfect" Chicken Salad. Red's notes in his chef book with a list of recipes titles, including "Pawfect" Chicken Salad.

"Did Addison steal your ideas?" I asked.

Beads of sweat popped up on his top lip. "Damn straight she did. Tried to pass them off to Sunday as her own. But Sunday knew better. She'd seen them before."

Speaking of Sunday, she barged inside. "What the hell are you doing?"

At first, I thought she was talking to me, until I saw Red flinch.

"She knows," he bellowed.

I shook my head. "I don't." I wasn't sure what he was referring to, but by the look of outrage on his face, I was going to deny everything.

Sunday marched across the hardwood floor. She slammed her oversized tote on the desk. "You're an idiot, Redmond. I'm so tired of cleaning up your messes."

"No one asked you to." His petulance was surprising.

My gaze swung between them. I half expected Red to stick his tongue out at Sunday like a four-year-old. And Sunday looked like she wanted to pinch some sense into him.

They sounded like me and my brother Mitch. Oh. My. Gosh. That was it. I sucked in a deep breath. I'd read everything wrong — their relationship and Red's notebook. His note didn't mean to meet *on* Sunday, it was to *meet Sun,* his sister.

The question was, which one killed Addison and possibly, Hudson? I needed to get out of there. I had no idea if one of them had a weapon, and I sure as heck didn't want to stick around and find out.

"I got your note, Cookie." Betty waltzed inside, with freshly applied plum eyebrows, her purse hanging on the crook of her arm.

Hell's bells, she had the worst timing.

"Betty, meet me back at the RV." My strained smile wasn't fooling anyone.

Betty continued to walk toward me. "Why do you look constipated? Are you confused again? First you want me to meet you here, now you want me to meet you back at the RV. Make up your mind."

Sunday pulled a gun out of her tote. "I've had enough of all of you." She waved her gun at Betty. "Stand next to your friend."

"What's going on?" Betty screeched.

My stomach tightened in fear. "You don't want to shoot us. This place is crawling with cops." And an FBI agent. I silently called for Grey, counting on him to still be in tune with me.

Betty scooted up against my arm, clutching her handbag. "I tossed the note," she whispered.

My stomach dropped. So much for Grey

showing up. It was up to me to get us out of here.

Red dropped the box. "Sun, this is a bad idea. What are you doing?"

She glared at him. "Exactly what you think. I'm cleaning up your mess again."

"I don't like them either, but we can't keep offing people," he argued.

Betty pointed at Sunday. "You killed Addison? I thought he did it? You weren't even here."

The siblings stared at each other. I wondered if there was a way to get them to turn on each other to give Betty and me time to escape.

"Yes, she was," I said.

They both turned toward me, with their backs to the door. Now that I had their attention, I had to keep it until someone walked by.

"She picked up Addison's SUV from the towing storage facility and brought it here that afternoon. There was plenty of activity that first day; it was easy to slip around camp unnoticed. She disguised herself wearing that ball cap, and snuck inside the spa tent from the backside."

Sunday arched a blond eyebrow. "Impressive. How did you figure that out?"

"I was with Hudson when your suitcase

exploded. I noticed the ball cap immediately. It didn't seem like your style. I saw the opening in the tent a couple of days ago. A guest mentioned he saw a young kid hanging out the backside of the spa. With your build, short hair, and hat, you could easily be mistaken for a boy. It was a genius plan. I don't know that I would have put it all together if Red wasn't wearing the cap."

Sure, I sounded brilliant now. Too bad I hadn't put all this together hours ago. Betty and I would be on our way back home if I had.

"Why was Addison meeting you at the spa? Why not at her tent? Or the kitchen?"

"She was never meant to be there. I was meeting him." Sunday sneered at her brother. "A total screw-up."

I nodded in agreement, even though I was completely confused. "I know what that's like. I've got a brother too. Mama's favorite."

Red charged up to her and wagged his finger in her face. "How was I supposed to know she followed me? What about you? I may have killed Addison, but you killed Hudson. *You* screwed that up."

"I'm holding a gun, you moron. Do you want me to shoot you?" She turned the handgun on her brother.

"Please do. Put us all out of our misery," Betty said wryly.

Red lunged toward Betty, crazy-eyed. I stepped between them without thinking. "Back off. She can't hurt you."

"Watch your mouth, grandma," Red commanded.

I had to admit, I was all kinds of confused as to what had really happened with Addison, but I couldn't concentrate on that now. Time was running out. Sunday was getting antsy, and Red had lost control. I felt Betty shove something in my back.

"Pepper spray," she whispered.

I gave a subtle nod, hoping she caught it. That was only good up to ten feet. Red was close enough, but Sunday wasn't. We needed to get the one with the gun first.

I continued to shield Betty with my body. "Look, no harm no foul. Sounds like you two have some things to work out between you." I inched toward the exit, pulling Betty with me. "If he's anything like my brother, this isn't the last time you'll be bailing him out of trouble. Look at him, he's not even grateful for all you do for him."

I reached behind my back and grabbed the can of pepper spray. I prayed to the good Lord, Betty was handing it to me in a way I could just aim and spray without shooting myself in the face.

Sunday stepped closer to Red. "She's right. I'm not doing your dirty work anymore." She slapped the gun in his hand. "You kill them."

What? That did not go the way I'd laid it out in my head. I told myself to breathe. This was not the time to panic.

"Good job, Cookie. At least we had half a chance with her."

One side of Red's mouth lifted in a sardonic grin. He turned toward us.

It was now or never.

I raised my arm and shouted, "Betty, drop." I felt her hit the floor behind me, at the same time I pressed the top of the can, sending a stream of liquid into Red's face.

He immediately fell to his knees, dropping the gun. "My eyes. Agh," he screamed, writhing in pain.

Betty scrambled for the gun. I prepared for round two if needed.

"What have you done?" Sunday yelled. "Redmond! Are you okay?" She raced to her brother's side. She didn't seem to notice his snotty mucus and tears dripping on her jeans.

Betty stood up, pointing the gun at the siblings. "Freeze, suckers."

"Police. Drop the gun." Detectives Finn

and Lark stood at the tent entrance, firearms drawn and pointed at Betty.

Betty slowly lowered the gun, then set it on the hardwood floor. "Where've you been? They were going to kill us."

I held out the pepper spray. "He'll need some water."

Lark kept his gun trained on Sunday. Finn covered a sniveling Redmond as she took deliberate steps in our direction. As soon as she reached the gun Betty had laid on the floor, she kicked it to the side for Lark to pick up.

Finn pulled out her handcuffs. Her eyes shifted in my direction, catching my attention. "I can't wait for you to get out of my district. Laguna Beach homicide can have you."

CHAPTER THIRTY-TWO

The next morning, we were safely tucked away in our beds in Laguna Beach. By we, I meant Missy and I. Grey had to leave town to tie up some loose ends on Asher's case. But not before he told me he was proud of my quick thinking, and made me promise to keep out of trouble. Just thinking about the pride in his eyes made me smile.

Back to Addison. It turned out she had taken the cufflinks as a bargaining tool. Asher had been following her, waiting for the perfect opportunity to retrieve them. When he'd found out she'd be the chef for the ARL function, he'd purchased an event ticket and got his cufflinks back.

Betty was relieved to learn the ashes in the urn weren't human. They were from Asher's first dog, Skipper. Betty was sure that meant Asher was redeemable. I was sure that still made him creepy.

As for what really went down with Sunday

and Red, it was hard to tell who was telling the whole truth and who was blaming the other for a bad plan gone awry. If I was a betting kind of girl, I'd place my money on Red. He was the one who'd suffered the most from the pepper spray. Spilling his guts was the natural conclusion.

He claimed Addison had stolen his plating ideas and was going to publish them in her cookbook. The USB, which Detective Finn had kept as evidence (the evil siblings were never going to find it), was the only proof he had those were his original ideas. The plan had been for Red to search Addison's tent, steal the flash drive, and secretly deliver it to Sunday. Later that day, when Addison couldn't produce the photos or the recipes, Sunday was going to call the whole project off, firing Addison. Then she'd give the pampered pet cookbook idea to her brother and find a new publisher.

The problem was, Addison had followed Red, crashing the party. They argued. Red lost his temper. He pinned her to the table and smothered her. Sunday claimed she tried to stop him. I wasn't buying it.

Sunday was the one who thought sticking a fork in Addison's neck would throw the cops off. She obviously didn't represent crime writers. Forensics would easily prove that was done after the fact. What was she thinking?

Poor Hudson had walked in on Sunday and Red when he'd delivered her suitcase. Not exactly sure what he'd walked in on, Sunday had convinced him to meet her on the trail so she could explain. She admitted to ambushing him, pushing him off the cliff to his death.

I was glad the whole ordeal was over and we were back to our normal lives. Although we never did find my brooch. I still didn't know how I was going to break the news to Caro.

After taking Missy on her morning walk, I ate a piece of peanut butter on toast and left for a quick run starting at 10th Street Beach. Don't get the wrong impression. I hated exercise, but I hated being out of shape more.

It was a dreary morning, with a canopy of ragged clouds and heavy fog encasing our seaside town. This type of weather made sunbathing impossible, but running comfortable.

I focused on the rhythmic tattoo of my running shoes slapping the wet sand, emptying my head of all the unanswered questions of where Grey and I stood. By the time I finished the last of my thirty minute run, I felt energized and happy, even though I had no idea if I had a future with Grey.

I was halfway into my fifteen-minute cool down when my cell rang. I thought for sure it would be my mama wanting to rehash the whole letter ordeal, for the twentieth time. But it was a local number I didn't recognize.

"Hello," I answered, trying to catch my breath.

"Is this Melinda Langston?" the man asked on the other end.

"Yes." I wiped the sweat from my forehead.

"I believe I have something of interest to you. You've recently lost a brooch?"

My heart about burst through my chest, and it had nothing to do with my run. "Yes. Do you know where it is?"

"Can you describe it to me?" the man asked.

I listed through the details like I had a hundred times before. Antique gold fruit basket, filled with rubies, diamonds, and emeralds. "Is that the brooch you found?" I held my breath.

"Yes, it is."

I exhaled in a rush. I spun around, excited, sand scattering from under my running shoes. "Thank God! You don't know how much this means to me. I can meet you

375

anywhere. Or if you'd like, you can stop by my boutique."

"That would work out wonderfully."

I checked the time. It was just after nine. "Say, in an hour?" I rattled off the address to Bow Wow.

"I'll see you there." He hung up.

I tucked the phone back inside my waistband pocket, a humongous smile plastered on my sweaty face. I raced home, and showered. I slipped on a pair of skinny jeans and my favorite cream-colored scoop-neck embroidered top. I hurriedly finished the rest of my morning routine, including a stop-off at the Koffee Klatch.

I arrived at the boutique just before ten. The shop didn't officially open until eleven, but I unlocked the doors anyway. I stashed my purse in the back office and booted up the computer.

I laughed, thinking about how Betty would be equally excited to know my family heirloom was back in my possession. She'd decide we'd have to celebrate. Knowing her, that would include flaunting the pin in front of Caro.

I practically floated to the register at the front of the shop. I turned it on and made sure there was enough cash to make change. Once the brooch was in my hand, I'd call

Grey and fill him in. I was lost in thought about what I would say when the doorbell chimed. I smiled brightly, eager to meet my Good Samaritan.

My smile faded into confusion. It was Mr. Swanson. He leisurely walked into my shop as if he'd decided to stop by to browse at the last minute.

"Mr. Swanson?"

"Hello. It's good to see you again." He ran his hand through his thinning gray hair as he surveyed the boutique. "This is quite the setup you have here."

"Thank you. I'm sorry, I'm just a little confused. You have my brooch?"

"I do." He nodded. "I didn't realize it was yours until Betty had asked if I'd seen it. At the time, I thought you had something to do with that poor chef's death, so I wasn't in a big hurry to reward your bad behavior. But then the police cleared you, and well, Patty insisted we give it back to you."

I moved from behind the counter. "Well, thank you for returning it to me."

"Hold your horses there, Missy."

The doorbell chimed. I turned to greet my guest, but the words died on my lips. There stood my cousin. Tall, beautiful, perfectly composed — and completely unexpected. She looked comfortable in her jeans and white, short-sleeved jersey tee. She glided toward me, never taking her brilliant green eyes off my face.

"Caro," I greeted. "You look lovely as always. Forgive me for being so direct, but what are you doing here?"

"I called her." Mr. Swanson wheezed out a laugh at my confusion. "Betty told me all about your feud and how much this ugly piece of jewelry was worth." He held up Grandma Tillie's brooch in his strong wrinkled hand like a prize waiting to be claimed. "Ladies." He eyed us both, making sure he had our attention. "The pin will go to the highest bidder."

Caro and I gasped.

A sly smile pushed back Mr. Swanson's timeworn wrinkles. "Let the bidding begin."

RECIPES

TOSS ACROSS SWEET POTATO CHIPS

These are easy-peasy homemade treats your dog will love. They're so quick and simple, even Mel likes to make them for Missy.

You'll need:

3 large sweet potatoes
Baking sheet
Cooling rack

Preheat oven to 250° F

Scrub those sweet potatoes. No need to peel.

Cut the potatoes into 1/3″ slices, no smaller than 1/4″. Keep in mind, the thinner the slice, the shorter the cooking time.

Place sliced potatoes on a baking sheet in a

single layer.

Bake for about 3 hours. Turn over after 1-1/2 hours.

Cool completely on a wire rack. Depending on thickness, this could take 30 minutes to 1 hour. As the treats cool, they will harden.

For desired chewiness: Baking 3 hours creates a soft, chewy dog treat. If your pooch prefers crunchy treats, bake for an additional 20-30 minutes.

Storing: Remember, these are preservative-free and should be refrigerated for no longer than 1 week. You can freeze them for up to 1 month.

LAMB KEBOBS
PAMPERED PET STYLE

There's no better way to pamper your pooch than with some "pawsitively" delicious lamb kebobs. You can whip these up in less than 30 minutes. Make sure the kebobs have cooled sufficiently before you serve to your pup.

You'll need:

2 lbs. minced lamb

2 cans (14 ounces) of green lentils, rinsed
    and drained
2 medium cucumbers
3 large handfuls of fresh spinach
Food processor
Cupcake tray
Cupcake liners
1/3 cup
Cooling rack

Directions:

Preheat oven to 350° F

Combine lentils, cucumber, and spinach
into a food processor. Blend until a rough
paste forms.

Pour into a large bowl and add the lamb;
mix well.

Scoop 1/3 cup of mixture and roll into a
ball.

Place in a lined cupcake tray.

Bake for 15 minutes or until golden brown.

Remove from pan and let cool on a wire
rack.

Storing: Keep any leftovers in the refrigerator for no longer than 1 week. You can freeze them for up to 1 month.

ACKNOWLEDGEMENTS

Although writing is a solitary process, we are blessed to not only have each other to navigate this crazy journey, but an amazing support group and loved ones to cheer us on.

We'd like to thank the hardworking team at Bell Bridge Books. Your support and marketing expertise means the world to us. To our extraordinary editor, Deborah Smith, we're so grateful that you continue to share your talents with us, making us better writers.

To Christine Witthohn, our agent at Book Cents Literary Agency, thank you for your mama bear fierceness and keeping us on track to achieve our career goals.

We can't fully express our gratitude to our wonderful readers. You are the reason we write. Your tireless enthusiasm for more Mel and Caro is what keeps us going. Thank you. Keep those emails, Facebook posts, and Tweets coming. We love to hear from you! If you haven't already done so, please visit our website and sign up to get updates: SparkleAbbey.com

ABOUT THE AUTHORS

Sparkle Abbey is the pseudonym of two mystery authors (Mary Lee Woods and Anita Carter). They are friends and neighbors as well as co-writers of the Pampered Pets Mystery Series. The pen name was created by combining the names of their rescue pets — Sparkle (Mary Lee's cat) and Abbey (Anita's dog). They reside in central Iowa, but if they could write anywhere, you would find them on the beach with their laptops and, depending on the time of day, with either an iced tea or a margarita.

Mary Lee Salsbury Woods is the "Sparkle" half of Sparkle Abbey. She is past-president of Sisters in Crime-Iowa, and a member of Mystery Writers of America, Romance Writers of America, Kiss of Death, the RWA Mystery Suspense Chapter, Sisters in Crime National, and the SinC Internet group Guppies.

Prior to publishing the Pampered Pets Mystery Series with Bell Bridge Books, Mary Lee won first place in the Daphne du Maurier contest, sponsored by the Kiss of Death chapter of RWA, and was a finalist in Murder in the Grove's mystery contest, as well as Killer Nashville's Claymore Dagger contest.

Mary Lee is an avid reader and supporter of public libraries. She lives in Central Iowa with her husband, Tim, and Sparkle, the rescue cat namesake of Sparkle Abbey. In her day job, she is the non-techie in the IT Department. Any spare time she spends reading, and enjoying her sons, daughters-in-law and five grandchildren.

Anita Carter is the "Abbey" half of Sparkle Abbey. She is a member of Mystery Writers of America, Romance Writers of America, Kiss of Death, the RWA Mystery Suspense chapter, and Sisters in Crime.

She grew up reading Trixie Belden, Nancy Drew, and the Margo Mystery series by Jerry B. Jenkins (years before his popular *Left Behind* series). Her family is grateful all the years of "fending for yourself" dinners of spaghetti and frozen pizza have finally paid off, even though they haven't exactly stopped.

In Anita's day job, she works for a staffing company. She also lives in Central Iowa with her husband and four children, son-in-law, grandchild, and two rescue dogs, Chewy and Sophie.

The employees of Thorndike Press hope you have enjoyed this Large Print book. All our Thorndike, Wheeler, and Kennebec Large Print titles are designed for easy reading, and all our books are made to last. Other Thorndike Press Large Print books are available at your library, through selected bookstores, or directly from us.

For information about titles, please call:
  (800) 223-1244

or visit our Web site at:
  http://gale.cengage.com/thorndike

To share your comments, please write:
  Publisher
  Thorndike Press
  10 Water St., Suite 310
  Waterville, ME 04901